Summer NIGHTS

ALSO BY JILL SANDERS

The Pride Series

Finding Pride
Discovering Pride
Returning Pride
Lasting Pride
Serving Pride
Red Hot Christmas
My Sweet Valentine
Return to Me
Rescue Me

The Secret Series

Secret Seduction
Secret Pleasure
Secret Guardian
Secret Passions
Secret Identity
Secret Sauce

The West Series

Loving Lauren
Taming Alex
Holding Haley
Missy's Moment
Breaking Travis
Roping Ryan
Wild Bride
Corey's Catch
Tessa's Turn

Haven, Montana Series

Closer to You
Never Let Go
Holding On

The Grayton Series

Last Resort

Someday Beach
Rip Current
In Too Deep
Swept Away
High Tide

Lucky Series

Unlucky in Love
Sweet Resolve
Best of Luck
A Little Luck

Silver Cove Series

Silver Lining
French Kiss
Happy Accident
Hidden Charm
A Silver Cove Christmas

Entangled Series: Paranormal Romance

The Awakening
The Beckoning
The Ascension

Pride, Oregon Series

A Dash of Love
My Kind of Love
Season of Love
Tis the Season

Stand-Alone Novels

Twisted Rock

Summer NIGHTS

JILL
SANDERS

Montlake
Romance

Published by Montlake Romance, Seattle
www.apub.com

Amazon, the Amazon logo, and Montlake Romance are trademarks of Amazon.com, Inc., or its affiliates.

ISBN-13: 9781542007573
ISBN-10: 1542007577

Cover design by Vivian Monir

Cover photography by Wander Aguiar

Printed in the United States of America

Summer NIGHTS

PROLOGUE

Zoey held her sister's hand more tightly as they walked across the large wooden bridge—walking toward the place they would be spending the next month, alone. In the sweltering heat of the swamplands in Florida.

Sure, their father had driven for over five hours to bring them to the gates of the camp, but upon seeing the mass of young girls and parents inside the large iron gates, he'd come up with an excuse about needing to get home again and had practically shoved them out of the car.

Since she was the older of the two, by twenty months, it fell on her shoulders to make sure they both were checked in to the summer camp.

"Aren't you even going to wave goodbye to Dad?" Her sister, Scarlett, nudged her.

Zoey's chin rose before she answered. "No." She tugged on her hand so Scar, as she liked to call her, would stay in step with her as she shifted the heavy backpack on her shoulder. What her little sister didn't know was that Zoey had overheard their parents talking last night. Not only was their father having an affair, but he'd confessed that he was in love with someone named Bridgette. Zoey's eleven-year-old blood boiled at the thought of their father betraying their soft-spoken mother in such a way. Also—BRIDGE-ette? Blech.

"Why?" Scar tugged on her hand, breaking Zoey out of the dark thoughts. Her sister was still at the age where she had to know everything. Zoey joked that *Why* should have been her middle name. Scarlett Why Rowlett.

"Because." She rolled her eyes as they moved down the neat gravel path that took them toward the main building of River Camp, the "exclusive summer camp for young girls from elite families."

Their mother had sprung it on Zoey and Scarlett during the last week of school that they had been accepted to attend River Camp. Which both of the sisters had loudly complained about until the very moment their father had dropped them off at the gates of the large facility.

"Why?" Scar's voice turned to a whine.

Zoey silenced her by tugging on her hand again. "Don't be a baby," she hissed. "People are watching." She nodded to all the other girls around their age.

River Camp "delights young women ages eight to twelve via hiking, swimming, paddleboarding, yachting, gymnastics, ballet, and equestrian activities." Or so the brochure her mother had given her said.

But Zoey knew what this really was. This was a prison for her and Scar while their parents tried to work on salvaging their marriage. But really, what would happen was their father would promise to change, as he always did, and then, once things died down, he would return to his old ways. BRIDGE-ette was not the first. Sneaking around on his family while tearing down their mother and making her believe it was all her fault was his MO.

As she looked around the open field, Zoey spotted the line they were supposed to be in and started across the grassy field. They stopped behind a tall blonde girl in cutoff shorts and a light-brown tank top with worn tennis shoes. Zoey tossed her bag down in the dirt.

"Listen," she whispered, turning to give her sister a shake. "Dad and Mom shoved us in this camp for one reason: to get rid of us this summer. So let's try to look at this as a vacation"—her eyes narrowed—"even if it's nothing more than a prison."

Scar shrugged and raised her chin, much like Zoey had done less than a minute ago. "Whatever." She smiled brightly.

Zoey wished she had the same way to turn off depression Scarlett had. Her sister was an abundance of joy and cheerfulness most of the time—when she wasn't asking questions, at least. Unlike herself. Maybe it was because Scar hadn't hit puberty yet?

Zoey watched as her sister's dark eyes traveled behind her. "Hi." Scar's smile grew bigger.

When Zoey jerked around, she almost bumped into the tall blonde girl, who was now smiling back at them.

"Hi." The girl looked between them. "Sisters, right?"

They both nodded.

"I'm Scar." Scarlett waved.

The blonde girl's eyebrows shot up. "Scar?"

"She's Scarlett," Zoey corrected. "I'm Zoey." She sighed as she silently wished the summer were over already.

"Elle," the girl replied. "Is this your first time here?"

Zoey nodded and stuck her hands in her jeans. "You?"

"Gosh, no—my grandfather owns this place. I've been coming here since I was born." She giggled and shrugged.

Zoey stopped herself from rolling her eyes once the girl's words sank in. Her family owned this place. It wouldn't do to make enemies of her on the first day—after all, it wasn't her fault they were stuck here.

"Cool," she said under her breath. But in her mind she instantly put Elle in the rich, stuck-up category.

Unlike the tomboy category, which she fell into herself. Girls who enjoyed being outdoors, wore torn jeans, and more often than not had a few cuts and bruises to show off from sports. Most of them either had short hair or tied most of it up in a ponytail, while the rest of it flew around crazily, like hers was doing currently. She reached up and tucked her dark locks behind her ears quickly.

Then there were the stuck-up, rich daddy's girls. Zoey's gaze ran over Elle—even though her shorts were cutoffs, they were name brand. Her sandals were designer too, and she had a very freshly painted pink manicure and pedicure on both her fingers and her toes. She wasn't quite the princess type but was somewhere close to it.

"This is Hannah." Elle stepped aside and motioned toward a blonde girl in front of her. "I was showing her where to check in."

Where Elle was tall and lean, Hannah was shorter and extremely petite. The fact that she was wearing pink shorts with a lacy cream top and white sandals and that her long blonde hair was neatly braided in rolls and tied with pink ribbons slotted Hannah instantly into that princess category.

"Hey." Zoey nodded, suddenly feeling extremely lanky.

"Hi," Hannah said. Zoey thought she heard an accent, but the girl hadn't said enough for her to be sure.

"Where are you guys from?" Elle asked as they moved another step closer to the check-in table.

"Jacksonville," Scar answered quickly. "You?"

"Here." Elle smiled. "Well, less than half an hour from here. Hannah's from Savannah, Georgia." Elle sighed. "I visited there once; it was beautiful."

"This is pretty too," Hannah answered. "The beaches, the water." She nodded across the green field to the small private beach that Zoey had been too busy moping to even notice.

Now, for the first time, she took a look around. Hannah was right: the place was pretty amazing.

"We should all bunk together," Elle suggested, to Zoey's surprise.

"Sure," Zoey said, thinking that it was probably impossible since she was pretty sure summer camps didn't work that way. Not that she'd ever been to one, but adults didn't usually listen to kids when it came to this sort of thing.

And besides, she'd probably never see either of the two girls again for the rest of their monthlong stay. After all, there were hundreds of girls running around the place.

"It's Hannah's first time too." Elle continued to chat easily as the line inched forward.

"My first time here. Last year I was in Europe," Hannah replied with a shrug.

Yup. Princess, Zoey thought, then had to catch herself when someone bumped her.

"Sorry." A soft apology came from behind her.

Zoey turned to yell at whoever had almost knocked her down, but then she noticed the worry and fear in the redhead's light-blue eyes and swallowed her retort.

"It's okay," she said instead. The look in the girl's eyes reminded her so much of their mother's after she'd found out about the cheating that Zoey doubted she could say anything harsh to her, even if the girl had knocked her over. She could see tears filling up the girl's blue eyes.

"Are you okay?" Elle asked.

"Yes," the redhead answered as she looked down at her feet.

"I'm Elle. This is Hannah, Zoey, and Scarlett." Elle motioned to each of them as she talked.

"Aubrey," the girl said, her eyes returning to her tennis shoes.

The four of them looked the newcomer up and down. Aubrey had fiery-red hair, the kind that models paid lots of money for, and skin like a doll Zoey had seen in a shop several years ago. Her clothes said she was borderline princess, but the fact that she looked uncomfortable in them had Zoey watching her more closely to see where she would land on her scales.

"We were going to bunk together," Elle continued. "Would you like to join us? There's room for one more."

Jill Sanders

Aubrey's head jerked up, and she took a moment to search their eyes. "Sure." She nodded. "Thank you."

They all moved forward. Hannah was next in line as Elle continued to ask questions and talk about all the fun they were going to have. Aubrey told them that she was from New York, but there was a slight southern accent hidden in her voice. When they finally stepped forward, Elle took control and leaned on the table.

She turned to the teenage camp counselor at the desk. "Hi, Carrie. This is Hannah Rodgers, Zoey and Scarlett . . ." She narrowed her eyes.

"Rowlett," Zoey answered.

"And Aubrey . . ." Elle motioned and waited.

Aubrey's eyes moved around, and for a moment it looked as if she couldn't remember her name; then she sighed. "Smith." Zoey's eyes narrowed as another mystery piece surfaced. Smith wasn't a hard name to forget.

Elle didn't seem fazed and turned back to the teenager sitting behind the desk. "They're going to be joining me in the River Cabin."

The older girl didn't even blink at the request. Instead, she checked off their names and then smiled up at Elle.

"Have you picked a name for your cabin team yet?" She leaned over the table as if eager to hear the answer.

Elle turned toward the four of them and tilted her head, as if thinking. Then she snapped her fingers and turned back to Carrie. "Wildflowers."

Zoey had to admit it was a good name. She hadn't thought Elle had it in her to find a perfect name for the five of them. The girls were all so different, yet looking across their faces, she was easily reminded of the flowers her father had given her mother for her last birthday. Uniqueness had its own beauty.

"I love it." Carrie chuckled. "Okay, you're all set." She wrote something down. "Go ahead, you know what comes next." She motioned Elle aside.

"Thanks." Elle picked up one of Hannah's bags. The fact that Hannah had three of them, to Zoey's and Scarlett's one bag each, confirmed the "princess" title.

"This way. We'll go drop off your stuff at the cabin, then meet up there." She nodded to a large field. Zoey thought of the softball fields with yearning. But this field didn't have any lines; instead, on one side there were wooden bleachers, and each end had wooden walkways around the green grass.

"That's where the campers meet up every morning before breakfast and events," Elle said as they walked down the pathway. "That's the main building. My grandpa lives on the top floor when he's here during the summers. He started River Camp back when my mother was my age."

Scar was lagging, and Zoey reached over to take her heavier bag so that she could catch up. She estimated the other four girls were closer to her age, eleven, while her sister had just turned nine. However, Scarlett was still taller than Hannah, but Hannah wasn't having a tough time keeping up with Elle's longer legs.

"That's the cafeteria." Elle pointed to a larger wooden-sided building. "The boathouse is down to the right. The horse barn is down toward the left. The main swimming pool is back there." She turned back around and motioned to the wood cafeteria. "There's a swimming pool house, so you can change and shower there instead of walking around in your swimsuit." She turned again, and Zoey thought that Elle was actually enjoying acting like a stewardess, waving her arms around and talking about the camp as if she had built the place herself. "All of the cabins are this way." She motioned toward another pathway. "There's twenty of them. Most of them will have at least ten girls, but I took the smaller one for us." She smiled. "It's the best one, closest to the water."

"Are there alligators in that?" Aubrey asked quietly from behind them. She pointed toward the water.

The entire group stopped and turned toward her. Aubrey's gaze homed in on the water beyond them. Then, as one, the rest of them turned to look out at the almost clear surface.

Zoey loved the water. Ever since her uncle had taken the family sailing one summer, she'd dreamed of learning herself one day. But with her father being busy all the time and her mother focusing on keeping the marriage together, she'd never gotten the chance.

"I guess so, but I've never seen one." Elle leaned closer. "Sharks too, I suppose." She started walking again. "They pretty much leave you alone—my grandpa says that they are more afraid of us than we are of them. Although, I had heard that someone living nearby lost a dog once—a gator got to it. Ten cabins are over there, and ten down this pathway."

Zoey stopped. "I thought you said we were going to our cabin. If they are all that way . . ." She tilted her head toward the paths that Elle had just pointed out.

Elle's smile grew. "The *other* cabins are that way. Ours is this way." She motioned. "Come on. Trust me."

Zoey looked down at Scar, who returned her glance, her eyes filled with curiosity. They all followed Elle as she continued to talk about the camp and her grandfather. The path narrowed slightly, then opened up to a clearing. A small river flowed from there into the larger bay. A small wood cabin painted a soft green sat on the edge of the water with a large deck that hung over the edge of the stream. Its tall pointed roof was accented with large glass windows that overlooked the water. Chairs hugged a gas firepit on the deck.

"This was my grandfather's first home. He lived here for almost a full year with my mom while the camp was being built." Elle smiled at them. "It's my favorite place in the entire world." She sighed.

Zoey set the bags down and looked around. She was in love. She had never expected to have anything in common with Elle, yet here they were, standing on a dirt trail, looking at a cabin in the middle of the forest as if it were the best place on earth.

When her mother had mentioned that they were going to be stuck in a camp for a full month, Zoey hadn't imagined she'd get so lucky as to stay in a place with girls like this. Maybe her summer wasn't going to be as bad as she'd thought after all.

CHAPTER
ONE

Ten years later . . .

Zoey hobbled off the plane with one crutch under her arm while she shifted her backpack onto her shoulder; she gripped the other crutch so she wouldn't fall flat on her face.

Having a torn ACL was no joke. Still, her injury wasn't as bad as it could have been. She held in a curse; she hated that the stupid saying was the first thing that came to mind when she thought of her pain. Sure, it could have been worse—death, dismemberment, or even going through a surgery would have been worse. But the tear had cost her the spot on her softball team. A team that had gone on to win the gold in Rio de Janeiro while she'd sat in the bleachers and cheered them on.

Stupid knee, she thought as she made her way down the stairs of the small plane.

A wall of moisture in the air hit her hard and fast; then the warmth of the sun broke through, which had her turning her face up to the sky and taking a deep breath. She loved the feeling of it.

"Zoey!" She heard her name and looked down in time to see a blonde mass of hair fly in her direction.

"Elle." She smiled and allowed her friend to wrap her arms around her.

"You're here," Elle cried and held on. "Finally!"

She allowed herself to enjoy the feeling of holding her friend again for a moment. Then stepped back. "Wow, you look amazing."

"Thanks, you look . . ." Elle's blue eyes flicked to her knee. "Like you're hurting." She reached over and took her bag. "Scar is already here."

"Yeah, she texted me." Zoey slowly followed Elle to the waiting car across the open cement lot. "Is everyone else here yet?"

"Hannah arrived yesterday; Aubrey is coming in later tonight," Elle answered as she tossed her bags into the trunk of the car.

"I'm sorry about your grandfather." She stopped Elle from getting into the car.

Her friend's gaze dimmed as tears threatened to fall. "Don't make me cry."

"No." She shook her head and, holding her crutches in one hand, touched Elle's shoulder, then hugged her again when Elle moved closer. She heard her sniffle, and for a moment, she let the memories of one of the kindest men in her life surface.

That first summer, long ago, she'd grown very fond of Elle's grandfather, or Grandpa Joe, as he'd liked to be called. He'd taken Zoey under his wing and had taught her everything she'd wanted to know about sailing that first year.

She'd spent more time on the water that summer—and many more after that, thanks to the old man—than she'd spent dreaming about missing softball.

"How are you dealing with everything?" Zoey asked after she got into the passenger side of the SUV, and Elle climbed in behind the wheel.

She took a deep breath. "I'm dealing." Elle sighed. "He was ninety-eight. We all knew it was going to be soon. Still . . ." She rolled her shoulders. "It's hard. He was like a father to me."

Zoey nodded, remembering the first time she'd met Elle's grandfather. The man had been tall—taller than even Zoey's father—but where her father had been stocky and his build had run to fat, Grandpa Joe had been lean. He'd had a white goatee and a full head of matching white hair that he'd sometimes kept in a ponytail. She'd instantly liked the older man and had seen the love and connection between grandfather and granddaughter.

In the past ten years, she'd seen him more than a dozen times. Each visit she'd grown fonder of him, and they had spent most of their time together on the water. It was all thanks to that man that her love for water matched her love for playing softball.

It was strange: That summer long ago, she'd never imagined that she'd stay in constant contact with the other girls, the other Wildflowers, as they called themselves. Especially since at first glance, none of them had had anything in common with one another, but by the end of the summer, they'd realized they were going to be friends for life.

Elle's name had fit perfectly for the five of them. They had been a group of wildflowers—girls from separate groups mixed together. The fact that they had connected so perfectly together had shocked all of them. But they had, and they had stayed best friends ever since.

They'd even returned to the camp the following three years. Once they were all too old to attend officially, they'd become camp counselors every summer until the camp had closed four years ago.

After the camp had been shut down, they had spent a week together each summer in the Pelican Point home that Elle's grandfather had bought in town so that Elle could have a stable home away from the camp.

The last trip the Wildflowers had taken together had been two years ago, when they had traveled to Cabo for a week of fun.

"I'm so sorry." Zoey reached over and touched Elle's hand.

Elle nodded and then sighed as she pulled out of the small airport and headed toward the small town of Pelican Point, Florida, population about five hundred. Elle had called it home ever since her grandfather had grown sick earlier that year, moving back from her short stay in Colorado.

"Do you miss the city?" Zoey asked, looking out at the green trees that lined the road.

"No." Elle smiled. "I had grown tired of it all, after breaking things off with Jeff." The fact that her friend still said her ex-fiancé's name with a groan told Zoey everything she needed to know.

At first, the other Wildflowers had been concerned that Elle would fall for her ex's same tricks this time. Her grandfather getting sick had been a blessing at first. Getting Elle out of Denver had been a necessity. She'd met Jeff, a lawyer from Denver, almost two years ago. When Elle had packed up and followed him to Denver, everyone had been concerned. Especially when she had canceled last year's planned trip together. She'd claimed Jeff had needed her to help on a big case, but the rest of them knew that the man had been secretly controlling her, urging her away from the love and support of her friends.

Now as Zoey ran her eyes over Elle, she could see that her old friend had finally returned to her normal self. "I'm glad," she said. "He wasn't right for you."

Elle laughed. "So far, I haven't found one who is." She sighed, then glanced over at her friend. "What about you? I saw a picture in some magazine of you and—"

Zoey groaned. "Stop!" She held up her hand, causing Elle to shut her mouth. "No, Roger is just a friend."

Elle's blonde eyebrows rose. "Are you sure, because that image looked . . . heated."

"He was helping me." She nodded to her leg. "I tripped on the corner of the rug." She closed her eyes and remembered bumping into one of her idols and having the man's arms wrap around her when he caught her. The fact that the man was one of the sexiest athletes in the world, and one Zoey had a major crush on, hadn't helped.

"Roger Holloway is . . ."

"Freaking amazing?" she finished. The man was a god in baseball. Of course, he was on the cover of Wheaties boxes as well as most major sports magazines. Meeting him when she'd been in Brazil had been the ultimate—that was, until she'd embarrassed herself by falling at his feet.

He had surprised her by knowing her name. Then amazed her even further by telling her that he had been sorry when she'd gotten injured and that he hoped she would make a quick recovery.

She hadn't realized someone had snapped a picture of the two of them, but she'd been thankful. That was, until the gossip had turned toward them having an affair. She knew that Roger's wife of almost four years was pregnant with their first child. Besides, Zoey was no Jezebel.

"And married," she finished off. "You know how I feel about home-wreckers."

"I know." It was Elle's turn to touch her hand. "How is your mother?" she asked as they drove through the small town of Pelican Point.

"The same," she sighed. "Scar's been living with her while I've been overseas."

"They're still in Jacksonville?" Elle asked.

"Yeah." Zoey rolled her shoulders, thinking about the loss of income she was now dealing with. She'd been hoping for the extra boost that the Olympics would give her career. All those advertising opportunities that her agent had lined up for her—if she'd been on the team when they had won—were now gone.

Elle seemed to catch on to her thoughts. "What will you do now?"

"I'm not sure," she said softly, looking out the window. "We were hoping to move Mom out of Jacksonville. It's not good for her there. Too expensive."

"Scarlett told me a little over lunch. But you know your sister . . ." Elle slowed the car down.

"Yeah." She smiled. "She only tells you the positive things."

"You two make a perfect balance," Elle added as she turned off the main highway and into the small town.

"You're staying in town?" Zoey asked.

"Yes, since Grandad shut down the camp, he moved us full time into the house here." She nodded to a large classic two-story home on the main street of town.

Elle's family had pretty much owned everything in Pelican Point. The town sat to the east of Pelican Bay, just off the Emerald Coast of Florida.

River Camp was a ten-minute drive along the water's edge and sat on the end of a small inlet, with one side facing the Gulf Coast and the other toward the bay.

Elle shut off the car and turned toward her. "Since my mother . . ." She held in the words, and Zoey took her hand. "Grandpa Joe was the only family I had."

"You have us now." Zoey smiled and pulled her into a hug as Elle's tears fell. She felt her own join her friend's.

A knock on the car window had them both jumping and laughing. Scar stood outside Zoey's door.

"Are you two okay in there?" Her sister reached for the door handle.

"Yes," Zoey said when she opened the door. Her sister stepped in and hugged her before she could get out.

"I'm so sorry about your injury," she whispered in her ear.

Zoey felt more tears threaten but sucked them in. "I'm okay," she assured her. "It's just a tear, and it was totally my fault." She tried not to rehash that night she'd disobeyed her coach and the rules, which had cost her everything.

"Yes, but it took the win from you." Her sister's eyes met hers.

"There's always four years from now." She smiled. "Help me with my pack." She motioned to her bag.

Scar took the bag and followed her into the house. She needed help getting up the stairs on the large front porch. That she couldn't climb four steps made her feel even worse.

The Wildflowers had spent a week each summer for four years in this house. As well as spending almost a full month together the year the four of them had graduated high school. Scar hadn't been able to attend that year, since she'd been in school for another two weeks, but the house was well known to Zoey. It was strange, walking into the place and knowing Elle's grandfather wouldn't be sitting in the old leather chair or standing at the stove, cooking one of his famous meals.

More memories of her time with Grandpa Joe surfaced. He had been a whiz in the kitchen. She'd never met a man who could cook before him.

Then she saw Hannah at the base of the stairs. She hadn't changed much; she was still petite and still a princess. Her long hair had darkened a few shades, but she still wore expensive clothes that Zoey wished she could fit into.

Hannah smiled and rushed forward to give her a hug as she entered the living room. "How's the knee?"

"Sore, but I'm here." She sighed.

"I know," her friend said, pulling back from the hug. "The place feels empty."

Zoey wrapped her arm around Hannah's tiny waist and glanced around the room. The four of them stood inside the living room, looking around.

"Remember the time he decided to teach us how to cook his famous chili?" Hannah said with a chuckle.

"You blew up the stove," Elle added, and everyone smiled.

"He went in his sleep?" Zoey asked, turning back to Elle.

"Yes," she said softly. "We had a perfect night before. I took him to the camp; we watched the sunset from the car. He told me the story of how he'd met Karin, my grandmother."

Zoey moved over to sit on the edge of the sofa while everyone else found a place to sit. Scar left her bag at the base of the stairs and sat next to her.

"And?" Hannah asked. "Go on."

Elle filled them in on how her grandparents had met and fallen in love. Then how her grandmother had died a few years after her mother had been born.

Elle had lost her mother shortly before they had met her at camp that first summer. She'd moved in to live with her grandfather full time that summer before they had all met.

"What about you?" Zoey turned to Hannah. "How are your parents?"

Hannah groaned and leaned back in the chair to prop her feet up on the sturdy coffee table. "The same."

Zoey hadn't been far off when she'd gauged Hannah as a princess that first day years ago. But instead of the spoiled princess that Zoey had pegged her as, she'd been the princess trapped in the tall tower by her evil parents—more like Princess Fiona in *Shrek* than Princess Jasmine from *Aladdin*.

"Do they still expect you to date only their picks?" Scar asked.

Hannah rolled her eyes. "They had a date set up for me tomorrow night. One of Dad's clients." She shivered. "They demand I live life the way they planned for me to. It's just one more way for them to control me. The last one they expected me to go out with was my father's age."

"Yuck," the three of them said together.

"When does Aubrey get here?" Scarlett asked.

Elle glanced down at her watch. "Soon. Her flight from NYC was delayed." She stood up. "How about we start cooking dinner and open some wine?"

Everyone jumped up, except Zoey. "I'll sit this one out. My meds don't mix with alcohol, and my leg won't let me stand for too long."

"Go and sit at the bar. You can supervise." Elle helped her up. "I've got soda as well." She ushered her to the bar top, then retrieved a Dr Pepper from the fridge and set it in front of her.

For the next hour, Zoey watched the women, her friends, the Wildflowers, work around the kitchen like chefs in one of the top restaurants in New York, gliding around one another perfectly as each one worked on her own task.

When a knock sounded and the front door opened, Elle called a welcome. Excitement filled the room as Aubrey joined them.

What had once been a skinny girl with too-long legs, porcelain skin, and flyaway frizzy red hair had turned into easily the prettiest of the five of them. Aubrey's red hair had tamed and turned a deeper shade, but her porcelain skin was still accented by mesmerizing crystal-blue eyes.

Not that the others weren't pretty; Elle still was tall, blonde, and busty enough to catch every man's attention—as would Hannah, the petite princess, with her blonde locks framing her face in perfect ringlets.

As Aubrey joined the others to finish up the meal preparations, Zoey watched them all closely. Her sister, Scarlett, who was the youngest of them at nineteen, had been graced with what Zoey thought of as all the best genes. Not only was she taller than Zoey, but Scar's lips were fuller and her eyes bigger and a lighter shade of brown, making them almost look amber. Only Scarlett's hair was the same as Zoey's—the Rowlett curse of wild hair they had inherited from their mother, whose hair had in the past years turned a beautiful shade of silver.

Aubrey filled everyone in on the latest news from her world while they finished dinner preparation. She was working in New York at a desk job that she hated but needed in order to pay the high rent of the very small apartment she kept so she could live close to her father and to pursue her love of all things art. Of the five of them, Aubrey was the only one with real talent for art. There were several of her paintings hanging up in the house.

Aubrey's father was one of the wealthiest men alive, but since Aubrey was illegitimate—the result of the much-older man seducing Aubrey's barely legal artist mother—her father had only cared for Aubrey while her mother was alive. She'd died shortly after Aubrey had turned eight, after which the man had started taking over her life.

However, now that Aubrey was a young woman and legally no longer his responsibility, her father had cut her off. Aubrey had fended for herself for the past few years.

"It's not like I want handouts," Aubrey said, sipping her second glass of wine. "Actually, it's quite the opposite. I hated when he took over my life. I was like a prisoner after Mom died." She shivered visibly and took another sip of wine.

They were sitting around the kitchen table, the grilled salmon all but vanished from each of their plates. Just like the food from the rest of the dishes on the table. The wine, however, had been refilled, as another bottle or two had been opened.

"I remember: he controlled your every move," Hannah said, "down to what you wore. Even my parents aren't that bad." She tucked her legs underneath herself on the chair.

Zoey silently wished to be able to move her knee that easily again. A stool held her poor leg out away from the table with an ice pack over it.

"So, I work." Aubrey waved her wine glass. "I go to school."

"You're still taking art classes?" Zoey asked.

"When I can afford them."

"What about the inheritance you received when you turned twenty?" Elle asked.

"I still have it. It's for emergencies only. It would only cover my rent and life for a couple months if anything happened to me." Aubrey frowned. "I dug into it for this trip, though."

Elle's eyes turned toward Zoey. "And yours?"

"My . . ." She had to think about it. "You mean the money our no-good father was forced to give us by the courts when he left our mother for a woman half her age?"

Scarlett stiffened, causing Zoey to take a calming breath.

"We still have it," Scarlett answered for her. "It's in a joint account, along with what money our grandparents left us when they passed. We've been using it to fix up our mother's place and get it ready to sell."

"She's moving? You're moving?" Hannah sat up straighter.

"We're thinking about it," Zoey added. She'd run the numbers over in her head on the long flight back to the States. Now, with her injury, there was no way she'd be able to go back to work at the sports center she'd been employed at for the past few years. She had been working part time with the director of teen sports before the Olympic tryouts. She'd quit when she'd made the team, since she would have to travel a lot. She had been in charge of everything from softball to volleyball to gymnastics. She loved her work, but with the injury . . . she glanced down at her swollen knee, which was frozen under the ice pack. Surely Brian, the owner of the center, would hire her back if she asked him?

Her sister was working at a local dance studio as well as at a local stable, where she exercised the animals and taught disabled kids to ride. With Zoey's busy Olympic schedule, Scarlett had filled in the hours by helping their mother a lot around the house and fixing things up around the older home she'd purchased after the messy divorce.

"Where would you go?" Elle asked, biting her bottom lip.

"Somewhere cheaper," Zoey answered quickly.

The room fell silent for a moment. "Let's clean up and move into the living room," Elle suggested as she stood up, then glanced down at her watch. "Actually, scratch that. I have a better idea. Why don't we leave this mess for tomorrow and head over to the camp? The main swimming pool is still in working order. We can take a dip and watch the sun set."

Zoey looked down at her leg and thought about taking off the brace and enjoying a swim.

"I'm in." She stood up and grabbed her crutches.

Less than half an hour later, she was floating in the chilled water while everyone else swam around her. Taking turns diving into the water or doing backflips.

Two empty bottles of wine sat on the edge, while a third was being passed around. Since Zoey wasn't able to drink, she was the designated driver. She'd been thankful it had been her left knee, so she wouldn't have to be chauffeured around until she healed.

It was fun to watch her friends and sister joke with one another as the wine flowed.

Somehow, they had all decided to forgo the swimsuits, and she didn't mind. Floating in the water naked somehow put her more at ease than wearing the one-piece swimsuit she'd packed. It was the most relaxing thing she'd done since before she'd hurt her knee.

The last time the five of them had gone skinny-dipping, they had almost been caught and had to scramble to cover themselves. This time was different; there wasn't a soul around the massive campground. Not to mention that the five of them were way more comfortable with their bodies than before.

"Are you still seeing that mechanic?" Zoey asked Hannah.

Hannah frowned and kicked her legs to keep her head above the water. "No, he was a cheater."

"Who would he cheat on? I mean, with a body like yours?" Elle broke in and shook her head, her wet, long blonde hair falling in her eyes. "Stupid man."

Zoey grinned. "I agree. You easily have the best ass in the pool."

"Hey! No, she doesn't," Aubrey said from the shallow end. "Do you know how many squats and lunges I have done over the years to get this ass?" Aubrey stood up and did a quick turn, then shivered and ducked back under the water.

"And it is a beautiful ass. Thank you so much for sharing." Zoey laughed.

Aubrey chuckled and splashed water at her.

"What about you?" Hannah turned to Elle.

"I'm not showing you my ass, pervert." Elle laughed too.

Zoey smiled and changed the subject now that Elle was light-hearted. "Why did you break things off with Jeff? I thought he was the one. I mean, he proposed and everything." She'd been dying to get more details on the breakup.

Elle glanced around as the five of them drew together in a tight circle, each one kicking to keep her head above the deep water.

"He turned out to be a jerk." Elle shrugged.

"Nope." Zoey shook her head. "Wildflowers don't keep secrets. Spill."

Elle sighed, then swam over so her feet could at least reach the bottom. "We got into a fight about how much time I was spending with Grandpa Joe."

"And?" Scarlett asked as they all moved to shallower water.

Zoey sat on the stairs, propping her leg up on the side of the pool. Elle moved over next to her, tucking her legs up to her chest.

"I caught him slipping his number to our waitress one night," Elle finally said. "She dropped the napkin, and I picked it up and saw his number on it."

"What an ass," Scarlett said easily.

"What is wrong with him?" Zoey asked, getting everyone's attention. "What? We've all been jealous of Elle's boobs since the day we met. I mean, what eleven-year-old has a rack? Then you went and grew them bigger. I swear, I followed you around one summer, eating and doing everything you did, just to see if you had some sort of magic formula to make them grow. It's unnatural." She nodded to Elle, who chuckled.

"Maybe it wasn't about the size of my boobs?" Elle said, a hint of sadness entering her voice.

"Jeff was a jerk. I never did like him. His eyes were too close together. Your babies would have looked cross-eyed."

Elle laughed. "Thank you." She smiled, and Zoey watched her wipe a tear away from her eyes. "I really thought he was the one."

"When you find him," Aubrey said, moving closer, "when we each find our own Mr. Right, we'll all know."

"And if any of us don't agree"—Zoey put her hand in the middle of them, letting it float on top of the water—"we each promise to not keep it to ourselves. Wildflowers first."

"Wildflowers first," they each said, placing their hands over hers.

They all smiled at one another.

"I'm going to miss this place," Zoey said out of the blue.

"What is going to happen to the camp?" Hannah asked, glancing around.

Most of the buildings were in major disrepair; the other swimming pool had been drained, and all the horses must have been moved or sold, because the massive barn sat empty. Even the boats and other watercraft had been sold off over the past few years or were in such a state that they would probably sink immediately if ever put back in the water.

Elle swam toward her. Earlier she'd done a fine cannonball, and she and Scarlett had taken turns doing flips off the diving board.

Now, all of them sat along the stairs or hung along the wall of the shallow end as the dark water around them stilled.

"That's kind of why I wanted us to be here." Elle glanced around, then nodded toward the sunset. "Remember our first night together here?"

"She's changing the subject," Zoey muttered. "That's never a good sign."

Elle chuckled nervously.

"We almost got caught naked in this very pool," Scarlett replied.

"Who's going to come around now and catch us?" Zoey said, motioning.

Elle looked around, and Zoey could see the sadness in her eyes, even in the darkness.

It was too dark to see much, since the sky was filled with the aftermath of a beautiful sunset and the pool lights were no longer powered.

"You're still stalling," Zoey said when it grew quiet again. She was worried that Elle had bad news; after all, her friend wasn't a "rip the Band-Aid off quickly" kind of person.

"What do you think of opening the camp again?" Elle finally blurted out.

"What?" Four voices rang out at the same time, causing an echo to bounce off the pool house's walls.

"You're going to open the camp back up to young girls?" Scarlett asked.

"N . . . no." Elle shook her head and scanned her friends' faces. "I'm thinking of turning it into a camp for adults. You know . . . snowbirds, retired couples. So, it would be open year round, not just in the summer."

Everyone was silent; the sound of crickets and frogs singing filled the night instead.

"Well?" Elle finally said. "Any thoughts?"

"You want to sink a bunch of money into this"—Zoey motioned around them—"what was once a summer camp for privileged girls, and turn it into a . . ."

"Getaway camp," Elle said with a smile as her chin rose slightly.

Again, the night grew silent.

"The land alone is probably worth a fortune in today's market," Hannah suggested. "You could always sell it?"

"I know, but I just can't see myself getting rid of it. Besides, Grandpa Joe wouldn't want that." Elle sighed.

"Would they all pile in ten people to a cabin?" Aubrey asked.

"Sounds more like a swingers' camp," Zoey added with a chuckle, trying to break the tension. "Isn't there one of those in South Florida?"

"No." Elle shook her head and rolled her eyes at Zoey. "I've been working with a local handyman, Aiden Stark. Grandpa Joe hired him a while back to fix up some things around here. He turned out to be an architecture student too and has a few great ideas about turning each cabin from sleeping ten preteen girls into housing one couple with their own bathroom and small kitchenette." Her voice grew with excitement. "Then, we'll turn the old dining hall into a game or sports room with a bar and grill off the back patio. We'll add a screening room for movies and turn the old meeting rooms in the main building into a formal restaurant-style dining room with the back patio for outside dining." She took a breath after her huge list and then sighed. "There's more, but"—she paused—"I can see I'm overwhelming you guys."

"So twenty couples, then? How will you make your money back? Charge them an arm and a leg per night? It will take forever to make any real money," Hannah pointed out.

"With the initial investment, Aiden can have more cabins built before opening day, so that we'd have thirty cabins to begin with. Then, if everything goes well, we'll keep building more. We have plenty of land," Elle said.

"We?" Zoey had picked up on the moment Elle had changed from *I* to *we*.

Elle swallowed and wrapped her arms around herself. "I was hoping, that is—"

"I'm in." Aubrey shocked everyone by jumping in. She'd even raised her hand, and when everyone looked at her, she tilted her head. "What? It beats freezing my ass off in New York. Besides, I've grown to hate that Big Stupid Rotten Apple." She chuckled and turned to Elle. "That is what you were stumbling toward, right?"

Elle nodded and looked around. "I crunched some numbers. If I'm correct, with all of us, we have just enough to open the doors of River

Camp next fall. With the money Grandpa Joe left me, plus another sixty thousand—"

"Sixty!" Zoey gasped.

"Twenty each—I figured you and Scarlett would split it, since I know . . ." She trailed off and shook her head. "What was left to you. I'll be throwing everything I have into it."

Zoey glanced over at Scarlett as she calculated.

"What about our mother? Can she stay at our old cabin?" Zoey asked.

"Yes." Elle smiled. "I had counted on that."

"What about us? Where are we expected to live?" Aubrey asked.

"The entire third floor of the main building where my grandpa Joe lived has enough rooms for all of us. The second floor would be updated with rooms for any employees who need to stay on campus."

"Other employees?" Scarlett asked.

"We'll need some help, and I figured most of them would be like us, also needing a place to stay. There are apartments in Pelican Point, but not near enough for the number of people I'm thinking we'll need. Most will drive in from other towns, since I plan on hiring local first, but—"

"With adults in the cabins, there's no need for camp counselors who stay in each cabin too," Hannah said softly.

"Adults are easier than kids." Elle smiled. "My main reason for the change. Anyway, the counselors, employees, and any others that want to stay during the week will all be housed in the main building along with us. There's plenty of room, even if we have to take up some of the first floor."

"I'm in," Hannah said, gaining everyone's attention. "Like Aubrey said, it beats what I have planned. Besides, I can't wait to see the look on my parents' faces when I tell them." Hannah's smile grew.

Elle's eyes turned toward Zoey, who said, "We were going to sell our mother's place anyway. Then we'll have to see if she is okay with moving here . . ." She flicked a look at Scarlett. "Well, what do you think?"

Her sister shrugged. "You've been in charge of all of this. I trust your judgment."

Zoey closed her eyes and mentally counted how much money was left in their joint savings account. By the time she opened her eyes, the last slivers of the sun's rays had disappeared over the water, leaving them in total darkness.

Her knee pain was minimal at this point; the cool water had alleviated some of the swelling, relieving her mind of the overwhelming pain, so she could work on calculations instead of focusing on the aches.

Deciding quickly before she could come to her senses, she blurted out, "Why the hell not—count us in."

CHAPTER
TWO

Over a year later . . .

Zoey stood and watched as an older silver truck stopped at the bottom of the stairs near the main building. She squinted her eyes from the bright sunlight overhead to see who was in it and watched not one but three almost identical men step out of the vehicle.

All of them were tall and dark haired and as muscular as Chris Hemsworth. Zoey took a deep breath and appreciated them for a moment as they walked toward her.

"Hi," the tallest of the three said. It was hard to tell at this point, but she imagined he was the eldest as well.

"Evening." She dropped her hand from shielding the sunlight, since they had stepped into the shade.

"Are you Elle Saunders?" the taller one said. There was no doubt, looking at the three of them, that they were brothers: they were all tall and curly haired, with deep-brown eyes and olive skin.

"No, Elle ran into town for a few supplies. Is there something I can help you men with?"

"We hope so. I'm Owen—these are my brothers, Dylan and Liam. We heard you are looking for workers?" he said as his eyes took in the freshly painted building behind her.

Zoey nodded quickly. "Yes." She'd helped Elle and a handful of others paint the massive building. So far, they had hired almost three full-time employees: head chef Isaac Andrew, head waiter Kevin, and full-time front desk manager Julie. There were also a few part-time employees who would fill multiple roles around the camp. They were still looking for employees to fill the camp-counselor role as well as others around the place. Employees who would oversee activities and keep guests entertained with fun events that they had planned.

She was officially filling the sports-coordinator role, while Elle had taken over as camp manager. Hannah had taken on the events-coordinator spot, Scarlett was going to help Zoey out with the athletics and equestrian events, and Aubrey had ended up being the director of counselors.

"You'll want to talk to Aubrey—she's the director of counselors." She started to motion to where they could find Aubrey but stopped when Dylan, the man with the widest chest, stepped forward and spoke.

"We have plenty of other skills. I'm sure there's plenty else we can do around here." His dark eyes scanned hers, and she felt her entire body heat. It was the way he was looking at her that stirred something deep inside her.

His hair was cut the shortest of the three, and she detected streaks of blonde. She doubted he'd had it bleached, since it appeared natural— too much time in the sun. Kind of like her own hair was at the moment. He had skin a shade darker than the other two as well, hinting that he spent more of his time outdoors than his brothers did.

She had been in the process of heading down toward the stables to take an early-evening ride on Duke, one of the horses they had gotten over the last year from a rescue facility nearby for the stables.

She and Scarlett had overseen the acquisition of each adopted animal to make sure they were of the right temperament. Elle had asked Carter, the official vet at the Alaqua Animal Refuge, to stop by a few times each day and act as caregiver to the beasts. Scarlett would fill the full-time role of caregiver once they officially moved their mother in to the small cabin on site. Carter had assured her that all the animals were perfectly fit, but Zoey liked having the excuse to ride them each night while she still could, before the guests started arriving.

The place was already booked solid for the first three months after they opened their doors. The handful of ads that Elle had running in travel magazines and websites had obviously done their job. There were a few articles about their background that had drawn a lot of hype.

"I'm sure Aubrey can . . ." She had started to wave them off when her walkie-talkie bleated.

"Zoey, whoever they are, deal with them. I'm stuck helping Hannah for the next hour," Aubrey's voice squawked over the radio.

Zoey held in a groan and gave up the thoughts of a peaceful ride before nightfall.

"Come on this way." She motioned toward the front door and glanced up at the windows on the third floor of the building. She thought she saw Aubrey and Hannah duck behind the curtains in one of the private rooms they all shared. The top floor used to be a private residence for Elle's grandfather, so there hadn't been the need to change much for the girls to take over up there. They had all moved in shortly after that first night, with the exception of Scarlett, who had gone back to finish helping their mother fix up the house and sell it. Zoey was excited that they had a buyer for the house, but it wouldn't close until the end of next month. But after waiting this long to sell her mother's place, the monthlong wait seemed doable.

The three men followed her back into the main lobby area, where Julie, their newly hired front desk manager, stood behind the counter-top working on the computer system that would check guests in.

Zoey noticed that Julie's eyes followed the men closely as they all walked toward the back office that she shared with Scarlett and Aubrey. Hannah, being the events coordinator, had her own smaller office, which was filled with items for events. Elle had a larger office at the end of the hallway, since she often had meetings and interviews to conduct.

"What kind of work are you three looking for exactly?" she asked, shutting the door behind them.

They exchanged glances. "Well, anything you have," Owen, the oldest, said.

"You're in luck—right now, we're looking for a bit of everything." She sat down and pulled out three standard job applications from the drawer.

"Sounds right up our alley." Owen smiled at her. "I think between the three of us, you can fill whatever jobs you need."

She ran her eyes over the three of them and, deciding that was probably true, stood up.

"We'll need each of you to fill out an application." She handed each a form. "I'll be right back." She knew it would take them a while to fill out everything, and she needed to tell Carter that she wouldn't make her planned afternoon ride. She wanted to make sure that he'd let Duke run free in the paddock instead, since the horse needed his exercise.

She shut the office door behind her and walked back to the main desk to use the phone there.

"Spill." Julie leaned on the counter, her dark wavy hair brushing her cheeks, and nodded toward the hallway behind Zoey.

Zoey had liked the shorter Hawaiian woman instantly upon meet-ing her. She had a sunny personality and was very organized, which was a must in the position she had filled.

"They're applying for work." Zoey shrugged.

"I thought we'd been invaded by the Hemsworth brothers . . . may I say, yum. You should hire them." She winked.

Zoey glanced down the hallway. "If they pass the standard background checks." She turned back to Julie. "Can you call Carter and tell him I won't be able to make my evening ride with Duke?"

Julie nodded. "Sure. Oh"—she snapped her fingers—"I almost forgot. You have a message from your father." Julie handed her a note, which Zoey shoved quickly in her back pocket. If only she could forget the note as quickly—she'd been avoiding him for the past few days.

For over five years her father hadn't spoken to either her or Scar. Now suddenly, the man was calling her every other day. Each message only read, Urgent, please call, and left his number. How had he gotten this number? She hadn't told anyone what they were up to, other than their mother, of course.

Rubbing her forehead, she desperately wished for that relaxing time she could have had riding Duke. Instead, she had three dangerously handsome hunks to deal with. She was reaching for the door handle of the office but paused when she heard whispers coming from inside.

As she leaned her head against the doorframe, she strained to hear what they were talking about.

She heard Elle's name a few times and the words "Get close to her" before she opened the door. Instantly, the three men glanced up and acted as if they were filling out the paperwork instead of talking about Zoey's best friend.

"Done?" she asked, scanning each of the men for any signs of discomfort. Seeing none, she narrowed her eyes and walked over to them.

"Yes." The one who'd caused her body to react stood up and held out his form. "Dylan," he reminded her and pointed to his chest as he smiled at her. "You are?"

She took his paper and scanned it quickly. "I'm Zoey. *Dylan Rhodes*," she read aloud. "What made you three come down here from Destin?"

"Jobs," the three men said together. His brothers handed her their paperwork.

"So, any unique skills you have that would help out?"

Liam had longer hair than the other two brothers, and Zoey was pretty sure he was the youngest of the three. He stepped forward. "I'm great with crafts. Give me some wood, nails, and a saw, and I can build anything. I'm also pretty handy with mixing drinks."

"Okay." She wrote a note on his application, knowing that they needed a part-time bartender. Right now, they had their eyes on someone, but she had a full-time job that paid a lot more than they could afford. "You?" She turned to the tallest one.

"Owen," he said; then his smile changed. "I have a strong head for business. I've added a few office references on my application, but I also worked as a waiter for a summer back in high school." The serious tone had her determined to watch him closely.

"I've done everything from zip-lining to solo parachuting." Dylan spoke up. "Anything outdoors and sports related, I'm into it."

"Thrill seeker?" she asked.

"You could say that." He shrugged. "I've also spent a summer working a zip line in Brazil."

She thought about this as her gaze ran over him. She'd been planning on taking on the zip lines herself, but if they hired him, it would open her days up to fill in at other places. "We've been looking for someone to take control of the zip line we had built. We have two runs: a beginner run and a more expert one."

"Sounds like I'm just the man you've been looking for." His smile almost knocked her on her ass.

She quickly turned around and sat down behind her desk before her knees shook and betrayed what just one look from Dylan was doing to her. *Damn,* she thought. Going an entire year without sex hadn't been a clever idea. She'd believed that putting all her energy into the camp was the best plan. Not that she'd had men knocking down her door, but still, she'd turned a few away in her attempt to stay focused.

"We'll run a quick background check online and call some of your references," she started, then glanced up at the trio. "Are you staying in town?"

"No, we're driving back to Destin tonight. If we get the jobs . . ." Owen's voice trailed off as if it were a question.

"There's available housing on site," she said. "Or apartments in town; take your pick. The employee rooms are on the second floor; you're welcome to one—that is, if you three don't mind sharing a room while you're here?"

"Sounds perfect." Dylan stepped forward. "We'd like a look around if possible?" His eyes scanned hers. "If you have the time."

She was in the process of waiting for the computer to boot up, since she was determined to run the background checks now, but the way his gaze tracked her had her shutting it down. She tucked their applications into the top drawer and locked it after deciding she could use a walk.

"Sure." She stood back up and prayed that her legs would hold her as she tried to avoid Dylan's focus.

"You're Zoey?" Dylan asked as she opened the office door.

"Zoey Rowlett," she answered over her shoulder.

"I thought so." Dylan fell in step with her. "Zoey Rowlett, pitcher for the Florida Gators." His smile grew, and for a moment, she thought admiration flashed behind those big brown eyes of his.

"Yes." She held in a sigh.

"I followed your career," he said, his brothers falling behind them as they exited the back doors of the building and stepped out onto the back patio. "I'm sorry you couldn't play in the Olympics. How is the knee?"

"Better." Wanting to change the subject quickly, she addressed the others. "We've stopped in the outdoor dining area. Through those french doors is the main dining hall. All meals will be served here. Each cabin has a small kitchenette, but for insurance purposes, only microwaves are allowed. Guests will enjoy some of the best food prepared by our very own four-star chef, Isaac Andrew."

"Really?" Owen jumped in. "You guys got Isaac Andrew? The host from the TV series?" He snapped his fingers as if trying to remember the name.

"*Making It Right*," Dylan filled in for his brother.

She smiled. "Yes, we did." She was still excited over the idea that Isaac Andrew had taken the full-time head-chef position. The man had arrived less than a week ago and was already turning the refurbished kitchen into something grand. He was working with Aiden on the designs for the dining hall and, thankfully, sticking within their budget while he was at it.

She turned and made her way across the patio. "The guest services, dining room, patio, and the main pool area are here. The left wing of the main building houses the local doctor's office; Dr. Lea Val will be the on-call physician. There's also a gym and a room for yoga." She glanced up. "The third floor is private." She turned and started walking toward the building. "The smaller pool is down the path a little way. There are two hot tubs: one at each pool." They continued on, and the men kept up with her fast pace. She found it almost ironic that she was now playing host, much like Elle had that first summer long ago. Only this time, she was just as proud as Elle had been.

"Nice," Dylan said beside her. "This all looks brand new."

"Yes, thanks to Aiden Stark and his crew," she said as they hit the first path away from the main building area. "They've spent the last year returning this place to its former glory. Not to mention morphing it into a camp for snowbirds instead of little girls." She knew that most of the costs had gone to all the rebuilds and cringed every time she thought of how much money was left over to actually run the place now.

"Is it true that you and the other owners, your friends, met at this camp years ago?" It was Owen, not Dylan, who asked the question.

She stopped in the middle of the pathway. There had been, over the past year, a few articles that had run about the friends and their plans. After all, they had decided not to spend most of their money on advertising the place, so they had, instead, spent time chatting with local travel blogs and relaying the story about the five friends pooling together. The story was a big draw, and they found themselves answering questions from travel sites all over the US.

The five of them had been interviewed more than a dozen times over the past few months. Each time, Zoey had had to suck it up and play the role of smiling camp owner. She couldn't wait to have the place open already so she could fit into the role she wanted as sports director.

"Yes, Elle's grandfather left us all this." She sighed and looked around, remembering how Elle had told them that night, in the pool, what her grandfather had given them. The man she'd known and loved and had even considered her own surrogate grandfather had thought of the five of them, not just his own granddaughter.

Shaking off the mood, she turned and started down the path again. "This is the new sports hall. Inside, there's a bar and grill where small plates can be ordered, and a full bar off the back patio. The place has pool tables, video games, will host the bingo nights—those sorts of things—along with a movie theater that seats thirty people." They turned away from the other building and continued down the well-manicured stone pathway. At night, bright LED lights lit up each walkway.

She showed them the boathouse and the stables, as well as the other outbuildings, including the zip line hut and the woodshop. Hand-painted signs that she had helped make marked each path and direction.

"Really?" Liam asked as his smile grew. "You have a full woodshop?"

"Yes, I'm sure we'll have plenty of guests who'll like craft time. If everything checks out, we'd be happy to ask you to manage this."

"I'd love to." His eyes turned eager. The fact that she could genuinely see excitement had her relaxing around the youngest brother.

They stopped at the water's edge along the private beach, where the soft sugar sand glimmered in the sunlight.

"Very nice." Dylan stepped closer. "Will you be putting in some waterslides out there?" He motioned to the small floating docks.

She turned to him. "Water . . ."

"You know, the blow-up kind you can find in the waters off Destin?"

She tilted her head and glanced out at the calm waters. "We could . . ."

"You have enough docks; why not add a slide?"

She hadn't really thought about it. Since they were catering to snowbirds, she had refrained from a lot of extra things like that, but now she made a mental note to look into getting a slide for the end of one of the docks. She could vaguely remember there being one when she'd been here that first year.

"You know," Dylan continued, "there was a nice clearing back there. I bet you could have a dry inner tube slide made."

"A . . . dry . . ." She looked up at him as he chuckled.

"It's a section you spread out on a pathway in mats, with bumper walls; then people ride down it in inner tubes. Kind of like sledding on an icy hill, only there's no snow."

She nodded. "We can look into it."

"There's a lot more around here you could do to entertain guests," he suggested.

She was already imagining the new changes he'd suggested.

He glanced around. "No softball fields?"

She smiled slightly. "No, but there are plenty of places around here to play." She felt her face heat as the meaning of her words sank in. She could have sworn his eyes heated and a slight smile lifted those sexy lips of his as he swayed slightly toward her before she turned away from him. "I'm sure you'll want to get back to town before dark."

She walked quickly back up the pathway toward the main building, too embarrassed to glance over her shoulder to see whether they were following her.

She was thankful when Owen fell into step with her and asked questions about the business side of the camp. Some questions she answered, since they were basic; others were more personal, and she remained silent. Questions about where the money had come from to do all the upkeep and the maintenance around the camp.

The questions weren't out of the ordinary, especially after he had mentioned that he had a head for business; still, until they were officially hired, she didn't like sharing too much information about their inner workings.

When they stopped in front of their truck, she turned to them. "Well, I should let you know later this week if everything checks out." She started to turn and head back inside.

"The doors open next month?" Dylan asked.

"Yes." She grinned.

"And you're already booked?" Owen asked.

"We are, for the first two and a half months solid."

"Then I suggest you let us know sooner. There's a lot we can do around here"—Dylan looked around—"things that you'll want done before bringing in your first guests."

"I'll think about it. Good night." She turned and made her way inside. When she shut the glass doors behind her, she watched the truck disappear down the long driveway.

"Wow, did you hire them?" Aubrey whispered behind her, causing her to jump.

"No!" She had her hand over her heart and took a couple of breaths before it settled back down. "You know, for someone as quiet as you, I think you should wear a bell around your neck." She wrapped her arm around her friend.

Aubrey smiled. "I ran them on the computer already; they're clean. There's nothing in the system for Owen, Dylan, or Liam Rhodes."

"Nothing?" Zoey's eyes narrowed.

"No. No criminal records, no warrants out for their arrests." Aubrey shook her head. "Hire them." Her eyes moved back to the doors.

"We should check their references," Zoey started.

"At this point we can't afford to be picky. We only have two more applications, and they want way more than we can pay them." Her eyes narrowed. "You did discuss pay with them, right?"

Zoey ran it over in her head and sighed. "No, I forgot. This is why I wanted you . . ." She stopped when Elle made her way across the floor.

"So?" she asked.

Zoey knew that if Aubrey wanted them on board, there was no use fighting it. Besides, the brothers were perfect. Even if Zoey had a nagging feeling that something wasn't quite right with them, they couldn't be picky at this point. They still needed people to help run the place, after all; as it was now, everyone was going to be working full shifts.

"If they'll agree to work for pennies," Zoey started, "then they're hired."

"Yay, us!" Aubrey shot a fist up into the air.

Sighing, Zoey shrugged. "It looks like we have three new sexy-as-hell employees."

CHAPTER THREE

One month later . . .

Dylan jogged on the path heading toward the main building as sweat ran down his back, soaking his T-shirt. He loved being in the outdoors. The smells and sounds of nature, the peace and quiet he found by himself in the wild—there was something innate and primitive, almost primordial, that pulled at him each time he stepped onto a trail.

The other added bonus of running was it gave him time to think about why they were there: to look for their father. The old man had to be hiding around here somewhere.

While they were becoming familiar with the camp and their jobs, the three of them had surreptitiously searched for any clues about their father. There were a few questions they needed answered without raising any alarms.

So far, he and his brothers hadn't learned anything new about the mechanics of the camp or anything deeper about the five women who owned and ran it.

Of course, their first task had been to blend in while getting close to the ladies.

Since they had moved into their room on the second floor, he'd been too exhausted after each workday to even think about sneaking around during his off time.

One thing he had learned was that Aubrey Smith, the official director of counselors, was a stickler for organization. She demanded that he account for most of his time. The woman was soft spoken, but when she looked at him with those blue eyes, he knew she meant business, and there was no way he was going to cross a redhead. Not after the last time he'd done so.

His mind flashed to his very first love. Amelia had been the first girl to cause his eleven-year-old heart to beat fast. It had taken him a full month to convince her to kiss him under the bleachers. The hell he'd gotten from her after she'd caught him bragging to all his buddies about it had lasted years.

He knew that of the three of them, Owen was the one who'd had the most time to look around. Dylan had been busy setting up the new inner tube slide and outdoor water activities.

Liam had been too busy to do any searching either, since he'd been in charge of the woodshop. His brother had spent most of his time getting everything ready before the official opening day as well as helping out on a few last-minute improvements like the slides.

They had finished setting up everything for the zip line. He'd learned the app system they used for scheduling tours. He and Liam had helped build the inner tube slide. It had taken some doing to go around a few trees, but in the end, they'd built almost one hundred feet of slide.

He turned down another trail and dodged a low tree branch as his mind worked the puzzle of what his father would have wanted with the camp or the women who ran it. Dylan loved taking time to run in the mornings when he could, but since he'd had a meeting that morning, he was enjoying the early-afternoon run instead.

Having these cutout paths to jog through the trees was a huge bonus. At his place, he normally settled for jogging on the asphalt pathway or some days even headed to the beach. Jogging on white sugar sand was a lot harder than it looked. His ankles and knees usually hurt after only a five-mile run.

Since moving into the camp, he'd taken to running every day. The exercise was something he'd deemed necessary. Running was the first step in keeping the promise of fitness he'd made to his heavier self at the tender age of eleven. Most days he'd try to beat the heat of the day before he went to work.

Suddenly, his mind homed in on Zoey and how she'd looked that morning during the meeting. He found it funny that a pair of khaki shorts and a T-shirt with a camp logo on it could be so appealing on a woman.

It wasn't as if he tended to gravitate to a type, but thinking about her, he realized she fit his ideal woman perfectly.

Her long, toned legs were tan and looked sexier in her hiking boots than any heels he'd seen a woman wear. Normally, her long dark hair was braided or tied up in a messy bun at the top of her head, making him dream about burying his hands in it.

It had been a while since he'd felt almost instant attraction for a woman, and knowing that this woman might hold clues as to his father's disappearance had him rethinking his options. Still, maybe making a move was the way to get answers from her?

He reached up with his forearm to swipe sweat out of his eyes and, while distracted, bumped right into a warm body as he turned a corner. Instincts had him reaching out and gripping shoulders before he toppled the woman over.

"Oh!"

He recognized Zoey's voice before he actually saw her face.

"Easy." He chuckled and held on to her more tightly to steady her, surprised at the pleasure of her soft skin under his rough hands.

Her hands ended up against his chest, sandwiched between their bodies. The fact that her shirt was as soaked as his told him that either she had been working out as well or she'd just taken a dip fully clothed. Feeling the coolness of her skin, he figured it was the latter.

"Don't you know you shouldn't go swimming with all your clothes on?" he joked as he smiled down at her, not releasing his hold on her. Not yet.

Her dark eyes narrowed as she glared up at him.

"I didn't . . ." She took a deep breath. "Sometimes having friends is too much work." She glanced behind her.

"Catfight?" he asked, his eyebrows shooting up.

"No," she almost gasped and turned her gaze back toward him. He could see there was humor in her eyes instead of anger toward her friend.

"Friends can be . . . challenging," he agreed as he grinned. "But the way you five interact, you're more like family." He thought about his brothers and how many times they had joked around, one of them ending up in the water against his will.

It was then that he noticed she'd paused. She'd probably become aware that he was still holding her close, their chests pressed against one another. Of course, he towered over her by a few inches, putting her breasts just under his pecs. Still, the feeling of them against his skin did something to him.

"You can let go of me," she said softly.

"I could," he agreed with a smile. "But you're cooling me off." *And heating him up,* he thought.

Again, her eyes narrowed. "What are you doing here?" she asked.

He glanced around; they were on the back path, the one that led from the smaller swimming pool area toward the docks. He'd been heading down that way at the end of his run to jump into the cool water at the small beach.

"Jogging," he answered, trying to make his tone easy. The nagging voice in his head called for him to make a move so he could enjoy it and possibly get answers from her. When she looked up at him, she tilted her head with a look that told him that that wasn't what she'd been asking. In reply, he smiled and pretended he didn't understand that her question was about him and his brothers being at the camp in the first place.

It was hard for him not to show everything to her in his expression, so instead he focused on his thoughts of desire for her. Letting his gaze heat as he watched her.

Then she glanced down at his hands, and he knew that she wanted him to drop his hold. He released her slightly so that if she really wanted, she could easily step away from him. The fact that she didn't move expanded his smile even more.

"What are you doing here?" he retorted.

She sighed. "You're playing a game." She finally took a step away, breaking their contact.

"Am I?" he asked, running his gaze over her.

She was dressed in bright-red shorts with a white T-shirt that had no doubt been fresh and dry earlier, but now, after she'd taken a dip in the water, the almost see-through material clung to her skin. The cream-colored bra she wore underneath did nothing to hide her peaked nipples.

His body reacted instantly, and then it was he who took a step back.

"Your shirt is see-through." He didn't know why he'd said it, other than the fact that his brain had stopped working since all the blood had fled it for lower ground.

She glanced down and then quickly crossed her arms over her chest. "God, I'm going to kill her," she moaned.

"Who?" he asked, still not in control.

"Hannah," she said between clenched teeth.

"Hannah? What did she do?" he asked, his eyes still locked to the spot where her arms covered her nipples.

"She pushed me off the dock and right in the water," she answered. She must have been talking, but his mind was too focused on that wet shirt and the toned skin underneath to hear a word. When her hand jerked up to less than an inch from his nose, and she snapped her fingers, he jerked back into the present.

"Huh?" he asked, shaking his head.

"Men!" Zoey exclaimed. "A pair of tits will turn them into Neanderthals." She spun on her heel and disappeared down the path quickly.

"Hey!" he called after her. "I resemble that remark." He smiled when he heard her chuckle echo back through the trees.

Suddenly in a great mood, he made his way down to the soft sand of the private beach, toed off his running shoes and socks, then dove headfirst into the clear waters of the Gulf of Mexico and let his body cool down.

He'd been on the swim team in high school, so as he cut through the water, he focused his mind on his form, trying to clear Zoey's sexy body from his brain and loins.

When he turned back and hit the beach again, Owen was sitting next to his shoes.

"Hey." He climbed out and shook the water from his short hair. His mind now clear from the swim, he knew he had to make a move on Zoey one way or another to get answers from her. His first thoughts were to grow closer to her—befriend her in hopes of gaining her trust—but part of him desired to make a different move. After all, it wasn't as if he'd be taking one for the team. He'd been thinking about her since the first moment he'd seen her standing on the steps out front. Now all he had to do was convince his brothers of the move.

"Hey." Owen's arms were crossed over his knees. He looked like he'd been sitting there awhile, as he'd removed his shoes already.

"What's up?" Dylan asked as he sat beside his older brother.

"We've been here almost a month and haven't found anything out about Dad or the money yet."

"So?" he asked. "Did you think we'd just come in here, walk up to Elle Saunders, ask her if she was Dad's mistress, and force her to confess to swindling our dad out of money?"

Owen sighed. "No, of course not. But"—he glanced around—"something's got to give. I mean, don't get me wrong, this place is pretty great, but not a million dollars' worth of great. Where did the money go? Did they spend it on fixing it up? Do they even have it? Or does Dad have it still? Where *is* Dad?" His brother ran a hand through his hair in frustration.

Dylan glanced around again and shrugged. "I can't see that it took that much cash to fix this place up. I mean, the cabins are cool, but from the pictures online of how the place used to look, I'd say less than a hundred thousand tops to overhaul the entire place. There's the staff, but most of them are part time or have donated their time, like the local vet and doctor."

"Yeah." Owen nodded. "Those were my figures too."

Dylan rested his arms on his knees. "So, what does the board expect us to do?" he asked.

"Well, until we figure this out, or until we find Dad . . . or he comes out of hiding, since he's done one of his disappearing acts again"—he shrugged—"I'm not sure what the board expects from us, other than we secure the finances they were hoping for. I think they've already decided to replace Dad."

"He's probably here." Dylan glanced around. "I mean, if he and Elle are—"

Just then they heard a noise behind them and turned to see Liam approaching from the path.

Their youngest brother settled beside Owen. Liam's hair was longer than Dylan's and Owen's at the moment. But the three of them could have easily passed as triplets.

"We were just talking about Dad. Do you think he's on the grounds?" Owen asked.

"No." Liam shook his head. "I've been all over this place—unless he's living in our old place across the lake." He nodded behind them. "I doubt he's around that place; it's probably been bought and sold a few times since we lived there."

There was only one private house within view of River Camp. The massive mansion sat across the bay's waters. Its white, gleaming windows were familiar to the brothers. They had lived in the mansion for a few years when they had been kids. It was one of the reasons they believed their father had returned and was staying around the camp somewhere.

River Camp sat directly in the middle of an inlet, flanked by the Gulf of Mexico on one side and Pelican Bay on the other. The camp had access to both waterfronts. The bay side held the boathouse and all the watercraft, including sailboats and docks and now the new waterslides. The gulf side held the private beach, filled with white sugar sand and chairs and umbrellas that could be set up once guests arrived. Now, however, the beach sat empty except for the brothers.

"I can look into who owns the place now and see if it's empty," Owen suggested.

"I don't think . . ." Liam started but then shook his head.

"What?" Owen asked.

"It's just . . ." Liam glanced between them. "I don't think Elle is Dad's mistress."

"What makes you think that?" Dylan asked.

"You tasked me with getting close to her," Liam said. "The way she acts; it's just . . . she doesn't seem like the kind of woman . . ." His brother looked frustrated, then sighed. "Just call it a hunch."

Owen interrupted him. "If she's behind Dad handing over close to a million for this place, then she's the kind of woman who can play men. She could even play you, baby brother. Maybe I should—"

"No," Liam answered quickly. "I can handle her."

"What about you?" Owen turned toward him.

"I'm getting closer to Zoey." Dylan smiled. "If she's hiding any-thing, I'll figure it out soon enough. How are you doing with Hannah?"

Owen frowned, and Dylan was reminded of the moment his brother had informed him that their family's company might be in real trouble. That their father had pulled out a lot of cash and had possibly invested his personal capital into a stranger's summer camp instead of his own family business.

"They aren't what we expected, but the fact remains: Dad might have invested in this place instead of Paradise Investments. A business he's run for over forty years," he reminded them. "The reason rests with one of the five women running the place. And seeing Elle Saunders's name in Dad's calendar was our first clue."

"Yeah, I'm on it." Liam nodded.

They had drawn straws as to who would get close to her. Since Owen liked to control everything, it had been the only fair way for Dylan and Liam to assert some authority over the situation. Liam had drawn the short straw.

Liam's only job was to get close to Elle, while both Owen and Dylan had two others. Dylan had chosen the sisters, Zoey and Scarlett, since he had felt an instant attraction to Zoey that first day. Owen had gotten tasked with Hannah and Aubrey.

So far, Dylan hadn't had a chance to say two words to Zoey's younger sister. The woman hadn't been around a lot. When he'd asked after her on the first day they'd arrived at the camp, Zoey had told him that she was out of town, dealing with a family issue.

"We have less than three days before guests start flooding in here—let's do everything we can to get some answers before then." Owen stood up and dusted the sand from his shorts.

Dylan stood, followed by Liam.

"So, we continue with our plan?" Dylan said softly. His two brothers looked at one another, then nodded. They didn't say anything else as they all took separate paths in different directions.

Dylan made his way slowly up the path toward the main building so he could change into some dry clothes.

He counted himself lucky when he came to the path intersection and noticed Scarlett walking toward the barn. He jogged toward her with a greeting and noticed that her steps faltered.

"Uh, hi." She met him with a slight frown.

"So you were out dealing with a family issue?" he asked.

She nodded. "It's all handled." She turned to go.

"Heading out for a ride?" He gestured at her boots and riding attire. The tan jodhpurs looked worn, as did her black riding boots. He could tell that she spent a lot of time on the back of a horse.

"Yes, did you enjoy your swim?"

He'd removed his shirt and had it bunched in his hands, but his shorts still dripped even now.

"Yes. I ran into your sister earlier," he said.

Here Scarlett relaxed slightly. "It appeared she had a swim as well." She giggled and bit her bottom lip as if to stop the sound from escaping.

He smiled. "From the sounds of it, it wasn't voluntary like mine."

"No." She chuckled. "Hannah and she have this . . . thing."

"Oh?" he said, curious.

She took a deep breath. "It was our second year here, and Hannah accidentally"—Scarlett air quoted—"nudged Zoey into the lake when she was fully clothed."

He thought he knew where she was heading with this. "So what? She nudged her back a few times?"

Scarlett smiled, and for the first time, he could see the resemblance. "Yes, and they've been nudging each other ever since. They usually sneak up on one another. It's almost as if they're still only thirteen." She chuckled.

He echoed her laugh. "Siblings." He shook his head. "Age doesn't matter. When you get around one another, it's like you're ten all over again."

Scarlett tilted her head. "Are you and your brothers the same?"

"Yeah." He nodded. "We have our own . . . quirks."

She glanced down at her watch. "I'm supposed to meet her down at the barn."

"I won't keep you." He turned to go.

"Dylan?" she said, causing him to glance back. The humor that had been in her eyes a moment ago was gone, replaced by something deeper. "Don't mess with my sister." The look in her eyes told him clearly that even though she was for the most part timid, she still had claws.

"I wouldn't dream of it," he answered and turned to go.

The rest of the evening, Scarlett's words played over and over in his head. It was strange; he'd only bumped into Zoey a few times since they'd been hired on. Each time, however, he had felt the growing attraction between them. Hell, everyone standing within shouting distance could feel it. The air had almost crackled around them that first day he'd been at the camp and had run into her at the docks. She'd just come back from a sail on the small sailboat.

He had watched the small white sail coming closer to the dock, where he'd been trying to get into the boathouse to look around.

He'd been lucky that he'd seen the boat in the reflection of the glass and had turned around in time to see her dock.

Walking over, he grabbed up her line and tossed the knot over the dock cleat.

"Nice day for a sail." He watched her tie off the rest of the lines.

"Yes, it is," she called back.

"Need help?" he asked, then held in a chuckle after her eyes traveled over him like she knew what he had been up to.

"No, I'm done." She moved to jump onto the dock, and he reached out quickly to help her. When she bumped into him, he almost toppled over.

"Easy," he murmured and made sure they wouldn't end up in the water together. He didn't expect the electrical shock just touching her skin caused, or the fire that spread in his blood as he held her.

"You're in my way," she warned, then easily sidestepped him and disappeared down the dock.

After a quick change of clothes now, he decided to head back out and see if he could find Zoey again. After all, her evening ride with her sister was probably coming to an end, since the sun had set already.

He hadn't expected to see a silver-haired woman walking down the path toward him. Her resemblance to Zoey was so uncanny that he stopped to say hello.

"You must be Zoey and Scarlett's mother." When her eyes lit up, he smiled. "Dylan C—Rhodes," he corrected quickly.

"Call me Kimberly." She took his hand easily. "I've heard all about you and your brothers."

"Lies." His grin stretched his cheeks. "Whatever you've heard."

She chuckled, the sound so much like Zoey's own laughter that he couldn't help smiling with her.

"I've booked a zip line tour with you for tomorrow." She looked over him as a mother would her own son. He fought the urge to squirm under her gaze. "I hope you know what you're doing."

Something told him she wasn't talking about his job but something deeper. Still, he decided to keep things light.

"I do. I spent a summer as a guide in Brazil; their zip line was ten times longer and higher," he assured her.

"Good." She sighed and glanced toward the main building. "I'm heading in for dinner. Care to join me?"

He shook his head. "Can't—heading to the barn to meet your daughter."

Her eyebrows shot up. "Like I said, I hope you know what you're doing." She started to move past him. "It was nice meeting you, Dylan."

"You too." He watched her stroll toward the main house, then turned back down his route.

As he approached the barn, he saw Scarlett leaning against the paddock railing talking to Carter, the veterinarian.

Deciding he didn't want to waste any time chatting with the two of them, he ducked into the barn to look for Zoey.

He found her in a stall, brushing a large cream-colored mare. Zoey was talking to the horse as if the creature could understand every word.

"So, you see," Zoey was saying, "that is why humans don't get to sleep standing up."

He must have chuckled, because her head jerked in his direction.

"Sorry." He stepped from the shadows and into the stall. "I didn't mean to interrupt your story."

He saw her tense, so he walked over and started stroking the horse's mane. The creature leaned into his shoulder while he scratched its neck. He'd visited the stalls a few times already and had even taken a ride on Duke, who had quickly become his favorite out of the half dozen horses housed in the barn.

"Lady, right?" he asked the horse, not the woman. When the horse gave him a quick nod, he laughed and hugged her.

"She does that to everyone," Zoey said, causing him to glance over at her.

"Jealous?" He smiled. Zoey gave a quick shake of her head, then walked out of the stall and set the brush down on the table.

"Why are you here?" she asked, turning around and almost bumping into him, since he'd followed her out.

"Is this a private club?" he asked with a hint of humor.

"No, I mean . . ." She motioned around to the trees, and then to him. "You and your brothers are up to something. I just haven't figured it out yet."

"We can't just be here for the work? We're doing pretty well at it, I think," he teased and smiled more deeply when her eyes narrowed. "How about a walk?" he asked.

He could tell she questioned it for a moment, but then she fell into step beside him easily.

"So?" she asked once they were outside and heading on the path toward the water of the bay.

"So?" He peeked over at her, but it was too dark to see that annoyed look he knew she got. The one he was quickly growing to enjoy too much.

"Are you going to tell me?" she asked. She pulled her arm free and stopped in the middle of the pathway.

"What makes you so sure we're here for anything other than work?" he asked.

"It doesn't add up. Since arriving here, the three of you have been sneaking around the place as if looking for something."

His eyebrows drew up, and he was thankful she'd begun pacing and didn't seem to have noticed.

"What makes you say that?" *Damn,* he thought. He'd have to warn his brothers to be more discreet.

"Every time I turn around, I bump into you or one of your clones." She ticked off offenses on her fingers. "Not to mention, apparently Liam gets lost so much that I keep finding him in different places. Yesterday he was in the main kitchen."

"Maybe he was hungry," Dylan said. The look Zoey gave him sent him into a smile again. "Or not." He held up his hands.

"Then there's Owen." She tilted her head.

"What about him?" He was almost afraid to ask.

"He has a head for business," she answered.

"Isn't that a good thing?"

"It is if he were applying for a job as manager of a retail store; instead, he comes all the way out here for a job as a camp counselor." Her voice rose slightly.

"We like to stick together"—he shrugged—"and we like the outdoors."

She gave a low growl and threw up her hands in frustration. "Okay, so it's a game. What are you, internet millionaires who do this for fun?"

He walked over to her and took her shoulders in his hands to stop her. "Zoey, what makes you think that there's anything more than three brothers down on their luck, looking for jobs that they could all enjoy?"

She sighed and relaxed slightly. The moonlight streamed through the trees overhead, giving her skin a glow. Her dark eyes searched his face, and he was grateful that it was most likely hidden in the shadow, since the moon was behind him. His eyes darted down to her lips, wanting, wondering what they would feel like against his.

"I will find out," she said slowly, breaking his thoughts. "I have a nose for things like this." She stepped back, breaking their contact.

He watched her turn away and head down the path and, for a moment, thought about following her.

Instead, he continued on his way and sat on the dock until his head was cleared.

When he returned to the main house, the lights were dark. Knowing the schedule of most of the employees by now, he wagered he had enough time to make his way into the office wing of the first floor without being seen. There was a new coded lock on Zoey's office door, but he'd paid attention when he'd followed Aubrey into the room the other day.

He punched in the code and smiled when the green button flashed and the door lock was released.

He glanced up and down the hallway before stepping into the dark room. He didn't even know where to begin looking. Should he chance turning on the computer? Since he didn't know any of the passwords, he doubted it would do him any good anyway.

He walked over to the file cabinet and pulled open the first drawer and realized it was full of HR folders with small labels for each employee.

Seeing his and those of his brothers, he pulled them out and glanced inside. Their initial applications were stapled to the back with a printout from a website. The background check using their altered names showed that they had no criminal history and no outstanding warrants and that their work history didn't have any grievances. It was a pretty basic search.

What it didn't show was the vital information, such as his family's wealth or the fact that he and his brothers had stock in their father's business.

He put the files back in place and scrolled through the rest of the files. When he opened the second drawer, he found what he'd hoped he would. Financial papers.

That was, until he looked closer. There were several folders, one for each major bill the camp accrued. Water, gas, electric—all the basic bills a business would normally have.

He shut the drawer and was just about to open the third when he heard a noise outside the door. Cursing under his breath, he looked around for a hiding spot.

Deciding in a heartbeat, he moved to the closet and shut himself in the tight space.

When he heard his brother's voice, he relaxed and began to emerge—that was, until he heard Elle's voice respond. Then he tucked back into the darkness and prayed that she had no reason to reach into the closet.

He leaned closer, eavesdropping.

"Is there a reason I keep finding you in the strangest places?" Elle asked, her voice laced with disbelief.

"Like I said, it's not a crime to go for a walk." His brother's voice sounded relaxed.

Dylan chanced a peek through the crack in the door. Liam was leaning on the edge of the desk.

Elle was standing in front of him, her arms crossed over her chest and a look of disbelief on her face.

"This makes it four times in six days I've seen you sneaking around after dark."

"Sneaking?" Liam's voice rose slightly. "If you consider an evening stroll sneaking, what are you going to do when guests start arriving and milling about?"

Dylan smiled. Liam was a sneak and, as the youngest of the three of them, had learned early on how to get out of any circumstance.

The fact that Elle remained quiet for a moment told Dylan that his brother had most likely smooth-talked himself out of this situation as well.

"Why were you out near the River Cabin?" she asked.

Dylan ran through the map of the campgrounds in his head and determined she was talking about the lone cabin that sat off by itself near the edge of a small stream. Every cabin had its own unique name etched in a wood sign that hung over its front door.

He'd learned the cabin in question had been remodeled like the rest of the camp cabins, thanks to his chat with Aiden, head of construction. But when he'd asked Julie if it was booked, she'd informed him that that cabin wasn't part of the rentals. When he'd asked her why, she'd only told him that it had been marked for private use.

Of course, the brothers had instantly decided that it would have been a perfect hideaway for their father.

Still, the place had been sitting empty so far.

"I saw a light," Liam said, earning Dylan's attention. "I thought someone might be messing with the place."

"No, no one is messing with the place. It's private," she said after a moment.

"Someone's living there?" Liam asked.

"Yes," Elle answered.

"Who?" His brother didn't miss a beat.

Elle shifted, and from his place in the closet, Dylan could tell that she hadn't wanted to answer. But after a moment, she threw up her hands.

"Zoey and Scarlett's mother." Elle started pacing. "Scarlett and Kimberly just got back from Jacksonville after selling their old home."

Liam was silent. "Why keep it a secret?" he asked.

Elle turned back toward him. "I'm not." She gasped slightly. "Why are you and your brothers sneaking around?"

"We don't sneak." Liam stood up and used his full height to tower over Elle.

"Still, either you keep getting lost or—"

"I enjoy evening walks in the great outdoors," Liam finished for her. "The three of us enjoy nature. It's one of the reasons we got jobs here."

There was another moment of silence, possibly as she absorbed that, before Elle finished. "Either way"—he heard steps toward the office door—"I'd appreciate it if you didn't go sneaking around the River Cabin. We've allowed Kimberly to rent it from us as a private home. She's a very reclusive person and doesn't wish to be harassed."

"I have never harassed anyone," Liam said after he'd moved toward the door. His brother stood in the entrance, looking down at Elle for a moment, then moved out of the doorway.

Dylan was lucky: Elle shut off the office lights and closed the door behind her.

He waited almost five minutes before walking out of the closet and leaning his ear against the door to the hall. He glanced back at the file cabinet and wondered if he should chance looking any more. Deciding not to push his luck, he opened the door and stepped out into the hallway.

"Well, well," a female voice purred behind his back, causing him to spin around.

CHAPTER
FOUR

Zoey's hand clasped Elle's, who was holding on to Hannah's. When Scar and Aubrey walked over, their hands were quickly taken up as well.

It was opening day. So much had gone right to get them to this spot in time, and so much was hanging on their success. Not only was money getting tight, but now they had a trio of spies in their mix.

One of the improvements Aiden had convinced them to begin with was a good security system. They had small cameras set up on every main building.

It hadn't been long after the brothers had arrived that she'd spotted them sneaking around. At first, she had gone to Elle in fear they were trying to steal; then Elle had convinced her to sit back and watch them.

For the next two nights, they had been glued to the computer screen, as if binge-watching their favorite shows.

Sure enough, once all the lights went off and everyone was tucked inside, the three brothers hit the trails, looking around, each of them taking part of the camp to search.

"It looks like they're looking for something," Hannah said, a bowl of popcorn in her lap as they huddled around the laptop. "*What* is the question." She sipped her wine.

"Something they could pawn for quick cash?" Aubrey asked as she reached for a handful of Hannah's popcorn.

Zoey watched the brothers more closely, her eyes zeroing in on Dylan, who was at the moment sneaking around the boathouse. Her mind returned to the first night after they had hired them. She'd found him by the boathouse after she'd returned from checking out the new-to-them sailboat. "No, they're looking for something specific." She squinted and wished that the camera's night vision was higher quality. "But what?"

"We can't afford to fire them," Elle said, biting her bottom lip. "Not now. Who would we get to replace them? Besides, they're building that slide thing."

"Dry tube slide," Zoey provided.

"Right." Elle nodded. "So, what do we do?"

"Two can play at the game of spying." Zoey smiled. "Why not let them sneak around? With us watching them, of course. We can each take a brother to watch." She leaned forward and opened her web browser.

"What are you doing?" Aubrey asked.

"Google search." She typed in *Owen Rhodes* and frowned at the eighteen million results that came up. Then she typed in each brother's name and the address they had put on their applications.

"Nothing." She frowned at the screen. "Even the address is just an apartment block."

"So? Have you googled yourself lately?" Elle sighed. "What did you expect?"

"I don't know, at least a Facebook link." She leaned back after flipping the screen back to the cameras.

"How about we each take turns watching them?" Hannah asked.

"Good idea—plus it gives us some time to figure out what they're doing here," Elle added.

"Here we go," Elle whispered, breaking into Zoey's thoughts.

"Ready or not," Zoey chimed in with a sigh; her nerves tingled as the first cars pulled into the parking lot at the edge of the field.

The covered parking had been one of the best ideas from Aiden. Since it had been a summer camp for kids before, most parents had dropped off their children. There had never really been a need for long-term parking.

Using the existing field that had been used for parking back when the camp had been open was obvious, but covering it with asphalt and adding the carport covers was a big bonus. One that apparently had been needed, since any car that pulled in parked underneath the shelters.

"Smiles," Elle said and squeezed her hand before dropping it.

The flow of guests coming in that first Friday morning warmed Zoey's heart and had her believing that they had all made the right choice.

Employees took care of the guests with alacrity, making sure everyone arrived at their cabins with all their luggage while giving them a quick tour around the grounds.

Zoey herself had a handful of guests to guide. First, she took a nice couple who had driven all the way from Richmond, Virginia. Mary and Luke Young were celebrating their fortieth anniversary.

They'd been one of the first couples to book and had requested the Love Shack—the cabin set off deeper into the woods by itself with a view of the bay.

The trek to that cabin was a little harder, and Zoey ended up driving them up on one of the many repurposed golf carts they had purchased from a defunct golf course across the state line. All the carts had been painted the camp's teal-green color and had the River Camp's logo on the sides.

Several of the carts bore **EMPLOYEES ONLY** signs; they used them to get around when toting bags or guests who required special help.

She took the pathways slowly and made sure to highlight all the attractions for the guests as they moved toward their cabin. The couple gushed about how their daughter and son had pooled together to purchase the vacation for them.

"Forty years together—that's amazing." Part of her questioned what it would have been like growing up with loving parents like this couple. What if her mother and father continued to look at one another like the Youngs were currently doing? Had her parents ever looked at one another like this? Of course, then her mind switched gears, and she started dreaming about looking at someone with so much love and admiration.

She watched as Luke reached up and placed his hands on his wife's shoulders. The simple touch said so much that she found herself glancing away as a slow pain spread in her chest.

"It's not long when you're with the right person," he said.

Zoey held in a sigh as more aches spread throughout her heart. She parked the cart in front of the Love Shack.

"Here we are—the Love Shack. It's all yours for your entire stay, which is . . ." She glanced down at their sheet and smiled. "A full month."

"Luke finally retired last month." Mary beamed.

Zoey climbed out of the cart and started to grab the luggage while Mark helped her.

"Go on in, it's unlocked," she suggested to Mary. "You'll want to set your own door code." The electronic keypad locks they had installed on each of the cabins could easily be reset at the end of each guest's stay.

"How wonderful. Mark's always losing hotel keys," Mary joked as she opened the door. "Oh my, how beautiful."

Zoey and her friends had been the ones to name them all. The cabin's unique wood exterior with its intricate carvings outside gave it almost a fairy-tale look. And as one of the newly built ones, off the main pathway, this cabin continued the romantic feel inside with creamy, soft colors and an elegant atmosphere.

"It's perfect." Mary walked over to her husband and gave him a kiss.

"We are fully automated in most things here, but there are some instructions on how to set your door-lock codes." She showed him the laminated card next to the door. "The camp schedule and list of available activities are on this computer screen by the door. You can book an adventure by clicking on its icon." She showed them on the screen. "If you want to cancel it, just click it again. It's pretty easy. There's plenty of other fun adventures to do that won't require booking. If you require daily maid service, click the icon. To order food service, you can review the menu here. And if, for any reason, you need to talk to someone, pick up the phone there. It will ring you through to the main building directly. Your son and daughter have requested your favorite champagne." She nodded to the back deck, where a bottle was chilling on the small table. "Enjoy, and congratulations on your forty years."

"Thank you." They both beamed as she exited the cabin.

The next couple she delivered to their cabin were the complete opposite of the Youngs. Judge Hogan from New York and his new bride, Sherry. The couple were a couple of weeks into their new marriage after two long years of dating. Zoey was pretty sure the engagement had lasted so long because the older judge had had to wait until his new bride was old enough to get married.

The woman couldn't be over eighteen. The extremely bleached blonde had a pair of impressive tits and a nose even younger than she was—Zoey could still see bruising underneath all the piled-on makeup—and, on her hand, a rock the size of Zoey's big toe.

Still, it wasn't Zoey's place to judge the couple, so she showed them to the Eagle's Nest, one of the new cabins off the beaten path again. This one hung up on the top of a small rocky hill and overlooked the white, sandy beaches of the gulf.

The cabin was more contemporary, designed with full two-story glass walls in the front and dark steel sides. A twisted staircase led to the massive second-story bedroom.

She explained the door locks and showed them the camp schedule and left as fast as she could.

When she returned to the main house, she needed a break and had Owen take over for her.

After making sure he was set to take the next couple who arrived for her, she walked into the lounge, a hangout area for employees. Food was always available—snacks or meals and drinks for all the employees. She grabbed a sandwich and a soda and sat down at a table next to Hannah.

"Well?" she asked her friend.

"Wow, talk about interesting." Hannah shook her head.

"What?" she asked, leaning forward.

"I just dropped off Barbara Collins and her new husband."

"Barbara . . . as in the actress?" Zoey leaned closer.

"Yes," Hannah almost squealed. "They officially checked in under the names Barb and Jamie Carter. But it was her." She smiled and took a sip of her water.

"Wow," Zoey sighed. "I never thought we'd get anyone famous—I mean, I'd hoped."

"Who?" Scar had sat beside her. "Who's famous?"

For the next half hour, they compared guests they had helped check in. Scar had had a couple from Idaho and one from Ohio.

"They seemed pretty boring compared to your couples," Scar complained. "I mean, Bruce Willis lives in Idaho. Why didn't we get him!"

"Maybe after lunch you'll have someone more . . . colorful," Zoey suggested. She glanced down at her watch and figured Owen would be done showing the couple to their cabin.

"I'd better go. I told Owen I'd meet him in five minutes." She got up to leave and spotted Dylan across the room.

Deciding not to get distracted by Dylan and his muscles, she darted out the side door and met Owen just as he was talking to a new couple. The woman was easily over fifty, while the man had to be in his mid-twenties. Her chocolate skin was wrinkle free, her outfit was to die for, and she could see why the younger man was drawn to the woman. She was stunning.

"Here she is now," Owen was saying as she approached. "Zoey, this is David and Rumi from Dallas."

"Hi," she said to them. "Thank you for filling in, Owen." He handed her their check-in sheet. "It looks like you'll be staying in the Tree House. It's one of my favorite designs. Looks like Owen has all your luggage loaded. Shall we head out?"

She watched the younger man help his wife into the back of the cart, then took the spot next to her up front.

"So, we've heard a few things about this place . . ." he started.

"Oh?" she asked, wondering who they had heard from and what they had heard, since this group comprised the camp's first guests.

"Is it true it used to be a summer camp for girls?" he asked, and she relaxed.

"Yes, actually, my four best friends and I met here when we were all younger."

"Nice," Rumi said from behind her.

"And we're the first guests?" David asked.

"Yes," she answered.

"Do all guests book for full months at a time?" he asked.

"Some choose our weekly rates instead, but for the most part, guests tend to book for a month at a time," she answered. "Especially during the winter seasons; we've already had several bookings for the full four months straight."

"What if we wanted to stay longer?" he asked, looking around as the cart turned off the main pathway toward the cabins. As with each couple, she'd driven them by all the basic amenities before heading toward their cabins.

"Normally, that might not be an issue; however, we're booked solid for the first two months," she answered.

"Oh." He slumped slightly.

"Don't worry—you'll have a full month's worth of fun before you have to go," she assured him.

"David likes to . . . play," Rumi said with a chuckle.

Zoey wasn't quite sure what to say to that, so she just nodded instead and talked about the swimming pools, the boathouse, and the stables.

"What about the staff?" he asked.

Again, unsure of what he was asking, she decided to be vague. "All of our staff are full-time employees. They're housed up at the main building," she finished as she parked the cart in front of the Tree House. It wasn't really a tree house but a tall two-story A-framed cabin set among the trees. The thick wood logs that had been used to build the place gave the entire log cabin an almost mystical vibe.

"Nice," David said as he helped Rumi out of the cart. It was then that Zoey noticed the woman walked with a limp.

"I'm sorry." She interrupted their motion. "Would you prefer a cabin without stairs?"

"No." Rumi smiled at her. "This is perfect." She looked up at the cabin. "Besides, David's around to help me out."

Zoey nodded and helped the man carry in their luggage, ran through the check-in speech, and left the couple to enjoy.

She made her way back to the main area and picked up her last couple of the day.

Trilla and Donni were not what she expected by just looking down at their check-in sheet.

Trilla was the older of the two, easily in her mid-sixties, while Donni, the younger of the pair, was in her mid-thirties.

She greeted them warmly. As she drove them toward their cabin, the Hangover, they talked about how they were from LA, where Trilla was an artist and Donni a dog walker. Trilla gushed about their wedding earlier in the year and even pulled out her phone to show Zoey pictures. Donni had been dressed in a beautiful white, flowing gown, while Trilla had worn a white tux. The pair were very cute together.

When they stopped at the base of the short path that would lead them to the Hangover Cabin, Zoey turned toward them.

"I hope you're okay for a short walk; your cabin is just up these steps." She motioned to the path.

"We are." Trilla smiled and grabbed one of their bags.

Zoey grabbed the other, but Donni stopped her. "Aren't you recovering from a pretty bad incident last year?" She nodded toward Zoey's knee.

Smiling, she answered, "Fully recovered, thanks." She took the bag.

"I didn't want to say anything, but wow, when we heard you were part owner in this place—well, let's just say, it sealed the trip for us."

Zoey smiled and moved toward the stairs. "Thank you," she said softly. She was uncomfortable with praise. Maybe it was because she hadn't gotten much of it when she had been younger. Her mother had been a "fade into the background" sort of parent, since her father had been so boisterous and domineering. But shortly after the divorce, she'd seen her mother start to come out of her shell.

The Hangover Cabin looked a lot like the Eagle's Nest Cabin, only instead of black steel outer walls and a second floor, the Hangover had large stone walls, and the entire cabin was only one level high. Most of that building hung out over a small hillside that overlooked the edge of the water. With the way the trees surrounded the place, Zoey could almost imagine the cabin on a hillside in Colorado instead of a few yards away from the sandy white beaches of Florida.

Zoey showed the couple around the cabin and went through the standard welcome package before leaving.

Then she took the pathway back to the main building slowly, since there was now the possibility of guests out and about on the trails.

When it had just been the five of them, they'd raced each other on the carts to see how fast they could go. Scarlett had almost toppled a cart over once.

When she returned to the office she shared with her friends on the main floor, she sat down and opened a soda and drank heavily. It was the end of summer in Florida, and there was a stream of sweat rolling down her back.

"So?" Scarlett asked her.

"So far, so good," she answered after another long sip. "Four couples are now getting settled in. What about you?"

"Three couples." Her sister smiled and nodded to her computer system. "We're already getting bookings for the zip line, tennis courts, trail horse rides, and sunset beach rides, and"—she clicked her mouse—"the sunset sails are already booked up for the week. If this keeps up, we'll have to have guests prebook some events when they schedule their cabins."

Zoey smiled. "We can talk about it during our meeting tonight." She turned and typed herself a note in her system to remind herself to bring it up.

"This system is a lifesaver," Scar said, clicking her computer screen again. "I'm booked solid tomorrow. How about you?"

Zoey looked down at her screen and enjoyed seeing the almost full days ahead of her, since her schedule was quickly filling up. Everyone was in charge of overseeing different events. Yet as it was now, they were all going to be spread pretty thin. Zoey worried that they would be running around the camp like a bunch of headless chickens. "I think we all are going to be very busy."

"Still, it's going to take a while to get used to staying this busy. Especially after this last year."

Standing up, Zoey figured she'd grab a snack from the kitchen before she left to make sure everything was in place for the first evening meal. Besides, she knew she'd find Elle and Hannah rushing around trying to make sure everything was perfect in the dining hall.

"See you later. I'm going to get a snack." She tucked her phone into her back pocket. Her schedule would buzz her half an hour before she was to be anywhere.

When she opened her door and stepped out, she noticed Dylan walking toward her.

Groaning inwardly as her body instantly reacted to seeing him, she pasted on a smile and tried to hide the heat she felt. "Sorry, I've really got to . . ." She tried to sidestep him, but he blocked her.

"Heading out?" He smiled.

"Yes, I was . . ."

"Good, I'll walk with you." He moved back to make room for her.

"I . . ." She tried to think of a reason to put him off. Other than the fact that she didn't have time to think about wanting him. How nice his hands had felt on her shoulders, or how sexy it was to watch his eyes heat as he looked at her. "Don't you have somewhere to be?" she asked.

He pulled out his phone and glanced down at it. "Nope, not until tomorrow morning. No one is keen on zip-lining the first evening they get here."

She shrugged and walked quickly toward the stairs. The fact that Dylan kept up with her was only slightly annoying at this point. She kept telling herself it was better to avoid him than to fight the need that surfaced whenever she was around him. He was an employee, which meant she had an obligation to keep things professional, since she couldn't risk everything they had invested by flirting with an employee. Even if she needed to keep an eye on him. His black polo shirt with the teal camp logo on it hugged his chest and arms like a glove. God, how she wanted to explore those muscles underneath. He wore khaki shorts and hiking boots and was the epitome of outdoor male sex appeal. She bit her bottom lip and dreamed about getting him naked as she rushed down the main stairs while he followed close behind her.

When they stepped outside, the wind was kicking up, and she could tell they were in for an evening shower. Keeping up her pace, she glanced over at him. "Did you want something?"

His instant smile threw her.

"I want lots of things," he said, which caused her to turn toward him. "Zoey, I need to ask you a question." She stopped at his words.

"Okay." She glanced up to see Ryan walking toward them.

Ryan hadn't been one of her hires—head waiter Brent had hired all the dining room staff, and Hannah had hired Brent. Zoey trusted Hannah's judgment completely in these matters. The woman oozed class and sophistication—everything River Camp wanted to project in the dining hall.

"Evening," Zoey started to say to the woman. But instead of walking by them, Ryan stopped, her arm locking into Dylan's easily.

"There you are," the woman purred. "I was hoping you'd stop by and see me again tonight before the dinner rush."

Zoey took a giant step away from the couple, as if someone had kicked her in the chest.

CHAPTER
FIVE

Dylan berated himself for falling into Ryan's trap. When he'd bumped into her the other night as he'd been coming out of the camp's office, she'd grabbed him.

"I don't know what game you're playing," she'd said, running her fingers up his arms, her nails scraping his skin. He'd thought about making some excuse for why he'd been coming out of the office, but then she'd smiled up at him and whispered, "Costa."

He'd frozen and glanced around, then pulled her into a small storage room.

"What do you know?" he asked.

She wrapped herself around him.

"Plenty"—she moved closer—"and unless I get what I want, so will Elle and the others."

He and his brothers hadn't thought of the possibility of running into anyone who knew who they were. After all, it wasn't as if they were famous, just . . . well known in some circles.

"What do you want?"

"I've been watching the three of you, closely." She tapped his chin. "It's simple," Ryan continued, tugging him closer to her in the small closet full of fresh towels. She wrapped her long arms around his neck and started rubbing her thin body against his. "Being on the arm of one of the Costa men, attending some of those fancy parties you always are invited to, will easily be enough to keep me quiet."

He gripped her arms and held her away from him. "I don't do blackmail."

He was clear enough, but Ryan shrugged and reached for the door and added, "Suit yourself; I'll just go find Elle . . ."

"Wait." He sighed and rolled his shoulders. "While we're here, our identities remain a secret?"

She smiled. "I'm looking for a little of what you have. I don't care about the people around here—I'm talking bigger than this place. I can wait a little." She tilted her head. "When you leave here, so do I . . . on your arm, directly into the spotlight. You'll take me to all the local events, where we can be seen together. You'll introduce me to the rich and famous." Ryan's dark eyes had sparkled with her smile, and as she'd moved back toward him, he'd stopped her.

"As I said, I don't do blackmail, but I'm sure we can work some other arrangement out."

Now, as Ryan rubbed her body against his in front of Zoey, it was obvious that the woman wasn't just a blackmailer: she was willing to force his hand.

"I'll leave you two . . ." Though Dylan was too busy trying to unwrap Ryan's arms from around him to notice the look on Zoey's face, he heard her tone clearly enough as she marched away.

"Later," he warned Ryan, then rushed after Zoey. He heard Ryan laughing behind him, and a rush of anger zipped up his back.

"Hey." He caught up with Zoey outside the door to the dining room. When he grabbed her hand, she jerked free.

"Don't." The single word loosened his grip.

"Let me explain . . ." he started, then groaned. "I can't explain, other than that I'm not with her."

"Oh?" Zoey's dark eyebrows shot up as her eyes traveled past him to where Ryan had disappeared into the back-kitchen door.

"No," he assured her. "I wanted to ask you if you could meet me, later tonight."

Zoey's laughter was quick and to the point. "There is no way—"

"It's not . . ." he interrupted, but he shook his head as a new idea intruded. "I thought you wanted to know why we were here." He paused when she touched his arm, stopping himself from smiling when he noticed her calculating her options.

"Meet me in the stables at nine," she finally said before turning around and disappearing into the dining room.

Glancing down at his watch, he smiled at the thought that he'd been able to spend more time with her that afternoon. He made his way to meet his brothers on the back trail, where they'd agreed to connect.

When he stepped into the clearing, he leaned against a tree and waited almost five minutes before Liam arrived.

His brother looked agitated.

"What's up?" he asked.

"There's this woman . . . a waitress, I think. She knows who we are," Liam said, shoving his hands into his shorts.

"Ryan?" he asked with irritation.

"How did . . ." Liam's brow furrowed. "She got to you too? She just basically attacked me and threatened to tell everything as I was coming out of the dining hall."

Dylan sighed and turned as Owen stepped out from the trees.

"We need to talk," Dylan told his brothers.

He quickly filled his brothers in, then took almost an hour to come up with a game plan with them. One in which Dylan didn't particularly like the role he was going to play.

Lying to Zoey while playing Ryan and putting her off was going to take some acting. He wasn't the actor in the family; Liam had those talents. But it seemed that Ryan had her eyes on him more than his brothers: she had only threatened Owen instead of kissing him.

Still, after plotting with his brothers, he filled the rest of his evening with a few more zip line groups until it was a quarter till nine, then headed out toward the barn.

When he walked in, he could tell Zoey was already there. He heard her soothing the animals.

He walked through the massive barn, noticing that all the horses were tucked away for the night. It appeared they were alone in the barn. When he stopped at the end of the stall she was in, he smiled at her riding attire, which was covered in mud as if she'd ridden through several large puddles. Her hair was braided, but several locks had fallen free and now fell around her face. It was obvious she and the horse had gone on a fast and wild ride.

"How was your ride?" he asked.

She glanced over at him. "Relaxing, even though I was working." She set the horse brush down and shut the gate to the stall behind her before she started walking toward the barn entrance.

He fell into step next to her. He could see hurt in her eyes and knew that he'd caused some of it.

"I know. It still gets me that I get paid to have fun." He shook his head.

She glanced over at him. "You get paid to show others a fun and safe time," she corrected him.

"Right." He nodded with a smile as his eyes ran over her face. Even with the hurt in her expression, he could tell she'd enjoyed the evening. "How much fun did you have on your sunset ride?" he asked.

She tilted her head. "I sat on Honey's back while a couple on their fortieth anniversary watched the sunset on the beach."

He stopped her from exiting the barn by taking her arm. "Zoey, I'm not with Ryan."

"Why would I care? We didn't implement any rules for employees in that . . ."

She stiffened, and all he could think about was having her look at him the way she had earlier.

He bent down and kissed her, stopping her words. The desire to kiss her had burned ever since he'd seen her standing on the stairs that first time.

He felt her shoulders tense under his touch, until he slanted his mouth over hers, slowly taking her soft lips. When he felt her relax, he moved a step closer to her; just one step had their bodies touching.

She was everything he'd imagined. Soft, strong, a perfect fit against him. He took the kiss deeper and felt her completely melt against his chest.

"Zoey." Her name escaped his lips as he moved them both until her back was against the wall of the barn.

However, when her shoulders touched the wood, her eyes flew open, and her hands snaked between them to push him lightly away.

"Don't." She shook her head, and he watched those dark eyes of hers change from passion to annoyance. "Were you even going to tell me why you're here?" She crossed her arms over her chest as if suddenly cold.

He sighed and ran his hands through his hair. It was on the tip of his tongue to tell her everything. But loyalty to his brothers and to his family came first. "I've told you: we're here for work." She started to move, but he stopped her. He didn't want their time to be up just yet. "I did want to talk to you about something else."

"Was the kiss to distract me?" she cut in, stepping out of the barn. He helped her slide the wood beam into place to hold the heavy doors shut.

"No." He looked down at her in the dark and smiled at the memory of her soft lips under his. "I kissed you because I've wanted to do that since the first time I saw you."

That seemed to throw her off for a moment.

"What is going on between you and Ryan?" she asked, changing the subject. "I don't let just anyone kiss me."

"Nothing," he admitted. But her eyes narrowed slightly, showing him that she didn't believe him. Again, he felt the need to explain everything to her. On this subject, at least, he could be open and honest with her. "She keeps trying to hit on me. After that little show this evening, she went and hunted down my brother Liam and did the same thing to him. Ask Elle—she was there."

"I will." She threw her chin up and started to turn away.

"Take a walk with me?" He reached for her hand, and when she didn't yank it back, he relaxed slightly. "We can head to the beach?"

"Okay," she said after a moment. They walked in silence for a while.

"So . . . your mother," he started. "I finally met her yesterday."

"Oh?" she asked, glancing over at him.

"Kimberly—she asked me to call her that." He smiled, remembering how nice the older version of Zoey had been. "Anyway, she was really nice. She said that she booked a zip line tour for tomorrow."

"She what?" Zoey turned and dropped his hand. "No." She shook her head. "Cancel it."

He chuckled. "She's an adult."

"She's my mother, and . . ." she began.

"What?" He waited.

"Frail," she finished.

The woman he'd met yesterday wasn't any more frail than any of the guests walking around the camp. "Zip-lining doesn't require many muscles, and everyone wears a huge harness. Besides, I'll put her on the beginning track. I'll be right there with her the entire way," he assured her. "She is living on the camp's grounds. There's a lot that she'll want to do. Should we stop her from swimming or playing a round of Frisbee golf?"

"No." She frowned and turned toward the beach. He followed her out onto the sand, then almost ran into the back of her when the moonlight bounced off very white, very naked bodies tangled together on a blanket in the sand.

"Oh!" Zoey turned and buried her face in his shoulder as she held in a giggle.

He blinked a few times before the scene finally registered in his mind.

"It's the Youngs," she whispered. "Go." She shoved him back a step.

He chuckled as he took her hand, and they sprinted back down the pathway until they were far enough away to talk.

"I swear." Zoey held her hand to her chest as she laughed softly. "I never expected . . . well." She shook her head. "I guess we should have planned for—"

"What?" He smiled down at her. "That couples like to have sex on the private beach?"

She giggled again and covered her mouth with her hands as she glanced back down the pathway. "Out in the open? There are other guests, employees." She motioned toward the pathway. "It's not all that private."

"Maybe they like that?" he suggested as he raised his shoulders slightly.

"Not the sweet couple I met," she gasped. "I just went horseback riding with them for over an hour."

"Then, they left the barn, stripped naked, took a dip in the gulf to cool off, and—"

She burst out laughing.

He enjoyed the sound. "It's only natural." He felt like a force was pulling him toward her. "I'm sure there are things I could do to help you forget . . ." Then, he bent his head down when she grew silent. His lips brushed against hers again. He took his time—enjoying his exploration of her mouth.

When he felt her pulling back, he let her go. He dropped his hands, even though they itched to explore, to touch her further.

"I'll never be able to look them in the eyes again." She glanced toward the beach.

"How about me?" he asked, brushing a strand of her dark hair away from her face.

"You'll find out tomorrow." She turned toward the main building with a smile.

His heart skipped a beat before he caught up with her and followed her back to the main building. His rooms were on the second floor and at the end of the left wing. Zoey was housed upstairs on the third floor and was only accessible by a smaller staircase that had a locked door at the top. From the outside of the building, he knew that that floor was smaller than the other two floors; still, there was close to a thousand square feet up top, to his estimate.

Leaving her to head up the other stairs without a kiss almost undid him, but she'd shaken her head when he'd started to lean in for one. She wouldn't allow him to kiss her in public yet. The fact that he wanted to told him he was slowly dooming himself.

"Night," he said, squeezing her hand before dropping it.

"Night," she said softly back.

When he entered the room he shared with his brothers, he was surprised to find himself alone.

Almost half an hour later, Liam entered the room, a smile on his lips.

"Looks like you had fun," Dylan said, relaxing back on his pillow.

"I did." He chuckled. "We caught a couple—"

"The Youngs?" Dylan jumped in. "On the beach?"

"What?" Liam said, then shook his head. "No, who are the Youngs?"

"Never mind. Who and what did you catch them doing?" he asked.

"You first," Liam said, toeing off his shoes.

"The Youngs, an older couple, on the beach—let's just say that the moonlight didn't enhance anything," he said quickly.

Liam shivered, then chuckled. "Okay." He sat down on his bed. "We caught a couple getting high."

"So?" He shrugged. "Wait, who is 'we'?"

"Elle and I. We were coming back from . . . well, whatever. Anyway, the funny part was, they asked us to join them, then asked if we liked to swing."

Dylan laughed. "It was bound to happen. I've heard stories. What did Elle do?"

"Turned a pretty shade of pink, then declined gracefully." Liam's eyes shifted away from Dylan's, and he could tell his brother was avoiding his gaze on purpose.

He jumped in. "You like her."

"What?" Liam pulled off his shirt and lay down on the bed. "Who?"

"Elle." Dylan sat up. "Liam, this is the woman we suspect Dad is having an affair with."

"I know," Liam said. Just then, Owen stepped in.

"You won't believe what happened to me tonight," his oldest brother said as he slipped off his jacket and shook water from his hair.

"Let me guess," Liam said. "You caught a couple doing something?"

Owen blushed. "I suppose it was bound to happen. Old people are horny as—"

"Who and what were they doing?" Liam asked, shifting in his bed.

"It doesn't matter. I also ran into Ryan again. What the hell does she really want from us? She wrapped herself around me and wouldn't let go." His brother looked pissed.

"To become the next Kardashian," Dylan said dryly.

"What?" Owen asked, sitting down on his bed. The room wasn't big, but at least it was cozy enough to have three beds fit in it.

"Fame," he answered. "Of dating a Costa. She'll probably do an interview from a local newspaper exposing us. I can just see it now:

'Wealthy sons of millionaire Leo Costa reduced to living in a single room. Forced to beg work from local seniors' camp. See how far the prodigal sons have fallen without the guidance of their father.' What's going to happen if we don't control the situation soon?"

"Damn." Owen slapped his shoes on the floor and ran his hands through his hair. "Now it looks like we have to come up with another plan." He turned to Dylan. "How did it go with Zoey?"

"As expected." He shrugged and tried not to allow his face to betray what he thought of their kiss. "How about you?"

Owen shook his head. "Struck out with Aubrey. She's just too . . . fragile." He threw his hands up in the air. "To be honest, I'm kind of afraid I'll either break her or piss her off by crossing her. I haven't figured her out yet."

"What about Hannah?" Liam asked.

"There's something more there." Owen swung his legs up onto his bed. "I'm not sure what it is, but she's hiding something. Trust me. I'll get to the bottom of it."

Dylan knew his brother would; after all, for the past year, he'd pretty much been acting as head of Paradise Investments, shortly after their father had started acting up. Whether it was a midlife crisis or he was hiding something, the three of them were determined to get to the bottom of their father's recent disappearances, along with the disappearance of most of the cash in his accounts.

Owen turned to Liam. "How did it go with Elle?"

"Like you said." Liam nodded at Owen. "There's something more there. I don't know what it is yet, but I can tell you this: if she is Dad's latest conquest, she's unlike all the others."

"What do you mean?" Owen shifted to look at Liam better. "She fits his type perfectly. Blonde"—he ticked off on his finger—"busty, young, has a business that needs funding."

Owen was right. In the past few years, their father had fallen for a certain type. The relationships usually cost him more money than necessary. Not that they didn't have it to spend, but still—all it would take was one who was smarter than the others to wipe out the family fortune. It was one of the main reasons they were here and so worried.

Liam stood up and started pacing. "She's smart. Smarter than what we've seen before."

"So?" Owen said. "It's either Elle or Hannah." He cupped his hands behind his head.

"You're being an ass," Liam said.

Owen glanced up at him. "This isn't a playdate. We're here to do a job."

"These are people's lives," Liam said, his voice rising slightly. "If they have anything to do with convincing our father to invest here instead of closer to home, why should we really care?"

Owen slowly sat up, his eyes flitting between Dylan and Liam.

"Because, no matter how you play it, almost a million is a lot to invest in a business that benefits someone other than family."

The room was silent. "It's not like it wasn't Dad's money to invest," Dylan said after a moment.

"No, but it was set aside for other things, and the board wants to know more. And since we can't get Dad to return our calls, we're here." Owen lay back down. "So, the question is, how do we deal with Ryan?"

That question had been running through Dylan's mind ever since she'd caught him. If she exposed them now, it could mean a change in the game—blocking their access to the camp and stopping them from getting any answers from the women about their father.

They needed to keep Ryan quiet if they were going to find out anything, but the only way to do so wasn't a line he was willing to cross. Not for her, anyway.

CHAPTER
SIX

Zoey showed up at the smaller swimming pool just before sunrise and stared down at the destruction in horror.

All the lounge chair pillows had been tossed around the pool deck or into the water. A few pool towels lay in a morass of beer bottles and plastic cups from the pool bar.

Already, the cleaning crew were taking care of most of the mess.

"So," Elle said, her arms crossed over her chest. "How do we prevent this from happening again?"

"I couldn't believe it when you called me." Zoey held in a sigh. Then turned to Elle. "You're the one that said adults were easier than kids."

Elle rolled her eyes just as Hannah, Scarlett, and Aubrey entered from a pathway. Each of them stopped at the opening of the pool deck as their jaws dropped.

"What happened?" Hannah asked quietly as she approached them.

"I'm not sure, but I was about to go view the security tapes." Elle turned, and they all followed her to the main building while the crew did their best to put everything back in order.

Even though the security system played on screens in all the offices with a simple log-in, to see the security history still took logging in to the main security system on Elle's computer.

When the five of them stepped into the office, Elle moved behind the desk and sat down.

"What are we going to do? We can't just allow this sort of destruction constantly. I mean, what if we have to buy new cushions, or what if the mess causes damage to the pool pumps? We can't afford to constantly fix things like that around here." Hannah thumped the desk.

Elle logged in and, after pulling up the correct file, hit the button, and the video began to play.

"We'll have to deal with it. We have a small budget for repairs, but most of the money is going into the new cabins and to pay what employees we have," Elle answered.

The five of them watched the scene unfold in fast motion.

First, one couple arrived at the pool; the time mark said a quarter past one in the morning. Zoey rolled her eyes when they immediately stripped off their clothes and jumped in. "Great, old-people porn," Zoey said under her breath, earning her a nudge from Elle.

The time mark showed that less than five minutes later, another couple arrived with a six-pack of beer. They quickly talked to the first couple, then stripped naked and jumped into the water.

"Seriously?" She groaned, earning her another nudge.

Now, as the tape sped up, four more couples arrived, all stripping naked and jumping into the water.

"Oh my!" Hannah said slowly. "Look, they're . . . swapping."

"What?" Aubrey gasped, then turned away.

"See, that's Elaine and Albert Tilton, from Houston, but Elaine is with Dane Juarez, while her husband, Albert, is with Sarah Juarez." She pointed to the screen, where two couples were making out. When everyone just continued to look at her, she sighed. "They swapped partners. Look." Everyone turned back to the screen.

"Thank god the water is dark enough that we can't see what was going on under there," Zoey said.

Then, to their horror, a couple jumped out of the water naked and laid the lounge cushions on the side of the pool.

Elle gasped and shut off the monitor, then turned to them.

"We're a high-end swingers' camp," she said under her breath as her face turned pale.

"Hey." Zoey walked over and took Elle's shoulders. "Maybe it was just a fluke?"

A low male chuckle sounded behind them. They had all been so engrossed in watching the computer screen that they hadn't heard Dylan enter the room and stand behind Zoey.

"I doubt it," he said easily. "Something like that doesn't happen naturally. They probably set it up before coming here. I doubt it'll be the only get-together while those couples are staying here."

Everyone in the room was looking at him, and he just shrugged. "What? Old people have sex drives too. You had to know this before you opened the gates."

"Sure." Elle rubbed her forehead. "It's just . . . well, we expected them to do that *inside* their cabins."

Dylan chuckled. "Look, no harm, no foul. You can probably put out a bulletin about destroying property. I'm sure everyone will obey the rules."

Elle nodded. "I'll send a text out to all of the cabin systems this afternoon." Then she turned to the computer. "I'm going to delete the footage and any more that may show up. I'll know, if word gets out about this, that it was you." She glanced up at Dylan.

Dylan laughed. "Yes, boss." He made a move as if he were zipping his lips.

"I need some coffee after . . . that show." Zoey motioned to the computer screen.

"More like a cigarette," Hannah said under her breath.

"I expect you'll hold what we witnessed with both the utmost respect and the privacy of our guests as your priority," Elle said to the room, but her gaze was glued on Dylan.

"Of course." His smile disappeared and he nodded.

Aubrey interrupted them. "Thank you. We appreciate it."

They all turned and left the office. Dylan followed them out.

"Coffee and food first; then we'll have our meeting," Elle said.

When he started to tag along, Zoey stopped him by grabbing his arm. "What are you doing here?"

"I was coming to see you."

"I . . ." She glanced around him and down the hallway, where Elle stood in the doorway to the dining room, watching them. "I have a meeting."

She started past him.

"Later?" he asked, his hand brushing hers. She held in a smile as she nodded quickly and then rushed to catch up with Elle.

"What was that about?" Elle asked, her eyes watching Dylan disappear out the back door.

"Nothing," she mumbled and nudged her friend into the dining room.

The five of them walked into the dining room at a quarter past six. There were a few guests sitting at tables, enjoying coffee and breakfast from the buffet.

Most of the staff enjoyed breakfast in the staff meeting room, where another buffet was set up for each meal.

However, this morning, they needed to have a meeting out of earshot.

"Let's take that table in the back," Elle said, motioning to the table by the large windows.

Everyone went through the buffet line, grabbed their drinks, and filled the table farthest away from the prying ears of the few guests up this early.

"So," Elle started. "First off, how can we tell which guests are here to . . . party, and which ones aren't?"

"We should have taken a better look at the video," Aubrey said.

Zoey chuckled. "Go on back tomorrow morning. I'm sure there'll be more to watch."

"I made a point to memorize most of our guests as Julie and her crew checked them in," Hannah surprised them by saying. "It's one way to be sure you're getting the right people to the right events later on without name-tagging everyone. I can write down the ones I know from the video."

Elle nodded. "Send it to us, only I'll compile a memo that I will send out to all of the cabins with our announcements." She stretched her arms. "I have no idea what it's going to say, but I think we should leave it as a reminder to be respectful of camp property. After all, swinging isn't illegal." She whispered the last bit.

Zoey chuckled again. "Sorry," she said when everyone looked at her. "God, how embarrassing was it to watch that in front of Dylan?"

Her friends erupted in laughter.

"Okay, now for the rest of today's business," Elle finally said as she pulled out her phone and started at the top of the list.

By the time they'd dumped their empty food plates into the dish bins, they all had an idea of what their days were going to hold.

Zoey headed straight for the pool area to make sure everything was back in order, since it was on the way to the zip line. Knowing her mother was going to be going out in less than half an hour with Dylan had her concerned.

She hadn't had time to call or text her last night, since she knew that her mother was always in bed no later than nine each night.

When she climbed the stairs to the small hut that marked the beginning of the zip line trails, Dylan was out front, sipping out of a thermos and watching her.

"Morning." He toasted her with his thermos. "Heard there was some . . . excitement at the pool last night."

Her back teeth clenched at his smirk. "Shut up," she hissed with a glare.

Dylan's smile widened, then fell quickly as he leaned closer to her. "Just an FYI: the cleanup crew found a lot more than soaked cushions and empty beer bottles. You might want to have a chat with them as well."

Zoey tensed. She hadn't thought of all the aspects of a sex party. There had probably been more used condoms and empty condom wrappers than there had been beer bottles.

"Ew"—she shivered—"gross. Let's never discuss this topic again." The memory of what they had seen on the computer screen threatened to cause her face to turn beet red.

Dylan's chuckle was one of the sexiest sounds she'd heard in a long time.

Crossing her arms over her chest to try to act casual, she decided to think about something else. "It's a beautiful morning."

Still, she knew that within the next hour or two, the heat would be in full swing.

"Come to put a halt to your mother's fun this morning?" He leaned on the railing next to her.

She felt how close his body was to hers and could even feel the heat radiating from him. Her first instincts were to pull away, but instead, she tilted her head and stayed where she was.

"If I asked you, would you turn her away?"

His dark eyes scanned her face.

"No." He shook his head. "I can't stop my father from all of his midlife craziness, and I don't think it's right for you to stop Kimberly's."

"The fact that you call my mother by her first name gives me more concern," she admitted.

"Hey, she's the one who asked me to call her that." He smiled. "Not Kim. Kimberly."

"My father used to call her Kim." She groaned.

"Used to?" he asked.

"Before he ran off with a woman a few years older than me." She leaned on the railing next to him.

"Ouch!" He shook his head. "Your mother seems like a wonderful woman. Your father must be stupid."

Zoey smiled. "Kiss-up." She nudged his shoulder with hers.

"It's the truth," he said as he reached up and brushed a strand of her hair away from her eyes. The move was so natural that she felt her breath catch in her lungs, waiting, hoping he'd make another move.

"What about your folks?" she asked, looking off over the tree line until her heart settled back down.

"Mom died shortly after giving birth to Liam."

"I'm sorry," she said, causing him to nod slightly. "What about your father?"

He sighed. "He's off sowing his wild oats somewhere."

"You don't know where he is?" She was shocked and straightened up as he shrugged. Then she remembered that, currently, she didn't know what her own father was up to.

"Not right now, no." He glanced around, and she could tell he was calculating something in his head. "Actually"—he straightened and turned toward her—"we had thought he might be here."

"Here?" She balked. But before she could ask him what he meant, she heard her mother's voice.

"This is a surprise."

Kimberly Rowlett was the most beautiful fifty-five-year-old woman Zoey had ever seen. Her mother's silky silver hair was the envy of any young woman trying to match it with dye nowadays. Though her mother's smile drew everyone in, she retained an underlying shyness as well as a touch of reserve that neither Zoey nor Scarlett had inherited.

"Morning." Zoey walked over and kissed her mother's cheek. "How are you settling in?" She'd only gotten over to the River Cabin a few times to help her mother unpack, since she'd been too busy preparing for opening day.

"Oh." Her mother waved her hand. "I'm almost done unpacking. How was opening day? Am I the only one this morning?"

"The only one who's early." Dylan smiled at her.

"My mother is always early to everything," Zoey teased her.

"As you should be." Her mother patted her arm. "Dylan has promised to show me a good time today." Her genuine smile always filled Zoey with more desire to protect her mom's instant innocent love for strangers. Dylan in this case.

"We have a good-size group this morning." He walked over and picked up a sheet. "Four couples and a last-minute sign-up for someone named Reed Cooper." Dylan glanced up.

"He's a local," Zoey filled in. "He lives across the water." They were deep in the tall pine trees, so the thick underbrush restricted their view of the bay. "We've made a deal with him," Zoey added, feeling the need to explain to her mother. "He's paying to use all of the facilities. Sort of like a private club." She leaned closer to her mother. "We suspect he's a spy for the government."

"Oh?" Her mother smiled. "Why?"

"He fits the stereotype." Zoey winked at her. "You'll see for yourself." She cocked her head at the man strolling up the trail. The fact that Reed Cooper was easily the best-looking man over fifty Zoey had ever seen wasn't the only positive thing about him.

He wore black, all the time. Today's black T-shirt hugged impressive muscles that rivaled Dylan's. His thick salt-and-pepper hair was neatly trimmed, as was the scruff on his face. Zoey doubted the man's sharp green eyes missed any small detail.

Right now, his scan took in Zoey's mother, and Zoey was pretty sure she heard her mother make a soft sound of appreciation.

"Yeah," Zoey said softly.

But the main reason Reed Cooper fit the spy mold was that he was a very silent, private man.

His massive mansion had caught her eye the first time she'd visited the camp. The place had always looked like it belonged in Hollywood instead of in the middle of swampland in Florida. He drove a fast sports car and had a speedboat that flew across the bay in a few minutes' time, and she'd even seen a helicopter take off from his place a few times.

After quick introductions, Zoey pulled her mother aside while the men chatted.

"Why are you doing this?" she hissed.

"What?" Her mother's eyes were still glued to the newcomer.

"Mom"—she dragged the word out and nudged her mother until her eyes focused on her—"zip-lining is dangerous."

"Then why do you offer it to your guests?" her mother retorted.

"You know what I mean," Zoey said insistently. "It's dangerous for you."

"No, it's not. Dylan has assured me that I'm perfectly safe—"

"I don't care what Dylan said. Scarlett and I talked about it. We don't want you—"

"Zoey Elizabeth." Her mother's tone stopped her cold. "I am fifty-five years old. I think I can assess what is good for me and what isn't. I've gone years allowing someone else to rule my life. I'm done with that." Her mother clenched a fist and shook it. "If I want to go skydiving, I'll go. The fact that my daughters think they know better than I do what's best for me is downright insulting."

Zoey noted that the men had stopped talking to witness the scene.

Narrowing her eyes at Dylan, she snarled, "You'd better watch out for her. If she hurts one hair on her head, I'll come after you." She turned on her heel and marched down the steps and didn't stop until she stood outside her office door.

Feeling as if she hadn't cooled off yet, she decided not to go inside and instead took a turn around the grounds to stop herself from strapping in next to her mother.

When she returned to her office, beads of sweat were rolling down her back, and she took a few moments in the bathroom to wash her face and cool off.

She was a little surprised to see Ryan Kinsley as she stepped inside. The woman had taken a seat across from her desk and was waiting for her. Zoey must have unlocked the office the first time she'd arrived and forgotten to lock the door when she'd gone for a walk.

"I'm sorry. Did we have an appointment?" She pulled out her phone and looked at her schedule.

"No." Ryan smiled. "I was hoping we could have a little chat."

"Oh?" Zoey shut her door and walked over to make sure that her drawers and computer were still locked. "What can I help you with?" She slid into the seat behind her desk.

"Actually"—the woman leaned forward, her smile widening—"I think I'm the one who can help you."

Why this woman believed she could help Zoey was beyond her, but she was curious and, since she had a few free minutes, figured she could at least listen.

Still, it weighed on her knowing that Ryan had thrown herself at Dylan and Owen. She'd confirmed with Hannah, who had witnessed the scene between Ryan and Owen.

"The woman practically threw herself on him," Hannah had told her. "I mean, it was almost a reverse Me Too movement moment. I talked with Elle about firing Ryan, but she assured me that unless Owen filed a complaint, the only thing we could do was have an HR talk with her about her actions."

"Did Owen want to file a complaint?" she had asked Hannah.

"No." Hannah had frowned. "He assured me it was just a one-off and acted as if he wasn't fazed by it. What kind of man has so many women throwing themselves at him that he no longer notices?"

Hannah's question had rolled around in Zoey's mind and played against how Dylan had reacted to Ryan. There was definitely more to the brothers than they were letting on.

"Oh?" Zoey said again and leaned back.

CHAPTER
SEVEN

By the time Dylan was officially done for the day, the dark skies had opened up, and the downpour was almost blinding him while he made his way slowly back toward the main building.

Zoey had consumed his mind for the rest of the day—endless images of the way she moved, the way her eyes lit up when she smiled. He couldn't explain how she drew him to her but knew that if things were different, he would have no problem exploring his feelings further.

He had just turned the first corner in the pathway when he bumped into a very wet and very angry Zoey.

"We seem to keep bumping into one another," he joked. His smile fell slightly when he noticed the look in her eyes. "What's wrong? I made sure your mother didn't harm a hair on her head."

"I had a very interesting talk with Ryan Kinsley this morning."

"Oh?" Instant worry flooded him. Glancing around for some sort of shelter, he realized that there wasn't anything around, short of returning to the small hut where all the equipment was housed.

"Yes." Zoey shifted, and he realized that the cream work shirt hugged her curves perfectly. His mouth went dry as desire for her jumped full force. "She actually warned me away from you."

"She . . . what?" His eyes snapped to Zoey's.

"She told me that if I didn't stop flinging myself at you, she'd tell Elle." Zoey's laugh burst from her. "First off, I have never flung myself at a man before. Second, like her warning me would make a difference." She paced in a small circle as she spoke, as if she were upset. "Next, who does she think she is? Like Elle has any power over me. Doesn't she know we're partners in this venture? I mean—"

"Why don't you fire her?" he asked, interrupting her.

She frowned. "We're not exactly bursting with options at this point."

"Is that why you hired us?" As an answer, she shrugged and avoided his eyes. "What else did she say?" He almost held his breath waiting for the answer.

"Only that I'd regret it." Zoey's eyes darted to his lips quickly.

"Would you?" he asked, his heart skipping at the heat that he saw in her eyes as she stood in the rain.

"What?" Her gaze met his.

"Regret being with me?" He waited for her answer, which seemed to take forever.

"No." She shook her head, then rushed up, wrapping her arms around his neck as her lips covered his.

Water rolled down them, turning into steam from their heated skin. He moved quickly, stepping until his back foot hit the stairs to the hut. Their lips hadn't broken contact, and Zoey was pulling and tugging his wet shirt up and over his shoulders.

After he unlocked the hut door, she managed to free him from the wet shirt, and her hands rushed over his skin.

"My god," she almost hissed as her eyes ran over him. "It's better than I imagined."

He smiled quickly, then pulled her closer to him. Her wet shirt hit his skin as he kicked the door shut behind them. Then he moved until her back was pressed against the door. His fingers dipping under her wet shirt as she scraped her short nails over his shoulders.

When he tugged her shirt over her head, she giggled slightly, and he watched as goosebumps rose all over her skin.

"Beautiful," he said softly as his eyes ran over her perfect body. Her cream-colored bra was as wet as her shirt had been, turning the material translucent. The waistline of her shorts hung low on her hips. He used a fingertip to trace from her chin, down between her breasts, and over her ribs and navel, stopping at the button of her shorts. His eyes moved up to hers.

"I've wanted you," he said.

"I know." She put her hands on his shoulders and pulled him closer, covering his lips with hers as he unbuckled her shorts. They slid down her legs and landed on the floor.

She kicked her feet free as he hoisted her up in his arms, pinning her back to the door again as their mouths fused together. Her legs wrapped around his hips as his free hand cupped her outside her silky panties that covered her still.

Her fingers fisted in his hair as her mouth demanded more. She tasted better than anything he'd ever had before. He knew he could spend hours exploring her mouth, enjoying the feeling of it next to his.

"Zoey"—he broke free—"I . . . damn." He remembered then that he'd forgotten to put some condoms in his wallet. Hell, he'd never imagined finding someone like her here.

Resting his forehead on hers, he sighed. He wanted her, bad. But—he glanced around the small hut filled with harnesses and carabiners—this wasn't the place he'd imagined being with her.

"Let's try this instead," he said, hoisting her up to the high countertop. Her eyes closed in pleasure when he slid her panties down her legs, running his hands over the smooth skin of her thighs. He took a moment to appreciate her beauty as she leaned back against the countertop.

Instead of dropping his own shorts and stepping between her legs, he knelt and covered her with kisses on her inner thighs as his fingertips slowly ran over her skin.

She propped her legs on his shoulders as he traced her skin with his tongue. When he slid a finger gently into her, she arched and cried out with pleasure. "Dylan." His name sounded like heaven, echoing in the small space.

"Yes." He smiled as his tongue darted into her.

Her fingers fisted once again in his hair as she moved her hips under him.

He couldn't help it; he wanted to give her everything but knew he wanted more of her himself. Savoring as much as he could, he relished the smoothness of her skin against his lips and hands.

When he felt her building, he dipped another finger into her heat and held on to her as she tightened around him.

If he hadn't been holding on to her hips, she would have slid to the floor of the hut.

"Easy." He chuckled and wrapped his arms around her more tightly. He felt her body cooling next to his and glanced down at her wet clothes. Then pulled his extra jacket from the hook behind the door and wrapped it around her instead.

"Sorry. I didn't think you'd want to put those back on." He nodded to the floor.

"Whose is this?" she asked, hugging the jacket to herself.

"Mine. I left it here the other night," he answered. "I didn't leave an extra pair of shorts."

Zoey chuckled. "I can survive with those." She started to pull him close, but he stopped her.

"Next time," he promised her. "Right now, let me just hold on to you." He kissed her slowly, letting their bodies cool down further. "She must have really pissed you off earlier," he said when he pulled away again.

"Who?" Zoey sighed and opened her eyes.

"Ryan," he answered.

"Oh"—he felt her stiffen—"not really. I mean, sure, I was pissed that she was trying to warn me away from you." She shook her head. "But it wasn't she who'd pissed me off when I walked over here."

"No?" he asked. "Then who?"

"I caught some more couples in the act." She sighed. "So, I went back to my office and did a Google search."

"And?" he asked.

"There's a few swinger sites that mention us. How can we be known for swinging when we just opened our doors?"

"It's the age range. You're gearing your camp to fifty-five and above."

"So?" She shook her head. "We're also more expensive than most places around here."

He chuckled. "Just because someone has extra money after their kids are grown and out of the house doesn't mean they only use it on cruises."

Her eyes narrowed, and she jumped from the countertop to pick up her shorts and shake them out before sliding them up her legs.

"Cold," she gasped as she buttoned them. "How is it that men know more about swingers than we do?"

"Men?" he asked, curious.

"You and your brothers seem to be experts."

He chuckled. "Not an expert, but yeah—we're guys."

She shrugged. "So what? Porn sites?"

He decided it would be best to remain silent on the topic. Sure, he'd learned early in his teens about internet porn. Hell, what boy growing up with a computer hadn't at this stage? But most women didn't like knowing that guys, every guy, watched porn ever in their lives.

"Okay." She started to pace the small space. "So, how do we turn this around?"

"Why would you?" he asked. "As long as you implement rules to respect the grounds, your clients are paying high dollar for cabins, fun, and exciting activities in and out of the bedroom." He smiled. "If it keeps the cabins booked, I say go with it. You might even want to add a condom vending machine somewhere."

Her eyes narrowed. "But . . ." She bit her bottom lip.

"I'm not saying you should go out and buy a full-size ad in *SwingersRUs*, but for now, let it play out. Who knows. Maybe after this first group, things will settle down."

She sighed, and he could tell she had hoped for the same.

"Have you eaten yet?"

Her eyes met his, and she shook her head. "No, I was too busy to eat dinner."

He held out his hand. "Come on."

She stopped and picked up her ruined shirt, wrung it out, and tucked it in the pocket of his jacket, then took his hand.

He locked up the hut again. The rain had lessened a little, so by the time they walked into the main building, they weren't completely soaked. At least not like before.

"I'm going to run up and grab a dry shirt," she said at the base of the stairs.

He glanced down at his own shirt and nodded. "Good idea. Let's meet here in about ten?"

What he wanted to do was follow her up the stairs and spend the night in bed with her, but he knew that just like him, she had roommates. Not to mention he had a lot of thinking he wanted to do about what sleeping with Zoey meant. He wanted to make sure he wasn't using her to get what he wanted. Something deep inside him didn't trust himself around her, and he needed to understand why that was.

They made their way up the first set of stairs; then she waved at him as he moved down the hallway, and she headed up the rest of the stairs.

He changed his shirt quickly, then opened his door to go meet Zoey, only to find Ryan standing outside it. Blocking her from walking past him into his room, he nudged her back and shut the door behind him.

"What do you want now?" he asked.

"You know what I want," she murmured as she pressed him against the closed doorway, stopping him from moving. Her fingertips dug into his arms as she held him there. He could have broken free, but he didn't want it to appear as if he were aggressive if anyone stumbled upon them. "You and your brothers are stalling about giving me a commitment for taking me with you when you leave."

"We're discussing it." He shook her off him and sidestepped until he was free of her hold.

"You have until the end of this month to choose. One way or another I'll get what I want, or I will tell them all I know about the Costa family." She turned to go. "Oh, and by the way, you'd better watch out for Zoey. She has a few secrets of her own." She disappeared down the hallway.

Meeting Zoey at the base of the stairs, he tried to act as if nothing had happened earlier. His body still burned for her, but Ryan had been the wake-up call he'd needed. He was here on a mission. To find his father and to find the family money his father might have invested into the camp. Getting close to Zoey could only mean one thing: getting the answers they needed. The attraction he felt for her couldn't go any further, not with the secrets separating them.

So, he kept himself in check as they ate dinner at a large table in a room filled with other employees. He knew a lot of them by name at this point, since he'd had to work with most of them.

When his brothers joined them, he wasn't surprised to see Elle, Hannah, Scarlett, and even Aubrey sit at the table with them.

The talk turned toward the weather; since the evening rain had continued on and off, they were all hoping the skies would clear by tomorrow, when everyone had a full schedule planned.

He listened to the five of them talk about what needed to be done over dinner. From his calculations, Zoey still had a few more hours of work to do that evening.

He'd considered himself clocked out after his last zip line tour of the day. Suddenly feeling guilty, he asked if there was anything he could help with.

Seven pairs of eyes turned toward him.

Shrugging, he sipped his soda to give himself a moment. "What? I'm done for the evening. I might as well—like, I can make the rounds instead of Zoey." He nodded toward her. "That way you can do all that other stuff on your list."

"It's not a bad idea," Elle said, glancing over at Zoey. A look passed between the two of them.

"I'm done for the night too," Liam chimed in. "I'll take your rounds around the boathouse, Scarlett."

"Why is it you five decided to play security at night, anyway?" Owen asked.

"We're not . . ." Hannah started, then sighed. "It's just an extra precaution we decided to try."

Dylan smiled. "What if one of you stumbled across another orgy in session?"

Zoey kicked him softly under the table.

"Another?" Owen asked, his eyes moving to Hannah, who quickly rolled her eyes at him. So he turned back to Dylan. "What is it with you and walking in on orgies?"

He nudged his brother under the table, earning him a glare from Owen and a look of questioning from Zoey.

"We didn't stumble across it," Zoey said.

"Just watched it on video the morning after," Dylan added. "What?" he said when this time it was Zoey who kicked him under the table. Rubbing his shins, he continued, "We're among friends here. Besides, the gossip has spread like wildfire around the camp."

"Okay." Elle stood up and took a deep breath. "I suppose we should have known it would get out. After all, after hearing what the cleaning crew had to deal with, the events at the pool were obvious. We're going to have to have an employee meeting, tonight." She caught Zoey's eye. "Let's say eleven? That way the kitchen staff has plenty of time to attend. We can even hold it in the dining room."

Zoey stood as well and took her empty plates. "I'll put out a bulletin." She glanced down at Dylan. "You and your brothers have just volunteered to make the nightly rounds for the week."

Dylan heard a groan, realized it was his own, and clamped his mouth shut. "Consider it done."

"Thanks," Owen said once the three of them were left alone at the table.

"For?" He swallowed the last sips of his soda.

"You're the one who brought up the orgy," Liam added and nudged him.

"Hey," he answered back. "This gives us an excuse to be out at night, and an opportunity to look around to see if Dad is hiding out somewhere—not to mention we can sneak around for more clues about the ladies. We can also take the opportunity to talk to some of the other staff without them around, to see if anyone knows something more."

His brothers were silent. "Okay, we'll meet out front in . . ." Owen glanced down at his watch. "Half an hour and make plans."

Dylan glanced at his watch, then got up, dumped his plates, and rushed to find Zoey.

He found her sitting in her office, typing away at her computer.

"Hey." He knocked on the open door. She glanced up at him and nodded. "I'm sorry about bringing the orgy up." He moved into the room as she continued to type. He sat down across from her desk and waited. When she was done, she glanced up at him. "Are you pissed? My brothers already knew about it—they helped the cleaning crew fix the cushions, and Liam had to fix one of the chairs."

"No." She tilted her head. "Like Elle said, we should have known word would get out. Employees have signed NDAs about our guests. Gossip is not tolerated."

"Ouch," he said under his breath, causing her eyebrows to shoot up.

When she stood, he watched the movement and remembered how her body had felt against his. It was hard to stop the want, but he kept telling himself he didn't want to use Zoey like all those women had used his father in the past. He was better than that. But as he watched her pace around the space, the way her hips swayed and the way her ass looked in those tight shorts sure made it difficult.

"We're trying to run a high-end business here. Something that hasn't been done in the States before. We're hoping to keep our clientele level high." She sat on the edge of the table and placed her arms across her chest. "If word got out that employees leaked gossip, I doubt we'd see the same quality as we have right now."

"I'm sorry." He reached up to rub her arm. He knew the right thing to do was to steer clear of her, but his desires were quickly winning out over caution.

"For what?" She placed a hand over his; the simple move caused his desire for her to triple. "Actually, I should be thanking you. We've been so busy we didn't think of heading off the chatter, before you mentioned something."

As he stood up, he watched her gaze heat. "We'll finish this." He leaned in and placed a kiss on her widening smile. "But for now, I have to go make the rounds with my brothers. Why exactly do you think walking around the grounds is a good idea?" he asked, his hands running up her sides.

"We're hoping that if they see that we patrol, they won't engage in . . . activities out in the open. I mean, when you go skinny-dipping, the last thing you want is security walking up." She laughed.

"Okay." He shook his head, then leaned in and kissed her again. "God, you taste so good."

She fisted her hands in his hair and pulled him back down for another kiss, which then left him vibrating the entire time he patrolled the campgrounds by himself in the dark.

They had agreed to divide the acreage into three different sections. He walked around the main building and headed down toward the boathouse, passing the pool and pool house. There were tons of people sitting out on the back patio under the awnings, enjoying food, drinks, and music from a local band that had been hired to play on the weekends. Since the rain hadn't really let up much, the dance floor was empty, but still, he was surprised at how many people tolerated the rain to be out.

He had pulled on a rain jacket and had a flashlight to see the way through some of the darker areas.

The pool was empty, thankfully, and he walked over to scan the pool house, which had a few guests still inside. He knew there were massage as well as sauna rooms near the back. He opened the door, stepped in, and looked around. It was the first time he'd been in here.

The front of the building was one huge glass wall, looking out to the pool and the water beyond. Large white-cushioned wood sofas faced each other, with teal pillows. Several guests sat sipping from water bottles, waiting for their massages.

"Evening." He sketched a brief wave.

"Evening," the guests said back, eyeing him as if he were a piece of candy.

There was a back hallway with several doors—each marked either SAUNA, CHANGING ROOMS, or MASSAGE ROOM. One of the massage rooms had a door hanger that said IN SESSION.

He was just about to turn around when the door opened, and a very attractive blonde woman stepped out in a black stretch tank top with the camp logo on it. Her arms were lavished with colorful tattoos, but her hair was neatly tied back, showcasing a clean and beautiful face.

"Hi." She ran her eyes up and down him. "Are you Wayne?"

"No." He shook his head. "I'm Dylan. I work here." He pointed to the logo on his shirt, which had been covered by the rain jacket.

"Oh." Her smile grew. "I'm Andrea. I come in occasionally and do massages here." She snuggled up to the door and licked her lips. "Maybe we can hang out sometime?"

Normally, he would have taken the woman up on her offer, but with his lips still vibrating from Zoey's kiss, he happily declined and stepped aside while a gray-haired man in nothing but a camp robe stepped through the massage doorway instead.

After the pool house, he made his way down to the dock and boathouse.

Here, he found the place empty and peaceful. The rain had slowed to a light mist in the air. Standing on the dock, he watched the dark waters and took in a deep breath.

Looking around, he realized just how amazing the place really was. When he turned, he saw all the lights of the buildings illuminate the night in the distance. From the docks, he could see the main building and the pool house. Each of them had strings of white lights hanging off the back over outdoor patios.

"Pretty amazing, isn't it?" someone said from the dark. He had to admit that he almost squealed like a teenage girl.

He didn't know how he'd missed the older man sitting at the end of the dock with his legs dangling in the water.

Now, however, Dylan could easily see the red, glowing tip of a cigarette.

"Sorry." Dylan moved to the end of the dock, and the smell of weed instantly hit him. *Not a cigarette,* he thought as he stopped beside the man. "I didn't see you there."

"No worries." The older man glanced up at him. "Medicinal." He waved the joint he was smoking. "Damn Parkinson's."

"I'm sorry," Dylan said.

"Thanks. This helps mask it, so I can do simple things like walk, talk, live." The man chuckled, then took another hit.

"I'm Dylan." He sat down next to the man and held out his hand to shake his.

"Ross." The man met his grip, and Dylan noticed a slight tremor in his hands. "Patterson. We're in the Refuge. Sorry—this was my wife's idea."

"Pretty good one, I'd wager." Dylan watched as the moon finally poked out from behind the clouds, the light reflecting off the calm waters.

"So far, so good." Ross took another hit. "We don't have many warm nights like this in Oregon. I would have killed for a job like this when I was your age."

"Oregon's nice," Dylan responded, remembering the last time his father had taken them on a ski trip to Mount Hood. It had been years since they had taken a trip with him anywhere. It was almost as if a switch had been flipped one year, and the interest the man had previously had in them had died down. They hadn't noticed it, until he'd disappeared this time.

"Yeah, this stuff is legal there." The man waved the joint.

"It is here too, with a medical card." He rested against the railing. "So I won't be running to the police, if you're worried."

The man laughed. "Son, at my age and my condition, I don't give a damn about spending the night behind bars." He sobered. "No, what I worry about is leaving my beautiful wife too early." He tossed the used joint into the water, where they watched it sink. "I waited too damn long in life to finally ask for her hand."

He held up his left hand so that the moonlight glinted off his wedding ring. "I met Lara almost ten years before I grew the balls to ask her out." He rested back, his eyes going to the stars. "Five more years before I asked her to marry me. I shouldn't have wasted any time."

"You have time now," Dylan said, feeling his heart break slightly for the man.

"She deserves more than a man like this . . ." He held up his hand, and it began to tremor. Dylan didn't know what to say. "Well." The man stood up slowly, and Dylan stopped himself from helping him move. "Son, enjoy what you have now. If you have a woman, and she's worth holding on to, don't take too long to do it. Night." Ross slapped him on his back and started strolling slowly, relying on a cane as he walked down the dock and pathway.

Dylan watched the man go and turned his eyes back to the water and thought of Zoey. If she was the one, would he let what was going on with his father get in the way? What if she did know something about where his father was hiding or about the missing money? Maybe the money hadn't gone into the camp at all? Would that change how he felt about her?

His first answer to all of it was no. Maybe it was the honesty he saw behind her eyes, or maybe it was just his libido answering for him, but either way, he doubted that she would ever intentionally do anything to cheat someone else. Even for the sum of money his father was worth. Zoey was better than that. Didn't he owe it to her to give her a chance to explain what she did know?

When he stepped into the dining hall five minutes before the meeting, he found his brothers leaning against the back wall and stood with them.

As Zoey followed Elle into the room, he watched her eyes scan the small group of full-time and part-time employees, then briefly rest on him before moving on.

"Thank you, everyone, for taking time out of your evening for this impromptu meeting. We've heard the rumbles of gossip flooding through the camp." A few chuckles and whispers echoed through the room. Elle held up her hand to stop the noise. "We get one shot at this. To make River Camp something great, something to be proud of. To keep the high level of clientele we're so excited to have now. That same clientele who pay us to give them our best experience and to keep their secrets. If we spread gossip around, we might as well toss all that out the window." The room was silent. "Every one of you signed an NDA. Each of us as well. We may not all agree with how our guests live their lives, but it's not up to us. What is up to us is how we respect their privacy and how we deal with the situations as they arise." Elle visibly relaxed. "We appreciate how each of you have handled things so far, and we expect from here on out that the gossip floating around will be squashed quickly."

At this point Zoey stepped forward and touched Elle's shoulder.

Elle continued. "From the sounds of things, we should be expecting more of these . . . parties. We didn't plan for them, but I still expect everyone to handle our guests with great esteem and kindness. Yet we have started patrolling the common areas as a deterrent for destruction. If anyone happens to come upon anything, you're to call the front office immediately instead of intervening."

Elle stepped back. "Thank you for your time, and have a good evening."

"Well," Owen said, straightening up. "That was fun."

"Yeah, just like all those times in the principal's office getting chewed out for passing notes." Liam chuckled.

Dylan corrected him. "You weren't in the office for passing notes. None of us were." He smiled. "Besides, I'd rather have those five chewing me out than Principal Bowers any day."

"True," Owen said, grinning. "That man's face always turned a nasty shade of purple when he was yelling at us."

Dylan laughed at the memory and decided to wait until Zoey was done so he could walk with her to the stairs.

Ten minutes later, she was finally free after talking to several employees.

"So?" she asked. "How'd we do?"

He took her hand in his. "Remind me never to get in trouble around here."

She stopped and glanced up at him. "Was it that bad?"

He laughed. "Being reprimanded is never a good thing." He pulled her to a stop and then, after glancing around to make sure they were alone in the hallway, bent down and brushed his lips across hers. "But if I do have to be chastised, I pick you to do it."

CHAPTER
EIGHT

The first week after opening day had been more of a success than Zoey could have even predicted. Sure, there were a few hiccups, but when the following Saturday rolled around, she was thinking the first pool party had been a fluke.

For the most part, it appeared that any extra activities now were being done in private.

Her mind quickly moved from her guests' sex lives to Dylan and what he'd done to her in the small hut.

She hadn't been back there since and doubted she could step foot in the place without thinking about him. To be honest, she couldn't go a few minutes without thinking about him anyway. When she lay in her bed at night, in the dark, that moment was all she could think about. There were times she could still feel his mouth on her, his fingers inside her. She'd thought about picking up her phone and texting him her feelings but then kicked herself for being too clingy.

They'd enjoyed a few more meals together, and she had seen him several times during the day when she'd been rushing one way and he'd been going the other. But since that first night, they hadn't been alone. She could feel herself getting more desperate for his touch, and each time she was around him, her body would jump on its own. She kept telling herself that her strong desire to be with him was nothing more than her wanting to get over the long sex hiatus she'd been on while focusing on getting the camp ready.

But the fact was, she kept reminding herself, he and his brothers had secrets, and she couldn't trust him, but her body refused to listen to logic. No, her body was telling her to jump the man and not just once. She knew it would take a while to get her fill of him.

Since they had set out to watch the brothers, they had caught them on camera moving around the entire campground. However, since they were now filling the role of security, most of their movements were within the scope of that job. They no longer tried to get into any of the outbuildings, and they hadn't been seen sneaking into any offices again.

She wondered if they had found what they'd been looking for. If so, wouldn't they have left already? Why were they still sticking around? She and the girls were strapped enough for help as it was, so she couldn't just boot three good workers out. Was Dylan making a move on her because he wanted something from her? She knew that was a possibility. Was she prepared to expose her heart to new pain if he just used her and left after he'd taken what he wanted?

She had just left a couple she'd had a session with in which she'd taught them how to play pickleball and was heading up to her rooms to shower and change. Glancing down at her watch, she gauged she had about an hour before she was due in the dining hall.

Seeing Dylan was part of her everyday life at this point. All she had to do was learn to control her desires around him. It was as simple as that, right? Elle had been right: two could play the spy game. She'd find out what she could about him, while taking what she wanted from him. After all, there was no point in denying herself: if he was willing to go that far, so was she.

She was heading up to change when she noticed Ryan hanging out on the landing. "Is there something you needed?" she asked. She wasn't in the mood to deal with the jealous woman right now, especially since Dylan had kept his distance from her over the last week.

"Oh?" Ryan turned around, as if she hadn't seen Zoey climbing the first set of stairs. "Evening." She tried to scan the room as if she were waiting for someone. Perhaps she was—the woman was wearing a tight black dress better suited for nightclub life than a camp in the middle of the wilderness.

She decided to call her bluff. "Are you waiting for someone?"

"Yes." Her smile grew. "Dylan was supposed to meet me for dinner." She glanced down at her watch.

Zoey almost laughed but then decided to hold back. "Well, have fun." She waved to the woman as she started to climb the next set of stairs.

"You know who he is, then?"

Ryan's tone stopped her, and Zoey glanced over her shoulder. "Do you?"

Ryan walked to the base of the stairs, resting her hand on the railing. She lowered her voice slightly. "Let's just say that the Costas are well known in most circles." Ryan smiled.

"I'm sure they are." She narrowed her eyes at Ryan's words. The "Costas"? "Have a pleasant night." She turned to go and felt her entire body vibrating. She didn't know what it was about that woman, but she couldn't stand being around her for more than a minute at a time. It might be the smile that never left the woman's lips and yet didn't reach her eyes.

What did she mean? she asked herself as she let herself into their private rooms. *Costas?* The name rolled over in her mind as she tossed her tennis shoes into the bin by the door. She moved through the living space to the bedroom she shared with Scar at the end of the hallway.

She opened her laptop and waited for the old thing to boot up; five minutes later the update screen popped up. Updates could take forever on the old machine. Why did it seem that every time she opened the damn thing, it needed updates?

Frustrated, she pulled off the camp shorts and shirt, tossed them in the clothes bin, and walked into the bathroom for a quick shower.

Thirty minutes later, after slipping on a simple cotton dress, tying her hair up in a loose bun, and putting on minimal makeup, she sat at her computer, which had finally finished the update. She did a quick Google search for Dylan and his brothers with the word *Costas*.

The screen filled with multiple articles about the Costa brothers, including images. Her mind snapped. They had lied to her, to all of them, about their last name. But why? She opened a news article and was just about to read through it when her phone buzzed.

Zoey, get down here now!

Elle's text had her jumping up and glancing at the clock. She was late; they were supposed to have met five minutes ago to judge the first River Camp talent show.

She shut her laptop screen, slipped on a pair of heels, and rushed down the stairs. When she reached the main dining room, she found she was entering right as Dean Wallis was too.

"Evening," his deep voice rumbled.

Dean was one of the counselors who filled in when they needed him during the day and as a waiter by night. The man looked as if he'd been carved from stone—shockingly good looking.

"Hi." She started to pull away, but he reached out and touched her arm.

"Zoey, right?" he asked.

"Yes. Dean, right?" He nodded. "I'm late." She glanced over to where Elle was already introducing the first act.

"Maybe we can catch up later?" he said smoothly.

"Sure," she said and rushed away, thoughts of Dylan and his lying, no-good brothers surging into her mind.

"Sorry," she muttered as she reached Elle, who had handed over the microphone to the first act: a woman who began belting out a Mariah Carey song—fairly well too.

"That's okay." Elle glanced up and down at her. "I like that dress." She reached up and tucked back a strand of Zoey's hair that had fallen loose from her bun.

"Thanks," she said, reaching up and fixing it.

The fact that Elle's elegant silver dress clung to her beautiful slim body made Zoey instantly feel like a sack of potatoes next to her friend. But she knew that Elle meant what she said and took the compliment with grace.

"Where's everyone else?" She scanned the room for Hannah. She wanted all of them together when she told them the news about the brothers.

"I'm not sure; they should have been . . ." Elle stopped. "Hannah's here"—she pointed toward the back wall—"talking to Aubrey."

The two of them were joined by Scarlett a few moments later.

"I have something to tell you," she said to the group. "Later," she added as the current act ended and they needed to introduce the next one.

Each of them took turns introducing the next acts. Some of them good; others not so much. The funniest one by far was the couple who did a ventriloquist act. The husband sat on his wife's lap, dressed as a dummy, while she spoke.

Still, it was tough judging them all—three acts ranked in her top list. By the time the last act exited the stage, Zoey's head was about to explode.

"I thought adults were supposed to be better at this than kids," Scarlett whispered in her ear as a man and his wife tried to juggle on stage.

Zoey chuckled. "Remember our first talent show?"

Scarlett hissed and rolled her eyes. "Don't remind me."

Elle nudged her. "Ready to vote?"

They had kept track of the acts and had scored each of them. Elle handed over her sheet, tallied the votes, and smiled.

"Ladies and gentlemen, we have ourselves a winner. Will Wendy Mills please come up?" The room burst into cheers.

Hannah handed the silver trophy to Elle, who passed it on to the woman who had played violin.

"Thank you." Wendy beamed at the crowd. "However, this really should go to Denise." The room exploded with more cheers. "No, really, it's not fair. I play for the Phoenix Symphony. I only got up here because Denise begged me to."

The room clapped again as Denise, the woman who had sung Mariah's "Without You," came on stage. The women hugged each other.

"Thank you," Denise said. "I'm sure we'll take turns sharing this over the years." She wrapped her arm around her friend. "Thank you, Wendy, for giving me the courage to find my voice again." She hugged her.

When the microphone was handed back to Elle, she waited until everyone had settled down. "Now, as we close out the talent portion of the evening, we'd like you to sit back and enjoy the talented Deb Marton." Elle stood back as the curtain on the stage lifted.

The pianist walked gracefully across the stage and sat at the black grand piano that stood at its center.

The room fell silent as the lights dipped, and the melody started to fill the space.

Elle turned to Hannah and whispered, "This was a great idea. How on earth did you pull it off?"

Hannah smiled and glanced out at the full dining room. "You have your talents, and I have my secrets." She winked. It was something that Hannah always said. Their friend had still never filled them in on how she managed to get famous people to do things for her.

"Speaking of secrets," Zoey whispered to Elle. "I found out that the brothers' last name isn't really Rhodes. I started to do a search on them before coming over here but didn't get far enough to find out anything deeper than a few social media links. I needed more time."

Elle turned to her with a slight frown. "Why would they lie about their last name?"

She shrugged. "I'm not sure, but I'm going to figure it out."

"How *did* you find out?" Hannah asked.

"Ryan."

"Why does that woman have it out for us?" Elle whispered back. Zoey shrugged again. "Did you know, she actually came to me and tried to convince me that you were hurting this business?"

"What did you tell her?" Zoey asked.

"I told her that you were the major shareholder keeping this place open." Elle chuckled.

"You didn't!" she said slightly louder, earning her a poke in the ribs from Hannah.

"I did," Elle said. She added after a moment, "I thought it would keep her off your back for a while. Our records are public domain, after all."

"Why don't we just fire her?" Hannah whispered.

"Because, unless you can find someone else to fill her place, we're stuck. Besides, Brent and Isaac are pleased with her work. We want to keep *them* happy most of all. We can't afford to lose either of them over this."

"Agreed." Hannah nodded.

"Besides, I'm curious what she'll do next. I mean, it's almost like watching a spider weave its web," Zoey joked.

"I doubt she's smart enough to have a plan," Hannah said under her breath, gaining everyone's attention. "What? I've run into her. She doesn't come across as the evil-genius type."

Zoey scanned the crowd and noticed that the three brothers were missing. Then she remembered that they were on security duty. "I'm going to go get some air, then head up and finish my search. I'll fill you all in when you get done."

"Okay." Elle squeezed her arm.

"Good job." Zoey hugged Hannah. "She's amazing, and everyone is loving the show." Everyone in the dining hall was glued to the performance.

Stepping out into the cooler night air, she took a few breaths.

"Nice night." The deep voice had her wincing and wishing she'd checked around before stepping outside.

"Yes." She turned to Dean. The man moved from the shadows, tossing down a cigarette butt onto the ground. She wanted to berate him about the butt as he joined her but held back.

"So, how about a walk?" he asked.

She had been planning on taking a short stroll by herself to think through everything she'd found out, but now she wanted to head back up to her rooms to continue the internet search and pack for her day tomorrow.

"Thanks, but I'll pass." She started to move on but stopped. "You're missing the show."

"I'm on my break." He looked down at his watch. "We're serving champagne and cake after."

"Of course you are." She sighed. "Hannah thinks of everything."

"You've been busy around here."

"Yes, all of us have." He was good looking, but the man who filled her mind was on a date with Ryan at the moment. As she thought more about it, she realized they were perfect for one another: they both surrounded themselves in lies and deceit. Feeling defeated, she allowed Dean to move closer to her.

"I like your hair up." He brushed a fingertip down her cheek.

"Thanks." She suddenly realized how tall he was—taller than Dylan by about an inch. Dylan's shoulders were broader and more muscular, or at least she thought so from what she'd seen of Dean.

"I really want to kiss you," Dean said, his hand moving smoothly around to cup the back of her head, nudging her a step forward as he leaned closer.

She didn't know what to do or say. It was more instinct that had her hands going to his chest and stopping him. The smell of cigarettes floating in the air still.

"Thanks, but . . . I'm seeing someone," she started, not knowing if it was true or not. After all, Dylan hadn't given her any commitments or promises. Not to mention he'd lied to her about who he was. Still, she was thankful when Dean moved back a step.

"Too bad." He sighed. "Why am I always too late?" He shook his head. "No harm?"

"No." She smiled at him, and he grinned back.

"Whoever he is, he's a lucky man," he said before he turned toward the back door and disappeared through it.

She was temporarily blinded by the bright lights as he opened the door but relaxed as the darkness once again enclosed her.

"Yes, I am." A voice caused her to jump and turn around.

With those words, Dylan emerged from the darkness. Her mind instantly compared the two men. Where Dean had been smooth, Dylan was almost predatory.

"How . . ." she started to say, but he didn't stop until she was in his arms and his lips had covered hers.

She relaxed into the kiss, enjoying the feeling of him next to her again. It was hard to explain, but he felt like home. She ran her hands over those shoulders she'd dreamed about all week.

"I've missed you," he said against her skin. "I know I just saw you earlier today, but it's been almost a full week since I've gotten to kiss you like this." His hands tugged her hair loose.

"How long were you standing there?" she asked, a little breathless.

"Long enough to see you shoot him down." He chuckled. "Thank god. I'd hate to have to bust the guy's nose."

She pulled back with a frown. "Why would you bust his nose?"

Dylan smiled quickly. "For hitting on my woman."

His woman? Did she want to be his woman? Her first emotion was anger at being likened to his possession, but then she saw the humor in his eyes and relaxed slightly. She knew the pain of being with a man who lied. Her mother had suffered through years filled with lies. Did she want that for herself? No. Lies had brought her nothing but pain in the past and would continue to do so if she allowed them to.

She shoved him slightly and took a few steps away from the building, heading down the main path toward the front. She could have gone through the hallways but needed the fresh air instead. Dylan easily fell in step with her and rested his arm over her shoulders.

"So, I hear you have the next two days off?" he asked.

"I do," she said, looking up at him. "I'm not your woman," she added for good measure.

He smiled down at her. "I'll be your man." He wiggled his eyebrows at her.

She stopped in the middle of the pathway and turned toward him. "What makes you think I want you?" Her eyes ran over him as his name, his real one, circled in her mind. Dylan Costa. Somehow it sounded better than Dylan Rhodes.

"You just blew off tall, dark, and broody for me," he answered.

She narrowed her eyes at him. "Maybe I was talking about someone else?"

He surprised her by stepping closer and kissing her again. "God, I've missed the feel and taste of you," he said into her hair.

She sank into his embrace for a moment, enjoying it—momentarily forgetting about his lies and the pain they had caused her and just taking in the feel of him holding her.

"I work tomorrow, but I have Monday off." He leaned back to look down at her. "Play hooky and spend the day with me?"

She thought about her plans to veg all weekend, alone. What if she found out more about the brothers? What would that mean to her? Maybe if they spent the day together, she'd have an opportunity to catch him in a lie or maybe even get a confession out of him.

"What do you have planned?" she asked, tilting her head.

He smiled. "I'll think of something." He took her hand and started walking again.

Since most of the guests were inside the dining hall enjoying the show, the pathways were empty, and Zoey didn't care if they walked hand in hand. After all, if she was going to play the game, she needed to convince him that she trusted him.

"Your mother came back for more zip-lining."

"I know." She groaned. "I'm afraid you've turned her into an adrenaline junkie."

He chuckled. "She's still on the beginner course for now. But something tells me that she'll be on the advanced course before too long."

They entered the front entrance to the building together.

"Zoey." Julie rushed after her as they started heading up the stairs. The shorter woman was a little winded. "Sorry," she said, glancing between Dylan and Zoey. "Your father's on the phone."

Zoey tensed and dropped Dylan's hand. "Have him leave a message."

"He won't," she said. "He's been on hold for almost ten minutes. He says it's urgent." She moved closer. "It sounds bad—he keeps trailing off."

Zoey sighed and glanced at Dylan. "I'll take it in my office." She started for the stairs. She'd been avoiding his calls. It had been almost five years since she'd last seen the man. To be honest, she didn't know why all of a sudden he was calling her so much. She'd believed that he'd forgotten all about her and Scar, that they were better off because of his silence.

"I'll see you Monday," Dylan called out.

She waved and continued down the hallway.

She answered the flashing line on the phone. "Hello?"

"Zoey?" Her father's voice sounded faint.

"Yes." She pushed the phone up to her ear so she could hear better.

"I was hoping to do this in person." And the line went so quiet that she wondered if he'd hung up. "I'm so sorry about leaving you and Scarlett the way I did." She waited, knowing that a simple apology wouldn't cover the pain and hurt that he'd caused. "I had hoped to have more time, but it just wasn't in the cards for me. Bridgette left me."

She smothered a laugh. "I'm surprised it lasted this long."

Her father's sigh assured her that her words had landed on the mark.

"I've changed things around. I only wish that I could help out more, but she took most of it. There isn't a lot left over. You and Scarlett have taken such good care of your mother. I'm so proud of what you two have done. I want you to know that."

Suddenly her mind snapped to what this phone call meant. "Dad?" She held the phone closer. "What's wrong?"

"Tell your sister I love her and I'm so proud of her, and . . ." There was a long pause. "Tell your mother that I never really stopped loving her."

"Dad?" Her voice rose slightly. "Where are you?"

"I'm going to hand the phone over; they'll explain everything." His voice had grown even softer. "I love you."

Zoey waited as the phone changed hands. A woman's voice came on the line. "Ms. Rowlett?"

"Yes?" She hadn't realized tears were sliding down her cheeks.

"I'm Elicia Rodriguez, your father's nurse here at Saint Mary's Hospice Care. I'm sorry to be the one to tell you, but he's been trying to get ahold of you for a few weeks now." Zoey thought of all the unanswered messages she'd gotten from him. "Your father was diagnosed with stage-four cancer a little over a month ago. We expect him to pass in the next few hours."

The phone slipped from her fingers and landed on the desk as Zoey's knees went numb, and she crashed down hard in the chair.

CHAPTER
NINE

When Dylan walked into his room after leaving Zoey, he found the space empty. His brothers were still at the event or were making the rounds somewhere, no doubt still looking for their father or any clues.

The problem was, now he was full of energy and didn't want to be stuck in the small room. He couldn't help it; being that close to Zoey had sent him into overdrive. He paced for about a minute before finally giving up and heading out into the night. He had too much sexual frustration pent up—the only way to expel it was by being with Zoey, or by taking a long hike. He didn't know where he would end up, only that he couldn't stand being cooped up.

Luckily, he was heading down the stairs at the same time Zoey was heading up.

"Hey." His timing was perfect. Then she glanced up, and he could see that something was wrong. He was beside her quickly, her shoulders gripped in his hands, as if he could draw her pain away with sheer force. "What is it?"

"It's . . . my father," she said softly. "He's . . . terminal. They said he'd been holding on, waiting to talk to me. The nurse seemed to think it would be soon. Within the hour. I think he might be gone."

"I'm sorry," he said as she buried her face into his shoulders.

"No." She shook her head. "He left us, years ago. He made his choice." She gripped his shoulders as he held on to her. "Why should it matter to me?"

"Because he's your father," he said, glancing up as a group of employees came into the main lobby.

Taking her hand, he guided her up the stairs, toward the private staircase that would lead them to the staff rooms.

He was thankful that she didn't argue with him about going into her space. Instead she unlocked the door with her code, and he followed her inside.

They stepped into a full apartment; the space was bigger than he'd imagined. A small living room with a gourmet kitchen sat off toward the side. A long hallway led off to what he assumed were their shared bedrooms and bathrooms.

Zoey walked over to the sofa and sat down, her eyes going to the large dark windows. He moved over and sat next to her, taking her hands in his.

"Where is he?" he asked.

"A hospice in Vegas," she answered. "His second wife left him shortly after he was diagnosed with stage-four cancer."

The lost look in her eyes almost undid him. He'd been missing his father for a few months now, worried about the man who had acted more like a brother than a father. Now, looking at the sadness in her eyes, he felt guilty for even being concerned for the man-child his father was. His father was no doubt holed up in some five-star hotel, sipping drinks by the pool and flirting with women half his age, while hers had suffered, and probably died, alone.

"Have you told Scarlett or your mother yet?" he asked. Her eyes slid closed, and he allowed her a moment to breathe.

"God, I . . ." Her eyes opened, and he watched them fill with tears.

"Hey." He pulled her closer and held on to her, smoothing her hair with a hand. He'd do anything at this point to comfort her.

"This is stupid. I hate the man," she said again into his chest. "He left us."

Just then, the door to the apartment opened, and Elle, Hannah, Aubrey, and Scarlett walked in, all laughing and smiling. Until they saw him sitting there holding Zoey.

"Oh!" Elle's smile grew. "Sorry." She started to back out, pulling her friends with her, and then Zoey straightened and glanced over toward the door, tears shining on her cheeks.

"Zoey?" Scarlett rushed forward. "What's wrong?" Her sister glared down at him as Zoey stood and hugged her.

"Scar, it's . . ." Zoey took a deep breath. "Dad."

The entire room went silent.

"He's dead?" Scarlett asked, searching her sister's face.

"I . . . don't know. He was in the hospice and . . ."

"Good." Scarlett raised her chin. "His new wife can deal—"

"She left him," Zoey murmured.

Scarlett was silent for a moment. "Still good—he deserved to die alone, after what he did to us." Despite the heat in her words, Dylan could see her eyes fill; she quickly dashed the moisture away.

"You don't mean that." Zoey took her by the shoulders and drew her into another hug.

He watched the sisters. Zoey's anger for her father was overshadowed by the loss of him, while Scarlett's contempt for the man who'd left them was right out front.

Dylan had never seen the two of them together before. Scarlett had almost two full inches on Zoey. Their hair was the same rich dark color, filled with lighter streaks from their time in the sun.

"I do." Scarlett nudged herself free from her sister's hold. "He lied to us for years. Having an affair with Bridgette. What he did to Mom was—"

"Unforgivable," Zoey finished. "But the fact remains, he was our father, and a pretty good one at it for most of our childhood."

"For you, maybe. My first memories of him were dropping us off at day care, probably so he could go meet Bridgette."

Zoey sighed. "I'm going to Las Vegas."

Scarlett's eyes narrowed. "I'm not."

Zoey nodded. "It's your choice." She rubbed her sister's back.

Scarlett softened. "Have you told Mom yet?"

"No. I'm going to go over there now." She glanced toward the door.

Dylan leaped in. "I'll walk with you."

"When are you leaving?" Scarlett asked.

"I'll try to book a flight for tomorrow." She rubbed her forehead and glanced toward Elle. "Do you think you guys can deal—"

"Go." Elle rushed to hug her. "Take as much time as you need. We've got this."

The other women joined the embrace as Scarlett remained off to the side.

"Are you sure you don't want to go?" Elle asked her.

Dylan watched Scarlett raise her chin. "The man could never be bothered to show up to one of our school events. Not once." She dashed a tear from her face. "He left us and our mother penniless. If it hadn't been for our inheritance from our grandmother, we wouldn't be here in this camp."

"If you change your mind—" Zoey started.

"Mom won't go either," Scarlett said, crossing her arms over her chest.

"I know," Zoey replied, then turned to him. "Ready?"

"Yes." They left the building in complete silence. He'd lost his mother long before he really could understand death. Sure, he grieved for the mother he didn't remember, but it was a selfish emotion, since he had no memories of the woman.

"Are you okay?" he asked as they climbed into a golf cart, with him at the wheel.

"Yes," she said after a moment. "You mentioned something about losing your mother?"

"When I was two." He wrapped his free arm around her.

"I don't even know what comes next." She sighed and rested her head on his shoulder as he drove the dark path slowly. "Like, how to set up the funeral and everything else that comes with it."

"What about your mother? Won't she want some say in that? After all, she was married to the man."

"No." Zoey shook her head. "Mom won't want anything to do with it. Not after . . . no," she added again and looked away.

"Then we'll deal with it," he said, causing her to glance up at him. "Together," he assured her. "I did some thinking, and, well, if my boss says it's okay for me to take a few days off"—he smiled down at her—"I can get my hands on a private plane. I have my license. All three of us do—our dad taught us to fly early on. Anyway, instead of booking a flight, I could take you to Vegas?"

He came to a stop in front of her mother's cabin, and he watched her bite her bottom lip as she thought about it.

"I wouldn't feel right about . . ." She didn't finish, since the front porch light flipped on, and Kimberly stepped out with a robe draped around her.

"Zoey?" Her mother stepped out into the night.

He sat in the cart as Zoey rushed forward and talked to her mother on the deck.

"Mom, it's Dad. He's . . . well, he's in hospice. They say he's been fighting cancer for months."

"Oh, sweetie." Her mother held on to her again as Zoey cried softly on her mother's shoulder.

When Kimberly noticed him sitting in the golf cart, she invited him in for a drink.

He followed Zoey inside and sat on Kimberly's sofa while she made up a pitcher of lemonade. Mother and daughter talked as he listened. Kimberly filled Zoey in on how to handle making arrangements for her father.

"I'll call around a couple places in Vegas tomorrow," Kimberly said, hugging Zoey just before they left. "I'm sure he had his desires already planned out. Your father was always very organized in those sorts of things."

"I'll call you when we get there." Zoey hugged her back.

"We?" Kimberly asked, glancing over in his direction.

"I offered to fly her to Vegas. I've been flying since I was sixteen," he added, unsure why he felt the need to supply reassurance.

"Oh, that's wonderful. I was worried about Zoey going by herself." Kimberly walked over and grabbed him into a sudden hug. "Now I won't be. She'll have you there with her. She's not a very comfortable flyer."

He nodded and took Zoey's hand. "We'd better head back if we're going to be ready to leave by morning."

Zoey hugged her mother one last time, and he heard her whisper, "I'm sorry."

When they arrived back at the main building, he followed her up the stairs, pulling her to a stop on the second floor.

"I'm going to go get some sleep. When do you think you'll be ready to go?" he asked.

She sighed heavily and rubbed her forehead. "How about seven?"

"I'll meet you here." He bent down and, before she could respond or pull away, kissed her softly on her lips. "I'm sorry about your father."

Zoey nodded before turning and heading up the rest of the stairs.

When he entered his room, he found his brothers fast asleep. After a quick shower, he pulled out his phone and shot off a text to Joel, the family's personal assistant, asking him to make sure the plane was full of fuel and prepped for the trip to Vegas. He also had the man arrange for a hotel, since he wasn't sure where in Vegas they would be.

He hadn't unpacked most of his own clothes, since they mainly wore camp uniforms. It took only a few minutes to stuff the rest of his small personal items into his overnight bag.

He crawled into his bed a few minutes later and soon drifted off to dreams about losing his own father.

When he woke, his brothers were already getting dressed.

"Going somewhere?" Owen asked, motioning to the bag he'd set at the base of his bed.

"Vegas. I'm taking Zoey there. Her father is sick." He sat up and stretched. When he realized conversation had ceased, he glanced around. "What?"

"Don't you think you're taking this a little too far?" Liam asked.

"Why? Because I'm helping her out during a rough time?" He pulled on his jeans.

"We're supposed to be finding Dad, not going off to Vegas for the weekend," Owen said.

"Damn it." He stood up, shoving his chest toward his brother, knowing full well that all the extra hours he'd spent outdoors had made him bigger than Owen. "If we can't be decent humans along the way, then we're no better than our father."

Owen took a moment, then sighed. "Go." He turned to head out. "Maybe you'll find something more about the money along the way."

Feeling a little defeated and a little grimy from all the secrets he was keeping from Zoey, he finished getting ready and met her on the stairs.

He should just come out and tell her everything. At this point, he knew things had progressed between them. Even if they hadn't technically slept together yet, he felt something stronger for her.

But he hadn't had the time to talk to his brothers about exposing their secrets yet. Which made him feel as if he were being pulled in two different directions.

He couldn't help being in a foul mood but tried to hide it as he went down the stairs. Apparently, he hadn't been successful enough.

By the time he'd put their bags into the trunk of her car, Zoey was watching him closely.

"I can book a flight, you know," she said after getting behind the wheel.

"No." He shook his head. "Let's go." He took her hand in his. "I'm in a foul mood because . . . well, brothers can be jerks." She was dealing with a sick, possibly dead, father, and he was bitchy about keeping a stupid secret from her. His problems didn't seem relevant at this point. Maybe his light tone would divert her.

"Are you sure?" she asked. "You're not upset about having to—"

He stopped her by leaning down and brushing his lips across hers.

"Yes, it's all arranged," he replied. "Let's head out. Everything's waiting for us at the Destin airport."

They both climbed into her car and drove in silence for a while as the sun rose. She pulled into a small café in Pelican Point for bagel sandwiches and coffee.

While they drove through town and ate in the car, they talked about that first summer at River Camp and how the women had all met and had grown into more than just friends over the years.

"I've seen it myself—you're more like sisters," he said.

"We call ourselves Wildflowers," she said as she pulled into the parking lot of the airport. "Each of us is unique, but we make a great bundle."

He interrupted her. "Long-term parking." He pointed to the underground parking area and added, "It must be nice, having extended family like that."

She parked and sat there for a moment. "I didn't know how lucky until last year, when we all came together for the camps."

"More on this later. I want to hear all about it, but for now, let's get in the air." He motioned.

"I have to be honest with you." She shifted in her seat. "I'm terrible at flying."

He smiled. "You won't have to. I'll do all the flying."

Her voice quavered. "You know what I mean."

Reaching over, he took her hand. "Trust me—this will be one of the smoothest rides of your life," he said, deepening his voice with a hint of a smile.

There was a moment of silence, and then she burst out laughing.

"Oh god!" she said between laughs. "That was just what I needed." She leaned forward and kissed him, then climbed out of the car and stood back as he took out their bags.

They made their way toward the private-plane-storage buildings near the end of the runway.

"Sorry for the hike." He shifted their bags.

"Don't be." She glanced over at him. "You're the one carrying all the bags."

He chuckled. "This is us." He motioned toward the Gulfstream his father had purchased for the three of them.

"This?" Zoey stopped. "It's huge."

He whispered, "That's what she said."

She slapped his arm playfully. "Whose plane is this, anyway?"

Shit—he hadn't thought that far. "A friend's. Come on, that's Joel." He waved to the family's general factotum.

"So it's his plane?" Zoey asked.

"No; he just made sure everything was ready for us. He's a friend of the family." He walked over and set the bags down and shook Joel's hand. "Joel, this is Zoey; Zoey, Joel." Joel was a few years older than Owen. He was shorter than the three brothers but could have easily passed for part of their family. His dark hair, tan skin, and dark eyes spoke of his Greek heritage. The fact that Dylan believed that Joel could be their father's son from a previous relationship had at one point weighed heavy on him. But now, years later, the brothers treated Joel as family, no matter if their father couldn't own up to the fact that he was.

"Nice to meet you. I'm sorry to hear about your father," Joel added to Zoey.

"Thank you," Zoey replied.

Joel turned to him. "Everything's arranged. Your flight patterns have been logged and are in the onboard system. Since you didn't know where in Vegas you'd be staying, I've booked you the rooms at the Bellagio."

"Thank you." He picked up the bags and turned to Zoey. "Shall we?"

She nodded, then turned to Joel. "It was nice meeting you."

"Same." He nodded. "Have a pleasant trip." Joel turned and started to walk back to the building.

"Go on in. I'll just walk around the plane and make sure everything looks good." Dylan set the bags down at the base of the ladder.

"Sure." She started to pick up her bag, but he stopped her.

"I'll get the bags—head on in." He started to walk around the plane for his normal preflight checks.

When he finally climbed up the ladder, he found her standing just inside, her eyes huge. "You're going to fly *this*?" she asked. "Alone?"

"No." He shook his head, then stowed the bags in the closet and hit the button to close the door. "You're going to be here with me," he added. "Come on up; I'll show you around."

"Wait. Up front? Have you flown this before?" she asked as he opened the cockpit door.

"Almost five hundred flight hours." He smiled and gestured for her to take the copilot seat.

"Is that a lot?" she asked as he settled down and put on his headset.

Glancing over, he said, "It's enough to promise you that this will be a good ride."

The corner of her mouth quirked. "Right."

"Put on your headset." He pointed to the headset hanging up, turned to prep the plane, and asked her, "Ready?" once he was done.

She wiped her hands on her jeans and reached down to tighten her seat belt.

"Yes," she finally said.

He called up to the tower and found out they were fourth in line for takeoff. He made his way toward the runway and joined the queue.

"Here we go," he said when it was their turn. After calling the tower again and getting clearance, he punched it. The acceleration forced them back in their seats as the engine noise rose, and the plane rushed down the runway.

He noticed that she remained silent the entire takeoff. That was, until he leveled off the plane.

"How are you doing over there?" Her fingers were gripping the armrests, and her knuckles were turning slightly white.

"Okay," she said in a tense tone. "I've never . . . sat up front and watched a takeoff before."

"It's a lot different than sitting in the back. We're going to be turning soon." He pointed to the computer screen. "The red line is our flight pattern; we're the blue dot."

He was happy when she looked over and watched their progress.

"Turning . . . now?" she asked.

"Yes—watch." He turned the wheel, and the plane tilted. He noticed that she didn't return to gripping the armrest with her hands; instead, her eyes remained glued to the screen.

Once they were on a straight pattern to Vegas, he relaxed back and flipped on the autopilot.

"Don't!" She jerked her head toward him. "You're not holding the wheel."

"It's okay—it's on autopilot. We'll stay stable and on course for the next few hours." He sighed and stretched. "Do you want some coffee?"

She shook her head, her eyes still glued to the computer system.

"Zoey"—he reached over, unbuckled her seat belt, then helped her up to stand—"it's okay. There's nothing but sky between us and Vegas."

He nudged her until she stepped into the rear of the plane.

"Sit." He motioned to one of the white leather captain chairs. "I'll get the coffee."

She sat, her eyes darting to the cockpit door occasionally.

"Are you sure it's okay?"

"Yes. I've done this so many times."

"It only takes one time for things to go bad," Zoey hinted.

His smile fell. "I know; that's why I'll be returning up front, while you rest back here. There are plenty of movies, or if you want, there's a full-size bedroom in the far back. You could get some rest."

"I'm fine," she said. "I'll be better when you have your hands back on the wheel."

He chuckled and handed her a cup and the thermos of coffee. "There are some sandwiches in the fridge, as well as snacks. Help yourself." He took a soda and a bag of chips for himself. "Relax. I've got this. Have fun. You've got your own private plane with, if I might say so, one of the best pilots around. I would have thought that flying was included in your list of fun."

She narrowed her eyes at him. "I prefer having fun when my feet are on the ground."

He went back in to babysit the plane. He checked on her a few times during the flight; each time she looked more relaxed than before.

The last time he checked on her, she was relaxing in the bed, fast asleep.

Looking down at her, he wanted nothing more than to crawl in bed with her, but they were less than half an hour out of Vegas, and he knew that the traffic in the air around the city of sin was something he'd need to prepare for.

Turning away from her was harder than he'd imagined. He was looking forward to spending a few days with her, even if they had to deal with the unpleasantries.

This would be his first chance to see her away from the camp and maybe get to know more about her. The thought tickled in the back of his mind about the possibility of seeing if she knew anything more about his father.

After all, she was bound to be different when away from her friends and work. People normally were. Besides, he knew she was raw from the news about her father. He hated himself, knowing he would be, in essence, exploiting her during a weak time, but thoughts of his father in the same situation loomed over him.

CHAPTER
TEN

Zoey woke when the plane tilted slightly. Then Dylan's voice came over the intercom.

"We're heading down into Vegas. I thought you might want to come up front to watch the landing."

She stretched her arms over her head, then rolled her shoulders. The first part of the flight had been pretty tense, until she'd sat in the back and told herself over and over and over again that it was safer than driving.

Now as she made her way up to the front, she wondered if the landing would stress her out as much as the takeoff had.

She strapped into the seat beside him, glanced around, and saw the city in front of them.

"It looks so different from up here," she said, leaning back in the seat.

"It looks cleaner," he replied with a grin. "Have you been to Vegas?"

"A few times. You?"

"Yeah." He checked the instrument panel. "Did your dad live here long?"

"He moved here after he divorced Mom and married Bridgette. She used to be a dancer, and after they married, she convinced my dad that she should return to it."

"What kind of business was your father in?" he asked.

"Investments, like his father had been." She had never really paid too much attention as a child. "I don't think I ever remember him working hard—you know, nine-to-five type of work. I know that he was always traveling, and when he was home . . ." She glanced out the window as the plane pitched slightly. Still, she didn't have an urge to dig her nails into the armrests like she had at takeoff. "Life was different."

"Did your parents not get along?"

"No." She thought about it. "Actually, it was the opposite. I never remember them fighting. They had what Scar and I liked to call 'polite disagreements.' My father never raised his voice, but his words could cut my mother down, just the same."

Dylan fell silent for a moment. "I heard someone say that Elle's grandfather took you in and taught you how to sail?"

She smiled at the instant memories and settled back in her seat. "He was really the first genuine father figure I'd ever experienced. Actually, I think that's true for all of us."

She was surprised at the bump when the tires finally touched the ground, and he taxied to the hangar—she hadn't even noticed the landing.

"That was a lot easier than takeoff. Will it stay here until we return home?" she asked as she followed him out of the airplane. She'd watched him shut everything down and had been curious as to what would happen to it next.

"Yes, it'll get serviced and given a full tank of gas for the trip home." He swung his bag over his shoulder and took hers after hitting the button to lower the ladder. "Joel's taken care of everything."

"Speaking of Joel," she said once they were in the rental car that had been waiting for them. "He seems to be really connected to your business."

"He is. Actually, he's an employee—my father hired him fresh out of school. He's been an asset as well as a friend of the family ever since."

"Is he . . ." She paused, unsure how to ask him if the man was related to him. Maybe he didn't even know the answer, but just by looking at them, it was sort of obvious. "Related?"

"We're not sure," he said. "But yeah, we get that a lot. Every time we ask our father, he looks like he's been hit in the gut."

Zoey nodded and leaned back in the seat as Dylan drove away from the airport. She couldn't explain it, but knowing she was going to be dealing with her father had wiped her out. Even after a full hour's rest on the plane, she could sleep for another ten.

"I thought we'd hit the hotel first, then have some food before heading over to the hospice," he said, glancing sideways at her.

She looked out her window and wished they were in Vegas for a good time instead of to bury her father.

She'd told the hospice nurse last night that she would be arriving today. The woman had assured her that they would take care of her father and let her know when he passed.

She'd received a call at a quarter past one in the morning that he'd passed away. She had cried herself asleep and hated that she'd shed a tear for a man who had only thought of her in his last days.

"Okay," she finally said. "I'll need to call my mother. We may be heading to a funeral home instead, if he was moved." She checked her phone, and there were a few messages she'd missed. She punched the phone and listened to them.

"Anything important?" he asked, pulling into the hotel's parking lot.

She shut down her phone and glanced up. "Mom gave me the information to the funeral home. Dad's being moved there this morning."

Every time she'd been in Vegas, she'd always stayed at the more basic hotels—MGM, the Rio—the kind that had been nice twenty or thirty years ago.

She'd walked through the nicer hotels but hadn't been to the Bellagio before.

"We can go upstairs and clean up, then eat something here in the lobby," he said, pulling her bag from the back of the car.

"Sounds good. Somehow the dry heat is worse than Florida's humidity."

"A lot of people think the opposite," he suggested as he held open the door for her.

They stepped into the lobby of the hotel, and she became too busy looking at the Chihuly ceiling and enjoying all the sights and sounds to chat with him anymore.

She stood back as he checked them in at the front desk. When he handed her a card key to the room, she suddenly realized that not only had they not talked about how much it had cost to fly them there and rent the car, but she hadn't even asked him about the hotel room's cost or arrangements yet. Had he booked her her own room, or did he automatically expect that they would be sharing one?

"If you keep the receipts for the trip, I'll reimburse you," she said as they made their way toward the elevators, avoiding the bellhops with a wave from Dylan.

The fact that Dylan shrugged made her eyes narrow. When they stepped into the elevators and he punched one of the top floors, she took a moment to look at him.

Who was this man, really? Why did they feel it was necessary to give them a fake name? She'd read more articles last night about the Costas. For the most part, the articles had all been fluff pieces about charities they hosted or dinner parties they had attended. She'd been too tired to do any deeper searching and figured she'd have some time on the plane, but there hadn't been wireless.

She gave him a sidelong glance and figured that she'd try the direct approach again.

"You're not telling me something," she said as the elevator started to move.

"Like what?" Was it her imagination, or did he look startled for a moment?

"You and your brothers show up, looking for work." She ticked items off with her fingers. "You instantly start sneaking around the camp." When he opened his mouth to talk, she raised her eyebrows, which shut his mouth. "You know how to fly a plane and can, within a few hours' notice, get one at a snap of your fingers to fly to Vegas, where your"—she air quoted—"'family friend slash employee' arranges our rental car and hotel."

She was interrupted when the elevator door slid open at their floor. She followed him down the hallway and stood back while he opened the door.

When they stepped into the massive suite, she turned on him.

"Okay, what the hell? Who are you? Really."

"Dylan Costa." The way he said it had her heart rate spiking. He might as well have just told her *Bond, James Bond* instead. He said his name like it explained everything. But it didn't explain why he'd lied to her.

When she planted her feet and crossed her arms over her chest again, he relented.

"Let's clean up and get something to eat; then we can talk." At the thought of food, her stomach growled, as if contradicting her desire to get to the bottom of things.

He started to walk past her, but she stopped him by placing her hand on his chest. A bad move, because just feeling those muscles under her fingertips accelerated her heart rate.

"Promise me you won't avoid answering any of my questions?" she asked a little breathlessly.

His dark eyes met hers, and he nodded slowly. She searched his face but couldn't penetrate his steady expression.

To his credit, there were two bedrooms in the suite: a long hallway with identical rooms sitting on either side. The massive living and dining area sat at the end of the hallway, filling a giant *U*-shaped room. Two small balconies sat on either end, with access doors from each bedroom and the living room area.

She could spend all day just watching the activity below—their room faced the famous fountains. She imagined the view at night would be just as amazing.

She dumped her bag on the queen-size bed and walked into the bathroom to clean up. Seeing the massive tub, she instantly wished for enough time to try it out before leaving but instead ran a washcloth over the back of her neck to cool herself down.

As they made their way back downstairs, she resumed her questioning. "Why did you all lie to us about your name?"

He glanced at the other couple in the elevator before answering.

"It was Owen's idea."

She realized he didn't want to go into it further, since the doors opened and a large group of people shuffled in, all with luggage that filled every inch of the elevator.

They walked through the crowded casino toward one of the restaurants and waited for a table.

When they were finally seated by a window, he said, "My family, the Costas, have a business. My father acts as the head of it, but my brothers and I are just trying to make our own way."

"So the plane belongs to your family?" She felt her stomach roll slightly. Was this mob money? The articles had all avoided mention of what the family business actually did.

When he nodded, she glanced out the window as more fear roiled inside her.

"Hey." Dylan reached across the table and took her hand. "I just told you that I come from a family with money, not mass murderers."

"To me, it's almost the same." When his eyebrows shot up, she said, "My father is Jean Rowlett." She waited until the name sank in and recognition hit him.

"I'm sorry." He squeezed her hand. "I hadn't made the connection. I think I understand—that is, if all the rumors are true."

"They are." She grimaced. "Just like the papers said—he left his wife and two daughters pretty much destitute. I was sixteen years old; Scarlett was fourteen."

"Didn't your mother fight it? I mean, with any divorce, if she had a good lawyer, she could have . . ."

"My father has many powerful friends," she said. "My grandfather, his father, had been alive back then and bullied my mother into signing a prenuptial before the wedding." She remembered the threats her mother had received after the divorce. "Then, she was practically forced into signing the divorce papers by my father"—she flickered into memories of the hell her mother had been put through—"in exchange for custody of Scarlett and me."

"Your father . . . blackmailed your mother? Using his own daughters as leverage?" he asked.

Zoey took a sip from her water glass. "Yeah—now you can understand why it's so hard for me to do this"—she glanced out the window—"to be here."

"I'm here for you." He squeezed her hand. "My family may have money, but we're not heartless."

But still, doubt was something she'd learned to live with ever since the day they were left with basically only their clothes on their backs and an old beat-up car they'd borrowed from a friend.

"What about your father?" she asked after their burgers arrived. "Does he always just . . . disappear?"

"He started the disappearing act just after Liam graduated high school. I suppose he figured he was finally free to travel and date who he wanted. At first, it was short trips," he said between bites. "A weekend in Paris or relaxing on a Mexican beach somewhere." He shrugged, then laughed. "We used to get into such trouble while he was gone." He chuckled as he looked out the windows. "Then"—his smile fell away— "the trips grew longer, and when he started dating women our age . . ." She watched his body shiver and knew exactly what he'd gone through, how it made you feel to know that your parent was attractive to, and attracted by, people the same age as their children.

She reached across the small table and took his hand. "I understand."

From there, as they ate lunch, the topic of conversation turned toward other family. She tried to dig a little deeper into his family life; instead, he gave her stories of the three of them growing up.

He told her of the times he and his brothers had gotten into trouble, and she was reminded so much of herself and the Wildflowers.

"One summer, we decided we all wanted motorcycles, so we borrowed a friend's new Yamaha. Owen rode it first without incident; then it was my turn. I'd never ridden a bike before." He chuckled. "I was twelve. Anyway, I pulled back on the gas and shot across the field, directly into the only tree, totaling his bike. Dad made me work all summer long to replace it."

"Were you hurt?" she asked.

"No—just my pride. It took me almost five years to work up the nerve to get on another bike."

Perhaps they *were* nothing more than brothers worried about their father and their family business. Even if she felt they'd gone about things the wrong way.

For a few moments, she almost forgot where they were, and why they were there. Then realization dawned on her, and she slumped in her chair and wished for a glass of wine instead of water.

"It hit you again, didn't it?" Dylan asked as he searched her eyes.

"Yeah." She sighed and thought about getting some fresh air before having to deal with the unknown. "How about we take a quick walk before we head over to the funeral home?"

Dylan waved the waitress over, but before he could slap down his credit card, Zoey paid with cash.

"I'm not going to have you paying for everything. And," she said after standing up, "I expect to pay you back for my share of the rest of this. Even if it ends up going back into your father's account."

"Fair enough." He took her hand, and they walked out of the building.

The hot air hit them, and she groaned. "I love the heat, but man, I miss the water in it." She felt like her skin was drying up with each step and wondered if the hotel had ChapStick to combat the dryness.

He chuckled. "Maybe just a short walk, then?"

"To the fountains and back?" she suggested.

Vegas was Vegas. The streets were crowded, but they still found a quiet place to watch the fountain show in the shade.

Her mind circled around all the information he'd given her about his family and why he and his brothers had lied to them.

She thought about some of the stupid decisions she'd made in her life and knew that she couldn't hold most of it against him. After all, she'd washed out of the Olympics and had been injured because of one bad choice she'd made.

"Shall we head out?" He held out his hand for hers.

She knew he was offering more than just his hand: he was asking her if she'd forgiven him. Looking into his eyes, she took his hand. His smile shifted something deep inside her, and as they walked back toward the rental car, she realized that whatever came at her on this trip, she was thankful Dylan was on her side.

As he drove toward the funeral home, they talked about her time at the Olympics. For some reason, the first year after her injury, the subject had been tender, but now she could see past all the inner anger she had been carrying around.

It was all her fault that she'd been injured. Sneaking out after they had officially qualified at the finals had been against the rules—she knew that—but she and her teammates had chanced it anyway to celebrate. Falling down the hotel's fire escape and landing wrong on her knee had stripped her chances of actually playing at the Olympics.

Still, as she talked to Dylan now, the only feeling left in her about her past was gratefulness that she'd gone as far as she had with her career.

How many people could say they had made it to the Olympics?

She hadn't been the only one who'd snuck out that night, but she had been the only one who'd gotten injured and disqualified. Which, in some strange way, had boosted her into the spotlight for a short time.

The image of her cheering on the sidelines, an ice pack on her swollen and bruised leg, was still used as the epitome of good sportsmanship.

"That's one of my favorites. Bad girl shows her support for her teammates." Dylan smiled over at her. "It was rumored that you hadn't been alone that night, sneaking out, yet you never tattled on any of your teammates. The photographer deserves a medal for capturing that moment."

She sighed. "My hair was a mess."

A burst of laughter escaped him. "I can't believe that you're worried about how your hair looked in such an iconic moment."

As they entered the funeral home, he held her hand. When they walked in, she explained to the woman behind the front counter whom she was there to see; then they were ushered into a back room.

A man came in and informed her that her father had chosen to be cremated, but there would be a small private showing of his body before they would cremate him later that day.

"We've done what we could to make the viewing more pleasant, but according to his lawyer, he didn't want 'a big fuss made over him.'"

"I'm sure it's fine."

"If you'd like, I'll take you back to him now." The man stood up, and they followed him to where her father was laid out in front of a row of chairs.

She reached for Dylan's hand as they made their way down the aisle.

Her father looked so different that, for a moment, she questioned if they had been shown to the right room. Then she looked deeper into his face and could see the man he had been long ago.

What could have been if he had been a better man, a better father? All the times she'd invited him to her games, and he hadn't even shown a hint of interest in her or Scar.

Tears streamed down her face, and she dashed them away with the tissue Dylan offered her. She leaned heavily on him and was thankful that she hadn't had to do this alone.

She knew Scarlett and her mother wouldn't have been able to deal with any of it. Her sister was more emotional than she was and remained very bitter about how things had been left between them. Whatever time their father had cheated Zoey out of, Scar's time had been even shorter. Maybe it was because Zoey had been older and had understood more, but Scar had taken their father's lack of interest harder than she had. She knew her mother had left that part of her life in the past and was better for it. Being here, now, might have set her back too far.

"Miss Rowlett." They turned and saw a younger man in a very expensive suit approaching them. "I was told you would be stopping by today." He held out his hand to shake. "I'm John Jackson. I was your father's attorney. I'm sorry for your loss. Your father was—"

Zoey tilted her head. "You don't have to finish that. I know exactly what the man was." She turned to her father again, her eyes dry at this point.

"Still, my condolences." He searched in his pockets and withdrew a card, which he handed to her. "While you're in town, if you could find some time to swing by my offices, we can go over his will. There are some papers for you to sign. Did your sister, Scarlett, make the trip with you?"

"No," Zoey answered, her gaze turning back to her father, the man who'd caused so much pain and distrust in the sisters. "I only came because there was no one else."

"I understand you've elected to follow his wishes as far as his cremation?"

She shrugged. "It's all arranged, which leaves less for me to do."

"Then I'll let you have some time. I hope to see you soon." He turned to go.

"Mr. Jackson," she called after him, and he stopped. "How much did his second wife take?"

The man's eyes narrowed. "Not as much as she wanted, but still, more than your mother got."

The fact that the man had been honest with her told her something about his character.

"We'll stop by your office tomorrow," she blurted out. "How about eleven?"

"I'll arrange for it," he said and turned with a wave and left.

"I can't stand lawyers," Dylan muttered.

"Not all of them are bad." She sighed and spun away from her father. "The fact that he was honest about my father told me more than I needed."

"Now what?" Dylan asked.

"He's had his . . . showing . . . ." She glanced up as a woman rushed into the room, causing Zoey's temper to rise. *Bridgette.*

She wore all black, with large crocodile tears to match her handbag.

"Jean!" she cried and flung—actually flung—herself on Zoey's father's still figure, as if she had just found out about his death.

"The second wife?" Dylan whispered.

"Yeah." Zoey really wished a glass of wine had rushed in instead.

"She's an actress, right?" His sarcasm caused Zoey to chuckle.

"Dancer," she corrected as the woman turned on her—her tears replaced with anger.

"Why didn't you call me?" Bridgette accused her, causing Zoey's eyebrows to jump up in disbelief. The woman had a lot of nerve, accusing her of not doing something she wouldn't have done even if her father *had* asked it of her.

"Excuse me?" she managed as Dylan's hand rested lightly on her arm.

Bridgette straightened and smoothed down her dress as if preparing to step out on a catwalk.

"You knew he was sick. You kept him from me during his last moments." The woman's voice vibrated with anger as she moved closer to Zoey.

"Step back, Stepmonster." Bridgette had better not mess with her.

Instead, she edged closer, sparing a quick glance for Dylan. "I could have comforted him"—her voice cracked slightly, and Zoey wagered it was a practiced move—"yet your family kept him from me, just as you forced him to divorce me."

A burst of laughter escaped Zoey. "Right." She yanked her arm free from Dylan's hold.

Zoey was shorter than Bridgette by almost a full foot, thanks to the extremely high stripper heels Bridgette was currently wearing. She had dyed her hair a bright blonde since the last time Zoey had seen a picture of her. It made her look younger than her almost thirty-five years. Until you saw her face.

"You and your sister manipulated Jean ever since the first day of our marriage." Her voice rose.

Zoey laughed again. "That's rich. Oh, but I forgot, so are you, after stealing all of my father's wealth. Tell me, how did it feel knowing that you ruined two young girls' lives?"

"I loved your father!" Bridgette screamed.

"You loved my father's money." Zoey hadn't been prepared for the slap, but as her cheek burst with the sting, it took her less than a second to explode.

If it hadn't been for the strong hands pulling her back, she would have annihilated the woman. She'd been in plenty of sports fights before and had a reputation for being able to hold her own. Taking on the one skinny bitch who had ruined her family's life had been a dream of Zoey's for years.

"Easy, tiger." Dylan's voice broke through the red haze flooding her mind. "I think we'd better go." He started tugging her toward the door.

"Yes, that's right, control your temper." Bridgette's smile told Zoey that this was the reason the woman had come today. To get a rise out of her. "I'd hate for anything else to happen to you. You're so fragile during this time, after all."

Taking a deep breath, Zoey stilled. "You're too late to get anything else from my father." She felt Dylan's hands relax on her arms. "He changed his will. He told me so himself."

Bridgette's eyes narrowed as she waited. "You're lying."

Zoey moved a step closer. "Why don't you crawl back into the hole you slithered out of? There's nothing else my family has for you."

She turned to leave but was quickly pushed aside by Dylan, who caught Bridgette as she flew toward Zoey. He forced her back a step, keeping his body between them.

"Easy," Dylan warned. "Assault is a crime."

Zoey took a step back. "What's wrong? Did I hit a little too close to home? It's always been about money, and you won't get another dime from us." She sidestepped another blow, took Dylan's hand, and walked out.

Sitting in the car, it took a few minutes for her heart rate to return to normal as Dylan drove back to the hotel.

"Wow," she finally said. "What a bitch."

He glanced over at her. "Are you okay?"

She leaned her head back against the headrest and touched her still-burning cheek. She'd had worse, and she knew her cheek wasn't what stung the most. It was knowing that her father had chosen to be with *that* woman instead of them. "I need a drink."

She heard Dylan chuckle. "You're in the right place, then. What place *doesn't* have a drinks special?"

"What do you say we go out, drink some drinks, lose some money on slots, and then find a place to dance?" She glanced over at him. "I have a strong urge to see you naked." She felt her body heating.

He smiled quickly. "It's your party."

"I want to call my family and fill them in. And get a shower, and a change of clothes." She looked down at the dark slacks and shirt she'd worn to the funeral home. She wanted to wear something bright and cheery, something that would prove to the world that she was alive.

CHAPTER
ELEVEN

Dylan almost swallowed his tongue when Zoey stepped out of her room an hour later wearing a short, bright-blue dress. He'd seen those legs in shorts for the past month and a half but never in a sexy dress and high cream-colored heels.

"Wow," he said as she did a quick turn. The skirt of the dress flared out and rose slightly higher, causing his pulse to jump even more.

"Like it?" she asked. "Elle forced me to pack it. Just in case I wanted a night out."

"God bless Elle," he said honestly as he wrapped his arms around her. She reached up on her toes and placed a kiss on his lips.

"Now, take me out and show me a good time." She pulled out of his arms, and he watched her walk to the door and wondered how quickly the night could be over.

They first hit the Bank, a nightclub in the hotel, for drinks and dancing. The place was packed with beautiful people, drinking and dancing to the music that was pumping through the massive place.

Dylan wasn't a dancer, but he figured he'd suck it up and do his best to have Zoey bump and grind up next to him in the tight dress she was wearing.

The dance floor was full, and several times he had to help guide her away from being knocked over. No matter what kind of relationship their father had been in, his respect for women had been strong and had carried over to his sons.

"Wow, that was fun." She sat down on the soft red cushions of a sofa and fanned her hands in front of her face. "I haven't danced like that since we went to Cabo."

"We?" He sat next to her and waved a waitress over to take their drink orders.

"Sure." She leaned her head against his shoulder. "Me and my sisters."

When the waitress made it over to them finally, he decided they needed food more than drinks. "How about we head out to grab something to eat?"

"Burgers!" She jumped up. "I'm in the mood for some red meat." She laughed and tugged him up.

"Sorry," he told the waitress and handed her a few bucks for her time as Zoey pulled him toward the door.

They ended up at a greasy burger place off the Strip, where Zoey swore that they had the best french fries in Vegas.

When their plates came, he had to admit she was probably right. They had fries and malts and talked until he glanced down at his watch and realized it was a quarter past three in the morning.

Steering them back toward the hotel, he realized that he had never enjoyed his time with anyone else before quite like being with Zoey. He'd spent plenty of time dancing and clubbing, but most of those times he'd dreaded it and had counted the minutes until he could leave. Tonight, they had easily spent more than two hours without him even thinking about the time.

As they rode the elevator up to their suite, she moved closer to him, running her hand over his button-up shirt.

"Do you know, when I saw you that first day, when you got out of your truck, I felt my heart skip a beat. Like it's doing now." Her low, soft voice did things to his system.

"I wanted you too." He ran his hands up her sides. "I want you," he corrected himself.

"Make me feel alive," she whispered before her lips crushed his. She pinned him against the elevator wall as her mouth moved over his.

When he heard the doors slide open, he glanced up and walked them out of the elevator with their lips still fused.

Without them stopping once, the door was open, and he'd made his way into his bedroom and removed his shoes. Then laid her down on the bed and covered her with his body.

She fumbled with each of his buttons, then pulled his shirt from his shoulders. Slightly digging her nails into his skin, she moaned as she explored him.

Her skirt hiked up as she wrapped her legs around his hips. Using his hands, he brushed his fingertips up her legs and marveled at the smooth, soft skin of her inner thighs.

"You're so soft," he whispered next to her ear. "So perfect." He trailed his mouth down her neck and felt her arch for him.

Her long dark hair fell around her shoulders and pooled on the pillow. He brushed it aside, then slipped the thin strap of her dress down her shoulder until it fell away, exposing her breast.

"Zoey." When she looked up at him, he knew he'd never wanted like this before. Never desired a woman more than he did now. She was more than he'd ever imagined he'd get in life.

"Dylan"—she shook his shoulders and brought him back down to her—"touch me everywhere." Her fingers went to the buckle of his slacks as their mouths joined again.

He helped her wiggle his slacks off his hips and legs, then settled between her legs to kiss her and run his fingertips over every inch of her perfect skin.

Once the blue dress was a pool on the floor, he looked down at the sexy pair of black underwear she wore and wished more than anything for the image to be embedded in his memory.

"I'll remember you looking just like this for the rest of my life," he said.

She smiled up at him and raised her hands toward him. "We still have some clothes on." She glanced at his boxers, then ran a finger across the line of her panties.

"My god." The words that escaped him caused a smile to spread across her face.

"Do you like it when I do . . . this?" She dipped a finger under the panties.

"Yes." The word burst from him, and he felt himself growing harder.

"More?" she asked with a smile. Not trusting his voice, he nodded. "Your turn."

He quickly jerked them down his legs, causing her to chuckle.

"That'll work," she purred, then moved her hands over the silk again. "I'm thinking that you like watching me go slower, though."

He nodded again as his eyes moved with her hands and fingers. When she nudged her panties off her hips, he watched them slide down her legs and felt a little of his control slide as well. She was more perfect than he'd imagined.

"Dylan, come here." She spread her legs, and he moved quickly again. He'd grabbed a condom from his nightstand and set it on the bed beside them. But he knew there was more of her he wanted to enjoy, *had* to enjoy, first.

Settling beside her instead of between her spread legs, he covered her complaints by kissing her until he felt her relax again. His hands moved over her as he took his time learning her curves and enjoying her softness.

When he cupped her sex, she arched up and made a sensual sound that had him smiling against her lips.

"God, I love touching you," he said, bending down and taking her nipple into his mouth. He brushed his tongue across the peak and had her moaning again. Her hands moved into his hair, holding him as she cried out with pleasure.

"Dylan, please," she begged.

When he slid a finger into her, she cried out once more, then turned slightly toward him and draped her leg over his hip, as if to drive him deeper. When she reached for him, it was his turn to groan.

"Two can play at the torture game." She smiled over at him.

"Witch," he said, then moved his hand and watched her eyes close as her fingers stilled. "I'm in control now."

He thought she'd relax back; instead her eyes flew open, and she flipped up to straddle him. Her hands cuffed his wrists and pulled them above his head.

"Who's in charge?" she challenged with a smile.

"You are," he said, his eyes going to her perfect breasts.

"I thought so." She leaned down to tease him. "Now, are you going to give me what I want?"

Since she was rubbing her hips against him, he would have given her anything at that moment.

"Yes," he finally groaned out after she nibbled on his chest and used her teeth on his nipple. "God," he growled. "Condom." He waved toward the bed.

He watched her open the foil with her teeth; then she leaned forward as she slid the rubber on him. When she slid down on him next, he arched up, his fingers digging into her soft hips, holding her still for just a moment. Holding on to the feeling as long as he could.

Then she started to move, and he realized he was doomed. He'd never experienced anything as amazing as Zoey before, and he doubted he ever would again.

He let her take as much control as he could stand but knew that she was building them up too quickly. When he felt he couldn't take any more torture, he flipped their positions. He hiked her legs up against his chest and began to move inside of her.

Her short nails scraped along his skin as she held on to him, her eyes searching his as he told her exactly what she was doing to him. As he kissed her, he felt her building and knew that he wanted to see how perfect she was during orgasm.

Leaning up slightly, he ran a fingertip over her swollen clit and watched in amazement as she burst around him. Her teeth trapped her bottom lip as she squealed with her release, her nails digging into his sides now.

The pain was minimal and actually aided in his own release. He held on to her as he felt himself spiraling out of control and then even after as he felt his heart and breathing return to normal.

"Wow." She sighed, her breath floating over his heated skin.

"Yeah." He nodded and tucked his nose into the crook of her neck, enjoying the smell of her hair.

"Can we do that again soon?" She ran her hands over his back.

"Sleep first, then . . ." He laughed.

"Yes, sleep first." She yawned. "But soon."

He nodded and rolled until she was tucked into his arms. "I hope you're a snuggler."

"I am," she said softly. "Dylan?"

"Hm?" He already felt himself drifting off.

"Thank you for today," she said as he floated to sleep.

He woke to the sounds of a toilet flushing and reached for Zoey. When he didn't feel her, he opened his eyes to see her standing in the doorway, smiling at him.

"Morning." She came to give him a kiss. The fact that she was dressed in jeans and a T-shirt depressed him instantly.

"Going somewhere?"

"I ordered breakfast for us. It should be here soon. I didn't want to answer the door in my birthday suit." She grinned.

"It would be the best tip the delivery guy had ever had." He pulled her down on his chest and kissed her. "I'm sure we have time . . ."

Just then there was a knock on the outer door, causing him to groan.

"I called earlier. I'm starving." She jumped up. "Come on, put something on. Then, after . . ." She leaned over and lightly tweaked his nipple. Then sprinted for the door when he reached for her.

"You are in so much trouble," he called to her as she exited the room, her laughter trailing behind her.

He was surprised at how much food she'd ordered until the smell of waffles and coffee hit him. He *was* hungry.

Once they'd depleted the tray, he wrapped his arms around her.

"What are the plans for today?" he asked.

She gripped him tighter. "Shower sex, then meet with the lawyer, then . . ." She shrugged. "We never did lose money at the slots."

"Sounds good." He started to walk her toward the bathroom.

"Can you arrange for us to go home tomorrow?" she asked as they moved into the bathroom.

"Sure," he said. "Worried about the camp?"

"It's opening month," she pointed out and then groaned softly when he pulled her T-shirt over her head.

She wasn't wearing a bra, and as he tugged her jeans down her hips, he noticed she wasn't wearing any panties either.

"I was in a hurry," she teased.

"So am I." He removed his jeans and pinned her against the bathroom wall. "Shower after," he muttered between kisses.

When he slid into her this time, it was like returning home. Being with someone when the connection was as strong as the one he felt for her sent him into a feeling of pure heaven.

After, they showered together, and he took her again as the water rained down over them. She disappeared into her own bathroom to dress and get ready to meet the lawyer.

Walking over, he shut the door to his own suite to call his brothers. Owen picked up on the second ring. "How's it going?" he asked.

"Good. How are things there?" Dylan listened to his brother rustle around, no doubt getting someplace he could talk without being heard, and then the line grew quieter.

"The same. Ryan freaked out when she found out that you'd taken Zoey to Vegas. Liam claims she practically attacked him."

"What did she do?" He sat on the edge of the bed, fully dressed.

"Apparently, she followed him on his rounds last night and threatened him. We have to get a handle on this woman." He could hear the frustration in his brother's voice.

"Yeah." He glanced at the closed door and thought of how to tell his brother the new developments. "About that . . ." He closed his eyes in frustration. "Zoey already knows everything."

"What?" Suddenly, a loud noise echoed over the line, and he figured that Owen had dropped the phone. He heard a muffled "Shit."

"Do the others know?" Owen asked when he came back.

"I . . . don't know." He hadn't talked to Zoey about it. "I'm not sure. We're heading over to the lawyer's soon. I'll find out."

"Yeah." The stress from Owen almost shot through the phone like lightning.

"Hey, don't worry about it. She knows and honestly wants to help us find Dad."

"You're a fool," Owen said. "She's played you, bro."

"I don't think so." He'd mulled the situation over for what felt like forever. "I really believe that Zoey doesn't know anything about Dad, or the money."

"If she's so honest with you, find out what she does know. Ask her if the camp received any big investors."

"Yeah"—he heard Zoey moving around in the other room—"I have to go." Taking a few deep, cleansing breaths, he stepped out of the room.

Seeing her standing by the large window, looking out over the Vegas strip, he knew he was right. The way the light hit her face and the look in her eyes when she turned toward him—he realized his brother was right. He was a fool, because he was in love.

CHAPTER
TWELVE

A few hours later, when they walked into the waiting room of the lawyer's office, Zoey gritted her teeth when she saw Bridgette standing next to the water fountain. She had hoped to avoid the woman again today but knew it was probably inevitable.

"Don't flip out," Dylan warned her quietly.

"I wondered if she'd be around." She turned to him. "Don't worry—she's just trying to get her hands on some more of my father's money. You know I don't care if my father left anything for me or my mom or Scarlett, but I hope to god he didn't leave her another penny." It was true. At this point, the woman was a leech, and Zoey was no longer willing to feed her needs.

"Ms. Rowlett," the receptionist said.

"Yes?" Zoey started to say, but Bridgette jumped in.

"Yes, that's me." Bridgette rushed forward as if her name had just been called for winning concert tickets.

"*Miss* Rowlett," the receptionist said more clearly. "Zoey Rowlett." She raised an eyebrow at Bridgette. "You'll have to wait here, *Mrs.* Rowlett."

Dylan followed Zoey into the office, where the lawyer from yesterday was sitting behind a large desk.

"Welcome." He waved them both in. "Can Sherri get you anything? Water? Coffee?"

"No, thank you," Zoey answered as she took a seat across from the man, while Dylan took the chair next to her. "Why is Bridgette here?" Could the woman actually have some official business here?

"I ran into her yesterday, and she demanded to be present during your father's reading of the will today, but since she isn't included in the will, she'll have to—"

Just then the door burst open.

"I demand you let me in there." Bridgette pushed past the secretary. "He was my husband. *My* husband!" she screamed.

The lawyer looked to Zoey. "It's up to you. I can have her removed."

Zoey was curious now. If Bridgette didn't have any legal grounds to be there, it might be a good thing that she hear it from the lawyer that her father had changed his will and left her nothing more.

"I don't mind." Zoey's grip on her bag relaxed.

"Mrs. Rowlett, please come in." The lawyer motioned to an empty chair.

Dylan stood up, gave her his chair, and stood behind her as the lawyer started going over the will.

Since Zoey had talked to her father, she knew that he had said that he'd left all his assets to her and Scarlett. But as she heard the lawyer confirm it all, for the first time, it really sank in.

Of course, she wasn't given much time to think about it since, hearing this news, Bridgette sat up slightly. "I object."

"You . . ." John Jackson sighed. "I'm sorry, Mrs. Rowlett, this is a reading of Jean Rowlett's will. We're not in court. There is nothing to object to."

"Yes, there is. I object to the will. It's a lie. Jean would never leave anything to his two . . . 'brats,' as he always liked to call them." Bridgette shifted, and Zoey realized that no matter what the woman said, she was determined to keep her cool. "So, I'd like to know what you can do to make this right."

To the lawyer's credit, the man didn't burst into laughter. Zoey was having a tough time not laughing herself. Dylan placed a hand on her shoulder when a giggle escaped her. The sound caused Bridgette to glare in her direction.

"I don't think you understand . . ." the lawyer started but was once again interrupted.

"No, I don't think *you* understand. I'm here to collect my husband's—" Bridgette began, but Zoey just couldn't let that rest.

"Ex," she added easily, which earned her another glare from Bridgette. "Ex-husband. You divorced him shortly after he found out that he was sick, or so he told me on the phone the other day, before he died."

The other woman ignored her and continued to address John Jackson. "I'm sure you see this all the time, so I'll want you to fill out whatever paperwork I need so I can turn his will back to the way it was before he changed it." She smiled brightly at the man as if she were used to using her looks to get her way.

"My god," Zoey started. "Does she actually think that's how things work?" Dylan just shrugged.

"Missus . . ." the lawyer started again. "I'm afraid that's illegal. Jean Rowlett changed his will after your divorce, when he was of sound mind and body. There's nothing—"

At this point Bridgette stood up. "No, I'm right." She leaned on the edge of the desk, her long manicured bright-pink nails almost scraping the wood. "Either you disregard this will, or you'll have a legal fight on your hands."

"Okay." The lawyer shifted. "You're well within your rights to contest the will. However, after a divorce, my advice is—"

"I don't care what your advice is. I want to contest the will." She straightened up. "So, get to contesting."

A burst of laughter escaped Zoey, which she tried to cover quickly by coughing.

"Um . . ." Mr. Jackson started, his eyes darting between Zoey and Bridgette. "That's not really how it works. I'm not your—"

"Do whatever it takes. I won't have her"—Bridgette pointed in Zoey's direction—"getting a dime of mine."

"Yours?" Zoey started. Again the woman narrowed her eyes in her direction. Then she turned toward her; Zoey was still sitting down, trying to remain calm and relaxed.

"You think this is a joke? Your father told me all about you two brats—how you ruined his life. How your bitch mother . . ."

Zoey stood suddenly for the first time as anger washed over her. The fact that, through the red haze of pure rage, it registered that Bridgette's smile had grown had her taking a few deep breaths.

"Easy," Dylan whispered as he moved next to her. "She's trying to rile you up, remember. It's a game to her." He nudged her back a few steps.

"You won't get a dime of Jean's. He wanted me to have it all—he told me so all of the time. That's why he left you and your bitch mother with nothing." The woman's smile was almost too much for her to take at this point.

"My assistant has called security," John broke in.

"Good." Bridgette turned back to the lawyer. "Have her removed. She's totally out of control. Look, she has to be held back to keep from attacking me."

Zoey relaxed even more when she realized it was true. Even though the place on her cheek still stung from Bridgette's slap yesterday, she knew it wouldn't do any good to let the woman win. Especially not in front of so many witnesses, and especially a lawyer.

"I don't think you understand," the lawyer said. "Miss Rowlett is here on legal matters. You are not. You'll need to leave the premises." He rose as two security guards stepped into the room.

"I'm not leaving. Jean was my husband."

"*Was!*" Zoey shouted as the two guards flanked Bridgette's sides and took her arms.

"You'll regret this." Bridgette turned toward her.

"I doubt it." Zoey felt her smile stretch her cheeks.

Bridgette didn't have a chance to respond as guards hustled her out of the room.

"That was fun," Dylan whispered to her.

It took a few minutes for things to settle down. Dylan fixed the club chair she'd knocked over when she'd stood up.

She took the bottled water that was offered to her and listened to the rest of her father's estate plans. In the end, she was thankful that he hadn't insisted she take over the family business; instead, he'd made arrangements for Mr. Jackson to oversee the liquidation of everything, including the home and cars her father had just outside of Vegas.

As they made their way out of the lawyer's building, Zoey was still running over everything in her mind and was fully prepared to encounter Bridgette again. However, when she slid into the passenger seat of the rental car without so much as a glimpse of the woman, she relaxed back in the seat.

"Damn." She rubbed her forehead. "I was really hoping to see her again."

Dylan smothered a laugh. "I think security made sure she was off the premises." He pulled out of the parking garage. "I bet she's pissed."

"You think?" She smiled. "God, I really hope so."

"Where to?" he asked, turning toward the Strip.

"I don't know." She tilted her head. "I'll want to call my sister and Mom, but"—she paused for a moment—"what's around Vegas? I've only ever been to the Strip."

His eyebrows shot up. "Have you been to the Hoover Dam?"

"No. I've seen it on TV and in pictures but haven't made the trip. Actually, I've never seen the Grand Canyon before."

"What?" He reversed direction and started heading out of town. "I hope it's okay if we spend the next two hours in the car."

She shrugged. "I've got nowhere else to be. I'll use the time to call everyone and fill them in."

"Go ahead, and I'll head out of town. Once we get in the canyon, you might lose the signal."

"Thanks"—she touched his hand—"for being there. I don't think I could have handled that by myself."

He reached up to cup her chin. "Anytime." He pressed a soft kiss to the side of her face.

She couldn't explain the emotions that rushed through her, so instead of focusing on them, she pulled out her cell phone and punched her sister's number first.

Deciding to keep most of the story to herself, she filled her sister in just on what their father had left them. Scar seemed only interested in the fact that they could then turn the money back into the camp.

"We're running low, according to Elle. Since we have the other two cabins being built, we may have to hold off on building the next two until spring."

"Things are that bad?" she asked as she adjusted her headrest. "What about everything we put into the place?"

"Elle says that out of our initial investment, only a few thousand dollars remain. And that's salary for employees."

Zoey knew that the initial repairs and improvements had taken the majority of the funds the five of them had invested.

"It sounds like Dad did us a favor in the end. You always tell me to look at the bright side of things."

"I know, but . . ." Her sister paused.

"What?" she asked finally.

"I just hate that it's coming from him. You know? After what he did to us, how he hurt us and Mom."

"I know," she agreed. "We'll talk about it more when I get back."

"How long are you staying?" Scar asked.

"I was thinking we'd head back tomorrow," she answered.

"Make sure you take some time to enjoy. These were supposed to be your days off, remember?"

She smiled. "I know. Thanks. I'm going to call Mom."

"No, don't. I'm heading over there to have lunch with her. I can fill her in. Go, enjoy yourself." Her sister paused. "Zoey? We did a little more background digging into Dylan and his brothers."

She watched Dylan, who was busy driving, but she knew he'd heard her side of the conversation.

"And?" she asked.

"From what we can tell, it looks like they are searching for their father. Hannah pulled some strings, and, well, there are rumored reports among the employees of the family business that the company's been in trouble since his disappearance."

"Thanks—we can talk when I get back," she said when Dylan glanced in her direction. "Bye." Scar hung up, and Zoey laid her phone in her lap.

"Want to grab some lunch on the way back?" he asked. "We can probably be back in time for you to lose some money in the casino later tonight?"

"Sure," she agreed, wanting to ask him more about his father but unsure of how to go about it.

"What other national treasures have you missed?" he asked as he drove the winding roads through the canyons.

She thought about it. "I've pretty much seen them all, with the exception of the Grand Canyon." She'd been watching the red hills fly by.

"Yellowstone?" he asked, glancing over at her.

"Family vacation when I was ten." The one time her dad had acted like a father.

"Did you get to see the statue of Christ the Redeemer on top of Corcovado when you were over in Rio?" he asked.

"We all took the tour."

It was strange—talking to Dylan, she realized that they'd had plenty of good times with her dad, before things had changed.

"Things started to slide downhill shortly after my twelfth birthday, when my father's company purchased a company Bridgette had been working at in Orlando. I remember my parents talking about it." She glanced over at him. "What about your dad?" She'd been waiting for the conversation to turn.

"Dad's business has always been steady," he answered, and she knew she'd have to press further.

"My father's business had at one point been one of the biggest banking investment companies in the United States. Or so he always told us. But things changed shortly after he started seeing Bridgette," she admitted. "With the destruction of our family, my father's assets took a dive as well. He sold off most of his big income properties and made some terrible investments"—the local papers had had a field day—"which caused most of his investors to jump ship."

"I'm afraid that's what will happen to us," Dylan confessed, causing her to turn toward him. "Dad's been known to take a trip or two, but nothing this long and never . . ." He stopped and shook his head. "Nothing this long."

She mentally kicked herself for waiting too long and not getting enough information from him. "We'll walk from here," he said. He turned off the car and glanced over at her. "Whatever happens, remember that your dad tried to make it right in the end."

"I know." She rubbed her forehead. "I should have returned that final call sooner." She'd been feeling guilty about it ever since she'd talked to him. "It's not right." She rested her head back against the seat. "I should have . . ."

Dylan's hand on hers stopped her from finishing the sentence.

"Hindsight . . ." He lifted her hand up to his lips. "Let's take a walk." He got out of the car and rushed around to open her door.

They spent almost a full hour strolling around the dam; the conversation was kept light and away from family, since she'd had enough to deal with earlier and didn't want to dig deeper with him at the moment. Instead, she wanted to enjoy her moment in the sun—time with him.

He opened her car door for her.

"Thank you, for today." She leaned on the open door and looked at him. "I'm glad you talked me into this. I wouldn't have known what to do by myself."

"You would have probably ended up in prison for attacking Bridgette," he said with a wink.

She laughed. "It would have been worth it." She slid into the seat.

"What do you say we try our hand at the slots?" he suggested as they pulled out of the town.

"I don't know . . ." She cocked a brow at him. "How lucky are you feeling?"

He reached for her hand. "With you by my side . . . very."

The drive back to Vegas didn't seem as long as the one to the dam. They pulled into the parking area of the hotel and decided to run up to the room so that she could change into more casual clothes before they hit the casino.

She took a moment to send off a text to her mom. She knew that, as much as Scar had wanted to distance herself from their father, their mother's feelings toward the man who had emotionally tortured and rejected her were stronger.

Did Scar talk to you? Everything is taken care of. Dad left us everything else, which is being deposited into a new account the lawyer opened in our names. Ran into #2, story to follow when we return tomorrow. Heading out to lose some of dad's money. XOXO

Her mom's reply was instantaneous.

Yes, Scar and I chatted. Have fun, sweetie. I'm so proud of you.

As they stepped into the elevator together, he wrapped his arms around her and kissed her, and she told herself to forget about finding answers to her questions. That for now, she needed to let everything go. She wanted to take this time for herself so she could enjoy just being with Dylan. She knew that he was right; with him by her side, they were really lucky.

They stepped out into the casino, and each of them bought a hundred dollars on the casino cards.

"It's funny—instead of getting cash, it's all done on credit cards now." She stuffed her card into her pocket.

"Don't put it in your back pocket," he said. "You'd be surprised at how easily someone could slide that from your jeans."

"Oh?" She chuckled. "I'd like to see . . ."

He stepped closer, his dark eyes locking with hers as he wrapped his arms around her. Then he was kissing her, and she forgot everything—even that they were standing in the middle of a very loud casino with hundreds of people around them, looking on.

"See?" He held up her card.

She snatched it back and frowned at him. "Like I'd let someone else do that to distract me?"

"Put it in your front pocket," he suggested and then took her hand as they started to stroll through the large rooms.

"What's your game?" he asked. "Tables? Slots? Poker?"

"Let's start with the slots. I've always wanted to try them."

He stopped her from walking away by tugging on her hand. "You've never played before?"

She shook her head. "The last time I was in Vegas, I was twenty years old."

"Then this calls for the big one." She followed him through the floor. They stopped at a large slot machine. The kind that took both hands to pull down.

"To pop your slot cherry"—he wiggled his dark eyebrows at her—"you have to play this beauty."

"Wow. I didn't know they made these things that big." She pulled out her card from her pocket.

"Wait." He stopped her, then leaned in and kissed her. "For luck," he said.

She swiped her card and pulled the lever. The dials rolled around; the first one landed on a one bar, and she felt her heart skip a beat. Then the second landed on a two bar, and her hopes fell. The third landed in between a one bar and a two. A loss.

"We still have all night." He stepped next to her. "What shall we do now?"

"How about those?" She nodded to the smaller quarter machines down the aisle.

For the next few hours, they sat side by side as they spent their money at the quarter slot machines and drank complimentary drinks.

"How much do you have left?" he asked.

"About two dollars. You?" She could tell he hadn't wanted to admit anything. "What?" She tried to glance at the machine he had been playing.

"I hit a jackpot of sorts and won eight hundred," he finally said.

"What? You did not." She pushed him playfully. "Why didn't you say anything?"

He shrugged. "It wasn't a real jackpot—just a small one. This machine pays out up to five hundred thousand."

"What?" She surveyed her own machine with a frown. "I didn't know they paid out that much."

"They do if you win the right way." He rubbed her hand. "How about we head out and grab some dinner. Then we can come back and try our hands at the tables?"

She tucked her two-dollar credit card into her pocket and strolled down the Strip with him to a barbecue place he'd talked about.

They listened to a band play and sat out on a patio as they ate ribs and sipped cold beer. They hit the card tables next, and she was happily surprised that she won her first hand at blackjack.

"Looks like you're good at this," Dylan said, tossing in a few more chips for the next round.

When she won the next hand, Dylan sat out on the next one. "It's obvious you're lucky at cards. How about a drink?"

"I could do with something sweet and strong." She smiled up at him and thought that description fit him perfectly as well.

"I'll be right back," he said.

By the time Dylan came back, a small crowd had gathered around her table to watch her.

"Looks like you're doing well." Dylan ruffled the stack of chips in front of her.

She was up by almost $200. He placed a kiss on the top of her head and set her drink down.

Yet this time, she lost both hands. Glancing up, she decided she needed to stretch her legs and make a bathroom run.

Some folks took her spot at the table after she turned in the chips to the dealer and received a receipt in their place.

"Smart." She tucked the receipt into her front pocket. "I was beginning to wonder how I was going to carry all of those chips around with me."

He chuckled and took her hand. "Need some fresh air?"

"I could use some." They made their way toward the doors.

Stepping out, she was thankful the evening had cooled off some. They strolled around the fountains once more.

"What's going to happen if you don't find your dad?" she finally asked, figuring since she was on a roll, she could gamble by asking him the questions she needed to ask.

He turned his eyes toward her. "We're not sure."

"Will your business suffer?"

"It could." He stopped, and she stood next to him. "I'd hate to think that what your dad went through could happen to us. I mean, as far as the business sliding. We need the income; not to mention, we were all looking forward to someday taking over the business together."

"But you don't currently work there?" she asked.

"No, which was a dumb move for us." She could see the frustration in his eyes as he reached down and took her hand in his. "Hindsight."

"The business relies on him that much?"

"No"—he angled his head toward her face—"but we relied on him. How about we get some gelato?" He drew her to a halt in front of a small shop.

She knew he was trying to avoid the topic. But later, as she stood in front of the fountains, eating her raspberry gelato with his arms around her, she could only think it felt so good, so right. When she turned to wrap her arms around him in turn, the slow kiss was just what she needed.

"I know you probably want to head back in and double your winnings, but . . ." He kissed her again. "I want you so bad." He rested his forehead on hers. "I've wanted you all day long."

"Take me upstairs." She reached for his hand. "I want to get lucky. Finally." He joined her in a laugh and started pulling her toward the doors.

They remained silent as they made it to the elevators, then stood back as several others exited on different floors.

When they were the last ones in the elevator, he moved to her, held her against the wall, and kissed her until her toes went numb.

Then he pulled her out as they made their way to the room.

When the door shut behind her, he pounced again, this time pinning her to the door and kissing her until she hoisted herself up, wrapping her legs around his hips.

"Dylan, I need . . ." she said against his lips.

"Yeah." He walked them backward and almost fell. Laughing, she held on to him as he carted her into the room and playfully tossed her down on the bed.

"Get down here." She motioned with her finger.

He smiled down at her and pulled his shirt over his head, then reached for hers. Sitting up, she allowed him to tug off her shirt and jeans.

"God, I could get used to spending my nights like this." He moved between her spread legs.

"Me too." She held on to him as he kissed her until her head spun.

When he slid into her, she felt her chest contract while all the emotions of the last two days rolled out of her. She used the energy to take what she wanted from him.

When she knew she couldn't hold back any longer, she arched and cried out his name.

She surfaced again when their bodies had cooled off, to the point that she tugged on the blankets and crawled under them. He followed her, and she wrapped herself around him.

She rested her head on his chest and smiled as she rose and fell with each of his breaths.

"Yeah, I could get used to this." She drifted off to sleep.

CHAPTER
THIRTEEN

Dylan couldn't help feeling a little guilty as he listened to Zoey breathing as they lay there. Guilty for using her the way he had that night. But his mind kept justifying it, telling him that she had wanted him too.

He ran a hand over her bare shoulder and closed his eyes at the wonderful feeling of her lying next to him. What was he going to do when they went back to the camp? How was he going to sleep without her in his bed? He knew that, with him bunking with his brothers and her with her sister, they wouldn't be able to be together at night.

His mind turned to their conversation over the past two days. They had talked about family. His and hers. It was strange how similar the last few years of their lives had been. All except for the fact that Zoey and Scarlett had been lucky enough to have Kimberly.

Did she know how lucky they were to have their mother?

It wasn't as if he'd lacked anything growing up. Their father had been very hands on when they had been younger.

He had been at every soccer or football game, not to mention every swim meet he'd had. Anything the three of them had asked for, they had been given.

Much like her father, his father had started acting up shortly after Liam's eighteenth birthday. He still found it hard to believe that it had been more than six months since he'd talked to his dad.

It would have been different if there had been a fight or an argument with any of them. Instead, one day he'd gotten a call from Owen.

"Dad's gone," Owen had said.

"Gone?" Dylan had instantly thought his brother had meant dead, and he'd swallowed hard.

"He packed a bag and left," Owen clarified, and Dylan relaxed. He was in the car and had almost jerked the wheel off the road when he'd heard the worry in his brother's voice.

"He's done that before."

"Yeah, but it's been two months," Owen added.

"Two months?" Dylan searched his memory for the last time he'd talked to his father. "How do you know it's been two months?"

"Because I'm the one who drove him to the bank."

"The . . . what? I lost you." He pulled into his condo parking lot.

"Dad asked me to drop him off at the bank. I thought it was for a meeting."

"And what? He wandered out of the bank?" he asked.

"Not before pulling everything out of the account and closing it."

"*What?* He closed—"

"I didn't realize he was gone until I stopped off at his place. Joel's been there, watching over the place. Dad asked him to."

"For how long?"

"Hello, McFly—two whole fucking months." His brother sounded irritated.

"Well, shit. Have you tried calling him?" He parked.

"Yeah, his cell has been disconnected."

"That can't be right," he answered. "I'm heading into my place. I'll call you when I'm upstairs."

"Better yet, meet me over at Dad's place. I called Liam," Owen had added.

Dylan had backed the car out. "See you in ten." He'd hung up.

That had been the first of many meetings between the brothers.

It had taken them almost a full month to find the calendar with Elle's name scratched in it. Another week to figure out who she was, and almost another full month to come up with the plan to pose as workers at the camp.

Dylan shifted and looked down at Zoey sleeping peacefully in his arms. He had lied to her, and for the first time since meeting her, it was eating at him.

He placed a soft kiss on her forehead and vowed to tell her everything when they returned to the camp, after he talked to his brothers.

The next morning, they woke early. They checked out of the hotel and drove down the street to eat breakfast.

He tried to keep the mood light, since he knew that the trip had been a tough one for her already. He had to admit it to himself: this had been the best trip he'd ever been on.

Of course, he'd never traveled with a woman before, but he had at one point had a live-in girlfriend. Which had turned out to be one of the worst ideas he'd ever had.

One day he'd come home from a short trip, and it had been apparent that his ex had thrown a party while he'd been gone. He'd been pissed and prepared to kick her out; then he'd walked into his bedroom to find her in bed with not one but two other guys, and a girl.

He'd taken a deep breath, woken the group up, and asked them all to leave.

After she'd moved out, he'd donated and replaced all his furniture in the condo. Hearing about the orgy at River Camp hadn't been shocking to him—not after what Amelia had done to him.

When he and Zoey arrived back at the airport, he ran through his preflight checks as she strapped into the copilot seat.

"Ready?" he asked as he looked over at her. Once again, she was gripping the armrests. "Do you want to sit in the back for this part?"

"No." She took a deep breath. "I mean, yes and then no. I trust you. Take us home."

After waiting in the long line, they were cleared for takeoff. Once they hit cruising altitude, he watched her relax slightly. Then they hit the Rockies, and things grew bumpy. He'd handled turbulence before, but holding on to the wheel now took all his concentration.

So when he happened to have a second to glance over at Zoey, he knew she wasn't going to make it unless he talked to her.

"Hey," he shouted through the headset, "it's just air." Seeing her glare in his direction, he sighed. "Okay, hot air with bubbles of chilled air. Remember, heat rises?"

"Yes." Her grip relaxed slightly.

"Good." He continued to tell her about the science of turbulence and what it did to the plane.

By the time the plane had smoothed out, she was a little more relaxed than before.

"I think we're out of the worst of it. Why don't you head back, grab a bite to eat?" he asked.

"I'm not leaving you . . ." she started.

"Hey." He spoke softly to her. "I'm kind of wanting a drink and a sandwich. Besides, I bet it would help to stretch your legs. I'll keep my hands here, if you help me out."

She nodded and got up, then disappeared into the back. He relaxed even more when she came back in with a sandwich and a soda.

"How are you doing?" she asked.

"I'm fine. How are you?" He hit the autopilot but stayed where he was just in case they happened to hit any more turbulence.

"I'm"—she looked like she was quickly assessing herself—"better. Thanks."

"Why don't you go back, enjoy the ride?" he suggested as he sipped the soda.

"No." She shook her head. "I'll keep you company this time." She strapped in again and watched him. "Talking to you helps."

The rest of the flight home, they chatted about school, then about the camp. She told him about the last year, getting everything ready for opening day.

"We were building the first of the new cabins . . ."

She had finished off her own sandwich, and they were almost half-way home, when he noted that she looked calm. She chuckled suddenly. "Elle and I had walked out one evening to go check it out. We had taken the flood flashlights so that we could see the place. When we got there, the construction door was locked. Elle had a set of keys, and when we opened the door, a large raccoon rushed out of the building. It scared us so bad we both screamed, and we swore they would be able to hear us back in the main building." She laughed.

"How did he get locked in the building?"

"Apparently, the little guy had climbed down the hole in the roof where the gas fireplace vent was going to be. It hadn't been installed yet, and he was looking for a nice place to nest for the winter."

"It must have taken a lot of funding to fix the place up. I saw pictures of how it was before . . ." He waited.

She was leaning back in the seat, watching the sky outside.

"Elle's the one who managed all of us coming together. We've all put everything we have into this place." She sighed. "God, I hope it stays this busy."

"It should," he said. "I mean, it's a great business plan."

She narrowed her eyes at him. "What exactly do you do for your family's business?"

He shrugged and avoided her gaze, embarrassed at how little he did around the company to earn multiple digits beyond what he earned at the camp handling zip-lining. "Whatever they need me to. Sometimes it's just to be the face; others it's to meet with potential clients."

"Your family's business is investments. Like my father's was, correct?"

He shrugged. "Not really. I mean, yes, to some degree." He wished they would change the subject but knew he couldn't at this point without causing red flags.

"R&R Enterprises purchased defunct commercial buildings and turned them around, or tore them down, and built something else that would make a profit. What does Paradise Investments do?"

He glanced down at the screen and gauged that they were almost an hour away from Destin.

"They purchase buildings."

"Dylan . . ." Her voice made his ears prick up.

"Most of the large condo buildings you see along the Emerald Coast are ours."

She remained quiet for almost a full minute.

"What kind of people invest in property that big?" she asked. "I would think that the business would hold its own."

"It does," he admitted. "But there's always more land and more buildings to put up."

"And you use investors?" she asked.

"Sometimes," he said. "If we want to stay on top of things, we use investors to purchase land along the coast. Or we buy the land from other investors by brokering deals." She fell silent again. "You don't have to sell your shares in your father's business."

She shook her head quickly. "No, but I'm not holding on to them. Besides, I've heard the business is struggling. It's a good idea to get out now."

He thought about what his father would do if any of them sold the family business. Then again, Zoey hadn't been raised to take over after her father passed away. The three of the brothers had been, with Owen acting as head.

If anything ever did happen to their old man, Dylan had no doubt that his brother would step into their father's role. As he already had.

"What now?" He started their descent.

"Now"—she shifted in her seat—"I let Dad's lawyer sell off his shares and put what money he had into the camp."

"So, you're here to stay?" he asked.

"Yes." She beamed. "I may not always live on site, but for now . . ."

He had to reply to the tower, then glanced over at her. "For me for now, I'll keep showing people a good time while flying through the trees. Ready to land this bird?" He turned the plane and lined it up with the runway.

"Oh god," he thought he heard her say as her fingers dug into the armrests again.

CHAPTER FOURTEEN

She realized quickly how great it was to be back on the ground as the plane came to a stop. When they pulled into the camp's parking area late Wednesday evening, she smiled when she noticed that her friends were waiting for them.

"So?" Elle asked after hugging her. "How did it go?"

"I'm tired." She twisted to crack her back.

"We hit some turbulence on the way home," Dylan supplied.

"Oh"—Elle hugged her again—"you need a drink."

"Does she know me or what?" Zoey was guided away from the parking area. She turned back to Dylan to wave. "Thank you."

When she walked into the third-floor apartment, Scar hugged her.

"Thank you for dealing with everything. I wouldn't have made it. You're so much stronger than I am."

She held on to her for a moment. "I was thankful I had Dylan there." She took a deep breath before leaning back. "I'll be honest: the hardest part of the trip was not punching Bridgette in the face."

Scar smiled and squeezed her hand. "I owe you."

A glass of wine was shoved into her hands as she was pushed onto the sofa.

"So"—Elle sat down across from her—"tell us everything."

For the next hour, she filled them in on their trip, making sure to leave out the parts about her and Dylan. Her mother showed up shortly after she'd arrived and joined the rest of them. She wasn't a big wine drinker but sipped a glass slowly as she listened to Zoey talk. She told them what had happened with Bridgette.

"I doubt that's the last we'll hear from her," Scarlett said from across the room. Her sister had her feet tucked up underneath her as she sipped on a glass of wine.

Zoey had downed the first glass as if it were grape juice—which, hey, it was—and now she took her time to enjoy her second glass.

"You're right," Zoey said. "Still, I don't see the woman coming all the way to Florida to give us shit."

They hadn't stopped for dinner on the way back from the airport, since she'd been eager to get home, and the liquor was getting to her. Reaching down, she picked up the bowl of potato chips that had been set on the coffee table. She thought quickly about ordering some dinner but then realized the potato chips would probably fill her up instead.

"Don't you remember?" Scarlett dug into the bowl and took a handful of chips.

"Hey!" She moved the bowl away.

"Share!" Her sister's eyes narrowed. "There's more, and even some brownies are left over."

"What happened?" She handed over the bowl to Elle, who waved for it.

"Bridgette threatened her," Scarlett said between bites of chips.

"It wasn't a threat," their mother chimed in, waving her hand as if to brush it off.

"Sure it was," Scar added.

"What happened?" Zoey sat up again. "When was this?"

"During the divorce. She showed up at the hobby store, back when I was working there to pay for all those legal fees." Her mother set her wine glass down. "She showed up and grabbed my wrist."

"And threatened you," Scar added.

Their mother shifted. "I told my lawyer about it, and he took care of everything. She never came around again."

"What happened next?" Hannah asked, taking a chip from the passed bowl.

"The divorce was finalized, and your father and Bridgette moved to Vegas." She picked up her glass and drank more wine.

"Did Dad really leave us everything?" Scarlett asked, getting up and returning with a plate of brownies.

Zoey grabbed two and bit into one before answering. "Yes. It's going to be a while before all of his holdings are moved or sold. Apparently, the board of directors forced him to retire shortly after . . . well, according to the lawyer, after Bridgett found her way into a board meeting and started making demands on them."

"She sounds like a charmer," Aubrey said from her spot across the sofa. Her auburn hair was piled on top of her head in a messy bun, and every time she spoke, more strands of hair fell around her face. Aubrey taught tai chi classes after the yoga sessions.

It was hard to believe it of her delicate friend, but Aubrey had earned her black belt in both tai chi and judo. She claimed she'd started learning self-defense when she'd moved to New York to live near her father.

"That woman was always a hot mess," her mother added, earning a round of chuckles from the room.

"Dylan had to hold me back from punching her, especially after she slapped me."

"What?" everyone in the room shouted at once.

"Didn't I mention that?" She sighed and rubbed her head. "Sorry, still shaking from the plane trip back."

"Is Dylan that bad a pilot?" her mother asked. Zoey glanced around quickly and realized that her mother was easily the best dressed in the room. While everyone else was still in camp attire, and Zoey had on wrinkled clothes from the long day's travel, her mother looked neat and stylish. Zoey knew that before she left the house, she always ironed her shirts. Who did that anymore?

"No." She shook her head and winced as the room spun. Taking another bite of the brownie to combat the wine, she said, "He was wonderful. He talked to me the entire time he was fighting to keep the plane in the air. He kept telling me it was like speed bumps. With my eyes closed, I could just imagine us rolling over them."

When she stopped talking, she realized five sets of eyes remained on her.

"Sooooo . . ." Elle leaned forward and poured more wine into Zoey's glass. "What's between you and Dylan?"

Not caring anymore, she chuckled and took another sip of her wine. Finally, she was relaxed.

"Whatever it is is going to stay between us for now," Zoey said. "I don't kiss and tell. Besides, my mother is here."

Her mother eased back in her seat. "I was just leaving. I have an early . . . something." She stood up.

"No," everyone started, but when her mother held up her hands, they stopped.

"It's time for old ladies to turn in anyway. Way past my bedtime. I'll see myself out." She turned to Zoey. "I like Dylan." She leaned down and placed a kiss on Zoey's head. "I'm happy you're back safe. Night."

She waved as she walked out.

Hannah picked back up once they were alone. "So, there *was* kissing."

"Ugh! When was the last time you kissed someone?" Zoey joked back. When Hannah's face heated, everyone's attention moved to her.

"Who?" they all demanded.

"Stop! We're talking about Zoey and Dylan, not me." Hannah held up her hands.

"Spill. Two nights in Vegas—there had to be sex," Elle said.

"I'm not telling." Zoey shook her head again. "Tell me what's happened around here."

"I've caught the couple staying in the Love Shack four times," Elle said, chuckling.

"Caught?" Zoey asked.

"Having sex," she clarified. "They just do it anywhere, like dogs." Elle groaned and flipped her blonde hair over her shoulder as she tucked her long legs up under her in the chair.

"Doggy style?" Hannah always looked like she'd stepped off the cover of a magazine. Even when she was wearing sweats and had her hair in a long braid.

"Well, no, but they were doing it in the boathouse; then, when I went in to check to see about a thermostat setting in one of the massage rooms, they were there on the table; and the other night they were in the morning yoga room rolling around on the mats." Elle groaned. "I've seen their asses more than I have my own in the past month."

Zoey laughed.

"Ewww, okay, item added to my task list: make sure to sanitize the yoga mats every morning before class," Hannah said, and everyone giggled.

"Where else have you caught them?" Scarlett asked, as if it were a game.

"The movie theater," Elle said, ticking off her two fingers.

"We caught them on the beach that first night," Zoey added with a smile. "Their fortieth anniversary."

"When I've been married to someone that long, I only hope we have sex like they do," Hannah added wistfully.

"I hadn't thought of it like that," Elle said as the room went quiet, and several sighs rang out.

"Any more orgies?" Zoey asked, breaking into the moment, and all the girls laughed.

"We think there was one in one of the older cabins last night. The cleaning crew was called out this morning, and I was made aware, discreetly, of the situation," Elle stated.

Aubrey jumped in. "Do you think that it's just a fluke?"

"What? That old people are horny?" Zoey chuckled and almost spilled her wine, so she set the glass down. "We're horny. I'm horny."

"So, something did happen in Vegas?" Scar asked.

"Not talking," she reminded the room.

Aubrey said, "It's not that bad. I think, after that first destructive party, we've learned to handle things better."

"I agree," Elle said. "I don't really mind. I mean, we all knew adults were going to be easier than kids, but we came into this with our eyes open. There were bound to be issues. The fact is, it was still a smart move. The numbers prove it."

"Like you said," Hannah replied, "there's more money with adults. The camp can run year round instead of just the summer months. We already have bookings through the holiday season." She smiled. "Who cares if every once in a while, things get a little . . . rowdy," she added after a moment. "We can deal with each case when it comes up."

"You're right," Aubrey agreed. "I mean, I think the worst has come and gone."

"We could always make a fortune selling condoms," Zoey added with a giggle.

"Or sell sex toys in the lobby," Hannah added, earning a look from everyone. "What? Don't pretend you don't each own a vibrator."

Everyone laughed. "Okay." Zoey held up her wine glass. "To River Camp."

"To the Wildflowers," Elle added. "There isn't a day that has gone by in the last eleven years that I've regretted bumping into the four of you."

"Wildflowers." Zoey held up her glass.

"Wildflowers." Everyone toasted.

When Zoey woke the next morning, it was to a pounding headache.

"Stupid wine," she mumbled as she slammed off her alarm clock.

"Shhh," Scarlett said from across the room and buried her head beneath the comforter.

Remembering it was Thursday, she groaned and got out of bed. She was due to teach the beginners-yoga class in less than an hour, which meant that her wine hangover had to go away fast.

Walking blindly into the bathroom after hitting the wall once and stubbing her toe twice, she pulled off her clothes and took a deep breath. She turned on the cold water and stood under it for a full minute while screaming in her head until the water heated.

By the time she stepped out of the shower less than ten minutes later, she was wide awake and ready to go.

Stepping into the yoga classroom, she smiled at the few guests who were already rolling out their mats.

"Morning," she said, getting everyone's attention. "Feel free to do some stretches while we wait for the others to arrive."

She took her time rolling out her mat and trying to warm up her muscles after the cold shower.

When she glanced up again, the room was almost full. Yoga classes were open to guests and employees if it didn't interfere with their schedules. Zoey took turns teaching with Scarlett and Hannah, while Elle had a ballet basics class.

Zoey got everyone's attention by turning on the light music that played in the background while she taught.

Starting with some basic poses, she called out each move and stretched as she explained the positions as she went. It wasn't until after her body had started relaxing more that she took a moment to glance around the room to make sure everyone was following along. Dylan was stretching off to the side of the room.

Seeing him expertly perform an extended triangle pose had her smiling. When his eyes met hers, he winked.

By the time the class was over, her body was limber, and she had built up a slight sweat.

"Hey," she said to him when she finally broke free from chatting with a few guests.

"You look amazing in that outfit."

She could tell he wanted to kiss her, because his eyes moved to her lips. She smiled and looked down at his gym shorts and T-shirt. "I guess no one has created a line of yoga outfits for men."

"None that I'd be caught dead in." He chuckled. "Have lunch with me?"

She thought about it. There were questions still left unanswered between them. "Where?"

"How about we meet at the docks?" he suggested.

"I'll bring the food. Noon?"

He nodded, then glanced down as his smart watch chimed. "I've got to go." He smiled. "It was worth waking up early to see you." He reached out and touched her shoulder. "See you at lunch."

She watched him leave and wished more than anything to be able to spend the entire day with him, but after yoga, she had to be down at the pool to help with a new water-aerobics class they were trying, then up to the volleyball courts to run a quick beginner's course. Her day was booked until around ten that night, since she had it on her calendar to help Damion take a few couples out on a sunset sail that evening. Damion was possibly the youngest staffer they had hired. Fresh from high school, the guy knew his stuff when it came to cleaning the pools and sailing.

She swapped out her yoga outfit for her swimsuit, jogged across the campus, and jumped into the water. She'd never done water aerobics before but had watched a few videos to ramp up.

As she was starting to work with the few women who had shown up, she glanced up to see Ryan sitting by the pool in her swimsuit. It was certainly a day for drop-ins.

However, there were rules as to what the staff could and couldn't do. Flirting with guests was strictly not allowed. At this point, Ryan was practically sitting on a guest's lap.

Since Zoey was busy teaching a lesson, she waited until the class was over to approach her. The woman was now lying in the sun alone.

"Ryan?" Zoey wrapped her robe around herself and pushed her wet hair over her shoulder.

Ryan glanced up as if she were being bothered. "Yes?"

The fact that the woman acted as if she didn't know who she was set Zoey's back teeth grinding. Taking a deep breath, Zoey sat on the seat next to her.

"I know you may not have read through all of the camp's rules, but fraternizing with guests isn't allowed."

Ryan sat up slowly and removed her sunglasses. "Excuse me?"

"I'm sure Mr. Longley was very flattered, but his wife may not be. I'd hate for there to be an incident, especially considering who his wife is." She got up. "I'll expect better judgment from you in the future."

"You bitch," Ryan hissed. "You know nothing about it."

"What I do know is that we implemented rules for our employees, and as one, you will either follow them or be asked to leave." She didn't give the woman a chance to respond; instead, she walked away from the pool area to get ready for the next part of her day.

She couldn't stop herself from vibrating with anger about Ryan. Who was the woman, really? After what she'd thrown at Dylan and Liam, Zoey had checked her references herself—all smaller restaurants in Destin. But they had all checked out.

Again, she was thinking she should fire her but wanted to run it by Ryan's direct supervisor, Brent, first. No use destroying restaurant service over one rude employee.

After a quick shower, she made her way to the kitchen to grab a sack lunch for her and Dylan and to have a chat with Brent.

"Hi, Isaac." She waved to the head chef as she stepped into the back room. The man, who was in his late forties and from Belize, was easily one of the best chefs she'd ever met. "Two lunch specials to go, if you have time."

"For you," he said with a wink, "anything."

"You're just saying that because I sign your paychecks," she joked.

"I'm saying that," he said, moving closer, "because you are a beautiful woman . . . who signs my paychecks." He laughed. "Who's the lucky guy?"

She glanced around. The kitchen was busy as usual. There hadn't been a time she'd walked into the place since they had hired Isaac that it hadn't been.

"Dylan," she finally answered in a low tone.

"Don't worry—your secrets are safe with me." He patted her hand. "Two lunch specials coming up." He disappeared just as Brent walked in from the front.

"Zoey, I didn't know you were back." His smile fell. "I'm so sorry about your father."

"Thanks." Brent was tall, dark haired, handsome as the devil, and totally in love with his husband of almost a full year. "How's Kevin?"

"He's good." Brent's smile returned. "He's taking our dogs out to the beach today. That man would make a great father."

"Not you?" she asked, leaning on the stool.

"Oh"—he waved her away as he worked on gathering his next order—"sure, I suppose, but some people just have it . . . you know?"

She nodded, thinking of her mother. She may not have been the best mother, but Zoey was pretty sure that any of her downfalls had been a direct result of her father. Which shifted her thinking toward Ryan and other people's downfalls.

"Brent, you hired all of your waitstaff yourself, correct?" she asked.

"Each one." He frowned quickly. "Is there a problem with one?"

"Nnn—no." She hesitated.

He stopped preparing the plate he had been wiping down. "What?" he asked with his hands on his hips.

"It's just . . . what do you know about Ryan, personally? I know her references checked out, and as far as I can tell, she's a good employee, but—"

"Ryan Kinsley?" Brent asked, and Zoey nodded. "Personally, not a lot. Work wise, yes, she's tidy, a strong worker, and, so far, has had no complaints against her."

Zoey sighed. "It's the personal side I have an issue with."

Brent made a face. "I'll keep a closer eye on her if you want."

"No, thanks. I'm sure my reminder today has done the job." She waved him off, not wanting to stir the pot too much. Although, if she knew Brent, he would be keeping an eye on Ryan anyway. "Go, serve your food."

She took the two lunches with her and made her way slowly toward the docks. She was almost ten minutes early but figured she could use a few moments to herself. She sat on a bench overlooking the water.

She was having a hard time opening fully to Dylan. She knew that in the past, she'd struggled with people like her father and Bridgette, and now Ryan had taken on that role. They were the sort who enjoyed and used the power they held over others. That was something that Zoey despised the most.

At first, knowing that Dylan had money had had her thinking that this was a possibility with him, but then she'd caught him helping an older man down the stairs near the pool, and she'd watched from afar how patient and kind he was with the guests.

Then, she'd watched him closely around the camp guests, since he'd helped her out with a few volleyball matches.

She'd enjoyed watching him interact with the guests and his enjoyment at being the referee for the "bubble soccer" match he'd organized a few days back. Seeing the guests run like hamsters in the massive transparent inflatable bubbles while trying to kick the soccer ball had been one of the best days of her life. Seeing Dylan laugh and joke as the guests bounced around the field had given her a deeper insight into the man.

"Harry, you're a cheat," Dylan had joked with one older man. The fact that he knew all the guests by name impressed her. "Is that how you convinced Pam to marry you?"

The older man had laughed and joked back with Dylan like they were old friends.

"No, it was my big . . . smile"—the man had winked—"that convinced her I was the man for her."

"More like your big wallet," someone else had joked. After almost a full week of watching Dylan, she had only seen a kind, caring man who loved to be outdoors.

"Everything all right there, missy?" an older black man asked her, breaking into her thoughts. He was walking by on the trail, smoking a thick, rich-smelling cigar.

"Yes, thank you." She smiled at him. He moved over and settled down next to her on the bench.

"Meeting someone?" he asked, looking at the lunches sitting beside her.

"Yes." She smiled. "How about you?"

"No, taking a stroll, just a moment to myself. After almost thirty years of marriage, I live for these times." He took another drag from his cigar. "I'm Chuck Vogel. You're one of the ladies that runs this camp, right?"

"Zoey," she offered up.

"Your sister's the one that showed us around the first day."

"Scarlett." She nodded. "How are you enjoying your stay?"

"Oh, just fine. My wife, Tina, loves this place," he added.

"How about you?" she asked, hearing the hint of longing in his voice.

"Oh, it's fine. I was just hoping to get out on the water for some fishing." He peered out toward the water.

Her eyebrows shot up. "I could easily arrange for someone to take you out."

"Would you? It's not on the approved list of activities."

"It's more of a suggested list than an approved one." She touched the man's hand.

"Chuck, are you stealing my woman?" Dylan's voice sounded from behind them.

Chuck laughed. "Hell, no, she's too bony for my liking," he said with a wink. "I'll let you two enjoy your lunch." He got up, grinding his cigar in his teeth.

"I'll have the front desk contact you to set up that fishing trip," she said.

"Sounds good—I know a few others that might want to tag along."

"I'll add it to the list of suggested activities."

Chuck laughed and waved. "You do that. Have a good day."

"Nice man." Dylan sat next to her. "What did you bring us for lunch? I'm starving."

"Didn't you eat breakfast?" she asked, then quickly realized she hadn't had time to eat anything more than a granola bar.

"I had an apple and a soda," he said as she handed him his bag. "Woohoo." He opened a small container of chicken parmesan. He pulled out a plastic fork and started in on his lunch. "What did Isaac make for you?" he asked, nudging her.

She opened her container to show him her favorite, tomato pasta salad. "Isaac is worth every penny we pay him." She took a bite and sighed.

"He packed me a brownie." Dylan pulled out the foil packet.

She looked into her bag and removed a large cookie.

"You should give him a raise," Dylan said through a full mouth.

"You're just saying that because you were hungry," she said.

"I'm saying that because he knows and remembers everyone's favorite foods."

"True," she agreed. "Scar was telling me that while we were gone, he made a special dinner for a guest who was celebrating her birthday—he actually called the woman's mother to get the recipe of her favorite meal, then made it for her."

"Pure genius." He waved with his fork. "It must have cost a lot to get him for the camp."

"It was all Hannah's doing," she admitted. "She pulled strings and got Isaac." She finished off her food, unwrapped the cookie, and took a bite.

Dylan had already finished his brownie.

"You must have had a decent chunk of money to start this place back up?" he said while looking out over the water. His tone was casual, but the question had something tensing in Zoey. Was he still trying to be sneaky and ask her about the camp's finances? They hadn't talked about it before, but several alarms went off in her mind as memories of him hinting at the cost of things surfaced.

She was about to ask him when she heard a noise and glanced up.

She had to blink a few times to make sure she wasn't hallucinating. There, a few feet away from them, a squirrel was hobbling across the grass, a full slice of ham-and-pineapple pizza in its mouth. The squirrel stopped for a brief moment, looked over at them, wagged its tail frantically, then continued on to disappear into the brush.

"Did you just . . ." Dylan motioned to the space.

"Squirrel. Pizza." She nodded.

"The animals around here are strange." He chuckled.

Then she laughed. "We'll call him Hamlet." They joked about other animal names, some of which included Crusty, Mozzarella, and her favorite, Slice. Her worries about him questioning her faded to the back of her mind as they finished their desserts.

Wiping the laughter tears from her eyes, she took a sip of her water and realized that he'd sobered.

"What?" she asked, instantly thinking he'd continue his line of questioning about the camp's finances. "What's on your mind?"

He turned to her. "Remember me telling you about my father?"

She nodded and relaxed a little.

"Well, he's off . . . on one of his . . . adventures. At least that's what we always called them. The times when he would disappear for months at a time."

"You're worried about him?" she asked, genuinely concerned, since she could see the worry in his eyes.

"Yeah, we all are; this time it's different."

"How long has he been gone?"

He sighed and put his water bottle aside. "Almost half a year."

"What?" She set the empty container and bottle on the bench next to her. "With no word from him?"

He shook his head. "The last we heard"—he turned toward her— "he was driving down here for a meeting."

"With whom?" she asked.

His eyes met hers. "Elle Saunders."

CHAPTER
FIFTEEN

Dylan waited and watched Zoey's brow furrow the moment his words sank in. Then she slowly stood up.

"Your father . . . had a meeting with Elle?" she asked. He stood up and followed her as she walked over to the edge of the water. "My Elle?"

"Yes. It was on his calendar." He stopped with a hand on the railing of the dock.

"Why?" She looked back at him and shook her head. "Why would he have a meeting with my Elle?"

He shrugged. "We were hoping to find out."

Suddenly, her eyes grew huge. "*That's* what you're doing here. Spying on Elle. You think she'll lead you to your father?"

He sighed and took her arm. He'd been debating telling her ever since their first kiss had rocked his world. He hated keeping secrets from someone whom he was slowly growing very fond of. Besides, he trusted Zoey and believed she really didn't know anything about his missing dad or the money.

"What do you think Elle did? Murdered him and fed him to the gators?" She jerked her arm away.

"No." He frowned. "We think our dad is in hiding somewhere, enjoying himself too much to be bothered with contacting his worried kids. Calm down." He gripped her shoulders until she turned and looked up at him. "If we thought he was in danger, there would be cops crawling all over this place."

She relaxed slightly. "Why would he have an appointment with Elle?"

"We assumed it was to invest in this place." He nodded around.

Zoey frowned at him. "We had a few silent partner requests. But Elle decided to turn them all down."

"Are you sure?" he asked.

She nodded, but he noticed it was a slow, unsure movement.

He pulled out his phone and flipped open a picture of his family. "Have you seen this man?"

The photo was of the four of them the last time they were together. The sun was setting on the Destin beach. They had their arms thrown around each other's shoulders.

"No, I haven't seen him." Her voice was low, and she looked out to the water. "I . . . have to go soon. I have a tennis lesson I have to teach." She walked over and tossed her trash into the waste bin.

"Zoey." He stopped her from leaving by taking her hand. "Can I see you tonight?"

Her eyes met his as she shook her head. "I have a sunset sail I'm helping out on. I need time to think about . . . things . . . I have to go." She turned and rushed down the pathway.

He stood there and watched her disappear toward the river instead of on the path that would take her to the tennis courts.

Tossing his trash away too, he started to make his way toward the zip line hut. He had a full schedule for the rest of the afternoon, and all he could think about was Zoey.

He was so preoccupied with running through what had just happened that he didn't see Ryan until it was too late.

"Dylan," she purred as she approached him. She was wearing the standard dining room work uniform, which consisted of a black button-up shirt, black slacks, and low black heels. "I was hoping I'd run into you. I heard you had yourself a little . . . trip"—her head tilted—"with Zoey."

"I took her to deal with her father's death." He started to move past her, but she grabbed his arm.

"Do you think I'm playing around?" Her voice sharpened, causing him to give her his full attention.

"No, Ryan, this isn't a game," he said.

"Good." A slow smile crept across her face, and suddenly he was reminded of the Grinch. She pressed her body next to his as she played with the collar of his shirt. "Since you're so keen on leaving, I thought we'd head out on that private jet of yours soon, maybe hit Paris." She sighed heavily, her breath falling over his face, and he thought he smelled a faint trace of vodka. "Then Milan; I've always wanted to go." She giggled as she scraped a finger along his chin, and he held in a cringe. "But for now, I think we should meet later so that we can discuss our . . . future." She brushed her lips across his chin, since he'd pulled his face farther away from hers.

He gripped her wrist and pulled it away so that she wouldn't leave a mark on him. "I can't. I've got to get back to work."

He wished he could stop stalling her and tell her where to go. After all, hadn't he pretty much come clean with Zoey? Zoey would certainly talk to Elle and the others. Which meant that Ryan didn't really have any leverage. But until he talked to his brothers again, he had to keep stalling.

"That's okay. I work until midnight too." She glanced down at his hand, holding her at bay. "How about after?"

He shook his head and said the first excuse that crossed his mind. "I'm helping out on a sunset sail. I don't know when I'll be back. Then I have an early morning . . ." He chose to leave it there, since the art of lying was to leave everything vague. Besides, he had thought about seeing if he could sneak in on the sail to be with Zoey: to have a chance to talk to her again and smooth things out.

She sighed and tried to move closer, but he still had ahold of her wrist and repelled her. When her lips formed a moue, he dropped her hand and stepped back.

"I have to go."

"Dylan"—she stopped him as his name echoed in the trees around them—"I won't be ignored." The last tapered off into a soft whisper as he continued to walk away from her.

Damn, he thought. Now his mind was full of how to deal with Ryan as well.

He tried to keep his mind focused as he flew through the trees on the zip line with the group of guests, but how Zoey had reacted to him over lunch kept resurfacing. Not to mention the threat of what Ryan might do.

On the last run of the day, he was surprised to see Kimberly in the group. He walked over to her and said, "I didn't know you were going to grace me with your presence today." He smiled at the older woman.

Kimberly beamed up at him. "I wasn't, until I had a . . . shall we call it *disturbing* . . . visit from my daughter around lunchtime." She touched his arm. "Can you fit me into the last run of the day?"

"For you, anything." He waved her into the group and started to go through all the standard safety procedures.

As the group set off, Kimberly held back until it was just the two of them in the first tower.

"I like you," she said, surprising him.

"Thanks—I like you too." His stomach had been roiling at the thought of what the woman was wanting to talk to him about.

"We all have our secrets." Her eyes assessed him as she tilted her head. He waited, holding his breath. "Zoey told me a little about yours. I want my daughters to be happy, both of them. You and your brothers . . . have a mission, and I understand that your father is important to you, and that's wonderful. But if you mess with my daughter . . ." She locked her harness carabiner into the line, then smiled over at him as she pushed off. "I'll mess with you."

He chuckled and called after her, "If I wasn't afraid of your family before, I am now."

He heard her laughter as she sailed through the air toward the next tower.

After that talk, the mood lightened between them. It was obvious that Kimberly seemed to be really enjoying zip-lining. He told her that the next time she came by, she could advance to the expert run.

She was happy at that news and told him that she'd schedule it for later that week. He was looking forward to seeing her again.

After Kimberly shed her harness with the rest of the group, and as he was cleaning up for the night, she stopped to chat with him again before heading out.

"You know, at my age—"

"What are you?" he broke in. "Thirty?"

"Don't interrupt." She patted his cheek. "I have a lot of regrets. I wouldn't change a thing in my past that would hinder me having my girls, but there's plenty I would change after. I stayed with a man who didn't love me. One who was spineless and selfish and wouldn't fight for me." Her lips turned down into a frown. "Something tells me you're not that kind of man."

"No, ma'am," he assured her.

"You know, it's a beautiful night for a sail." She looked toward the horizon, then turned and walked away without another word.

He must have sat there less than ten seconds before he tossed the rest of the harnesses into the shed and locked it. He'd been building up the courage to head to the docks before she'd said something to him. He knew that he'd have to arrive early to finish cleaning up the mess in the morning, but he didn't care. His only thought was of being with Zoey and getting a chance to talk to her.

He arrived just as the last of the guests were climbing aboard the largest of the two sailboats docked by the boathouse.

Zoey was helping a couple onto the boat and stilled when she noticed him walking toward her.

She was wearing a pair of white shorts with the teal camp shirt, and her dark hair hung in a long braid down her back. She looked like she belonged in an ad for sailing.

"Hi. Is there room for one more helper?" he asked one of the mates, avoiding Zoey's gaze.

"Sure." The man smiled and shook his hand, then stood back and motioned for him to release the line from the dock.

When he stepped onto the deck of the boat, Zoey narrowed her eyes at him and whispered, "What are you doing?"

"Taking an evening sail." He smiled. "It's a perfect night for it. Don't you think?"

She sighed and moved to help the staff as the boat made its way out of the slip.

"You can pour the wine and hand out the beer." Zoey motioned toward the cabin. "Everything you need is down there." She had turned to pull on a few ropes when Damion called out to her.

He'd never really gotten into sailing, and if he'd been honest with himself before he'd jumped, he would have questioned his sanity for working for his first sail.

Sure, he'd been in plenty of boats, but they had usually been speedboats, where he had been driven through the waters.

As the sailboat slowly made its way out of the small mouth of the river and into the bay, he tried pouring wine into glasses, spilling more than he'd like to admit. He handed out cold beer to some of the men, all while trying to keep his balance and not fall overboard. Only a very low railing of a single rope was keeping him on the sailboat, which had him watching his step and holding on to anything he could to keep from falling out. It wouldn't do his ego any good if he had to be rescued in front of Zoey.

He knew that he needed to fill in his brothers on what had been going on, but at the moment, his only thoughts were to smooth things out with Zoey. He hated seeing the worry in her eyes as she worked around the sailboat. All he wanted to do was soothe her and assure her that he hadn't thought she had anything to do with his father.

Most of the guests were sitting on the deck of the boat, watching the sunset or chatting with their loved ones. The fact that they all looked very relaxed had him questioning if he was the only one having a challenging time walking around. There were five couples in all, with Damion at the wheel, while Zoey rushed around the boat pulling on ropes and making the sail fill with air.

As they entered the larger water, the sky changed to more vibrant colors as the sun set. The sail caught a burst of air and started to move the craft across the bay more quickly.

He approached Damion and watched Zoey work.

"Pretty impressive, isn't she?" Damion asked, looking over the hull of the boat.

Dylan's gaze shifted to where Zoey stood, smiling at the horizon. "Yeah," he agreed.

Damion's chuckle had him turning toward the man. "I meant the boat."

"I'll be honest: I'm more of a flying man than a sailing man," Dylan replied as he held on.

Damion slapped him on the back. "We all have our faults." The fact that the man was standing like he was on a dock instead of a rocking boat made Dylan feel self-conscious.

"How does she know how to do all of that?" He nodded toward Zoey.

"She went to summer camp," Damion added and glanced behind them. "Every summer since she was ten."

"Right." He nodded. "I didn't know they taught kids how to sail, though."

"They did." He frowned down at her. "But since she and Elle were friends, Elle's grandfather taught them all." Damion shifted slightly, and the boat tilted a little. "At least, that's what she told me."

Dylan stood back and let the man steer the boat. He refilled more wine glasses and handed out more cold beers and waters, but he wished for only a moment with Zoey.

Just as the sun was finally disappearing, he noticed that she was standing alone at the front of the boat.

He made his way up there and leaned against the rope railing. "You're pretty impressive."

She glanced over at him. "Thanks. I'd rather be on the water than in the air." She glanced up toward the darkening sky with a smile.

"I guess this is one of those areas we'll have to disagree. I love flying; I haven't officially made up my mind about sailing yet, but . . ." With one hand he held on to the ropes as water sprayed them both.

Zoey's laughter as the water soaked them was pure heaven. He grinned and wrapped his free arm around her.

"Then you're doing it wrong." She moved closer to him. "Here." She reached up and raked her fingers through his hair, messed up from the wind and water, then steered him around until he was facing the direction they were going. "Look out, over the horizon. Feel the wind on your face, the smell of salt water." She rested her head against his chest and just watched the horizon. "Feel the boat move under you."

He did as she requested, and for the first time during the trip, he relaxed and enjoyed the rocking of the boat. Wrapping his arm around her waist, he held on to her and let everything go. All his worry about his father, the family business, everything. The only thing that consumed him now was the air, the water, and Zoey.

Turning toward her, he smiled down at her.

"I've changed my mind," he said and brushed a strand of her hair out of her eyes. "I'm sorry about earlier. I should have told you everything in Vegas."

Her smile fell. "I knew there was more to you being here. I shouldn't have freaked out. If it helps, we can all help you look for your father?"

He shook his head. "No, I would prefer my brothers don't know that I told you anything."

"Why?" She turned slightly toward him.

"They think . . ." He shrugged. "It wasn't in our plans to bring the enemy into our fold."

She laughed. "I'm not the enemy. Neither is Elle or anyone else at the camp."

"For now"—he took her hand—"until I tell my brothers, can you keep it between us, and your mother?"

She laughed. "I wondered if this was her doing, you being here." Damion was calling her back to work, but she stopped before she left him. "For now, I'll keep this to myself. But talk to your brothers. I don't keep secrets from my sisters for long," she warned him and went back to work as the sailboat was turned back toward the camp.

He made his way to the hull so he could grab a fresh bottle of chilled wine. He stepped into the small space, only to come up short when he noticed a naked couple having sex on the small table.

"Oh!" He turned around quickly, noticing that the couple didn't even stop or slow down with him standing there. "Sorry." He climbed the ladder, chuckling.

"I thought you went down there to get Mrs. Bowman more wine?" Zoey asked when he almost bumped into her.

"Um, I think I'll wait awhile . . ."

"What?" She frowned at him and began to go belowdecks.

"I wouldn't . . ."

But it was too late—Zoey gasped and then turned around and rushed back up. "My god, is there any place those two won't do it?" She rolled her eyes with a grin. "Yeah, give them a few minutes."

"It's probably the motion of the ocean." He wiggled his eyebrows. "Or there's some sort of reverse mile-high club." He tilted his head in thought. "Below–sea level club?"

Zoey burst out laughing. "Aqua sports."

He laughed with her and enjoyed the sight of her smiling in the dim light from the strand of lights hanging from the mast of the boat.

She disappeared again to help Damion, and he waited for the couple to finish below.

By the time the sailboat had moved into narrower water, the couple was back up top and holding on to one another like they'd just survived the sinking of the *Titanic*.

He spent a few minutes cleaning up the plastic wine glasses and beer cans, then helped Damion tie off the boat as Zoey ushered everyone off.

"Want to walk me back?" Zoey asked him as they made their way down the docks.

He held out his hand. "What I'd like to do is find a quiet, secluded spot where no one will walk in on us and make love to you all night." He drew her closer at the end of the dock and kissed her.

"Sorry," Damion broke in. "I'm just going to . . ." He moved around them and waved. "Night."

"That was fun," he said sarcastically and took her hand again. "Now I know why the Youngs like it so much. Know of any place we could be alone for a while?"

She fell silent for a while, then tugged on his hand until they were heading down a narrow pathway.

"What's this way?" He frowned when the path lights disappeared, and they were enveloped by full darkness.

"Follow me," she whispered as she moved a tree branch aside. "Trust me."

Less than five minutes later, they came to a clearing. There, on the edge of the water, sat a small cabin. A lot of construction material still littered the small place, and most of the siding wasn't finished yet. A large construction trash bin sat a few feet away from the front door, along with a locked container, most likely full of tools and more materials.

"It's one of the new cabins. It's not done yet, but they delivered the bed while we were in Vegas." She smiled up at him.

He leaned down and kissed her. "You're a genius."

Stopping on the front porch, she entered the code on the door's keypad, and the door slid open. Once inside, she turned on the lights, and he took a moment to appreciate the beauty of the place. And then, in a moment, she was pressing him against the door as her mouth covered his.

She tugged his clothes off him; then he stood frozen in place as he watched her shimmy out of her shorts and T-shirt. It was easily the sexiest thing he'd ever witnessed.

"May I say . . . you're amazing." His gaze tracked and appreciated every curve of her naked body.

"You're not so bad yourself. Tell me you have a condom in those shorts." She nodded to the shorts she'd tugged off him.

He bent over and pulled out the foil package. "We're stuck with only one." He frowned.

"We can make it last." She took his hand and walked across the room toward the bed.

CHAPTER
SIXTEEN

Zoey could feel herself burning hotter than ever before for Dylan. As his hands moved over her, inside her, she felt her skin radiate. Short of ripping off his clothes, her fingers had moved as quickly as possible until they were both naked.

His mouth caressed her, and she enjoyed the warmth that he caused. When he slid a finger into her, she cried out his name and held on to him. The width of his shoulders and the weight of him pressing her into the new mattress were glorious.

When she reached for him and wrapped her fingers around his length, it was his turn to groan. Her name burst from him when she pushed him lightly back onto the bed and leaned down to take him into her mouth.

"My god," he moaned as his fingers settled in her hair.

When he placed his hands under her arms and pulled her up, she smiled down at him.

"Had enough?" she joked.

"You are dangerous," he growled.

Reaching over, she took the condom from him, and when she finally glided it onto him, she watched his eyes go darker and knew that he was on the edge of his control. Smiling down at him, she slowly slid down as the last strands of her own control snapped.

From there it was all speed, all a blur of passion and pleasure. She'd never experienced anything like Dylan before, and that fact scared her. Was scaring her even more the longer she had time to think about it.

They built together, and as she gripped his hands in hers, they fell together. Their bodies stilling as one as enjoyment spread through and radiated between them. She fell onto his chest, her breathing labored as their body heat began to cool. Yet as she lay wrapped in his arms, so many questions surfaced.

She had been upset when he'd hinted that Elle had had anything to do with his father's disappearance. She'd rushed to her mother's cabin after Dylan had told her that his father had set up a meeting with Elle.

One of the first rules of the Wildflowers was that they didn't keep secrets. So why hadn't Elle told them about a meeting with Dylan's father?

Zoey had told Elle about the brothers' use of a fake name the night of the first talent show. They'd had plenty of times to talk about it since then. What was Elle hiding from them? Had she really had a meeting with their father? What about? She'd been so worried about her friend knowing something more that she hadn't realized how it had looked to Dylan.

Ever since Vegas, she'd believed that he was being truthful to her, or at least, she felt that when she asked him something, he responded with truth. Whether he'd offered everything he knew was a different matter, but for now, she trusted him.

Still, for almost a full hour, her mother had comforted her about her doubts.

"Mom, I just don't know if it's wise to get into a relationship with someone who lied right out of the gate."

She held in a yawn. "I had a condo in Jacksonville, by my mother's old place."

"So the three of you packed up everything and moved here for this?" he asked.

"You're either all in . . ." She yawned loudly this time. "Or you're out . . ."

His hand started to rub her shoulder, and she felt herself drifting off, listening to his heartbeat, with his warmth surrounding them.

She woke in the middle of the night, surrounded by darkness, unable to focus on what had startled her awake.

"I think it's a bear," Dylan whispered in her ear.

That sent her heart jumping. "In the cabin?"

He chuckled. "No, just outside." He nodded to the large windows.

She'd been so consumed with desire for him that she hadn't realized that the window coverings hadn't been installed yet. What they had done earlier would have been on clear display to anyone who happened to pass by the cabin.

Her face heated, and she covered herself with the sheets a little more.

"Easy," Dylan said. "I don't think he wants in. It sounds like he's going through the trash outside, though." Dylan shifted, and suddenly she was alone in the bed.

"Dylan!" she gasped.

"Shh," he said from the darkness. "I'm just looking out the window."

She waited, now sitting straight up in the bed with the sheets around her shoulders as she counted heartbeats until he returned to her side.

"Well?" she said after a moment.

"I can't see anything." She felt the bed dip and reached for him.

"It's okay," he chuckled. "I doubt bears know how to open doors."

"Haven't you seen the videos where they get stuck in people's cars? How did they get in the cars? They opened doors." She glanced toward the front door. Suddenly, her thoughts zoomed across the room, and her eyes froze on the closed front door. "I didn't lock the door." It came out as a whisper.

He sighed and disappeared once more; this time she counted his footsteps, and when he returned to the bed, she relaxed.

"Okay. The door is locked. Feel better?" He enveloped her again.

"Yes." She relaxed as his hands moved over her.

"We still have a few hours before sunup," he said, brushing his lips across her bare shoulder.

"Mmm." She arched and gave him more room to roam. "You only had one condom."

"Like you said, there are plenty of other things we can do." His hands moved lower, and she forgot all about the bear outside the cabin.

She'd never enjoyed sexual play as much as she did in the darkness of the cabin. His hands moved slowly over every part of her, as she returned the favor.

When he started exploring her with his mouth, for a split second, she wondered how she could hold on to that moment for the rest of her life.

They dressed as the sky outside the cabin started glowing orange with the sunrise.

"Lunch today?" he asked as they walked out of the cabin.

"I can't . . ." She stopped and gasped at the chaos around them. It had been almost two hours since they had heard the noises outside, yet still, the first thing through her mind as she stepped outside had been to look for a bear. But this level of destruction was . . . something.

In all her years attending camp, she'd never stumbled across any dangerous wildlife, though she knew there were more than just bears out there.

"Did the bear do all that?" she asked, staying on the top stair of the deck.

"I'll go check it out," Dylan said, turning to her. "Stay put."

She watched him approach the spot where all the construction material had been stored. A small trailer held the tools for Aiden and his men. The door rested open, and tools were strewn all over the ground, as if someone had thrown them around.

A large construction dumpster sat next to it, full of building materials, only most of them now littered the ground. The place was a complete mess.

Dylan approached the dumpster with caution; when he turned the corner and disappeared from her view, she instantly worried for him.

When he came running back toward her, yelling, "Get in the cabin," she moved quickly. Her fingers fumbled on the lock.

When she glanced over her shoulder, she saw a black mass behind Dylan gaining speed and screamed as she fumbled again with the door handle.

He was beside her before she could get the door opened and shoved her inside. They shut themselves in and quickly bolted the door as he leaned against it, breathing hard.

"It was there," he said between deep breaths, "near the dumpster." He hung his head down with his hands on his knees to slow his pulse.

"What are we going to do?" she asked, glancing around the cabin windows, worried that the massive bear would bust through one of them at any moment. "Do you have your phone?"

He straightened up to pat his pockets, then groaned.

"I was kind of in a hurry to close up shop yesterday—I think it's sitting on the countertop at the zip line hut." He leaned against the door. "Does that thing work?" He nodded to the telephone that each cabin had to contact the main building.

She rushed over and picked it up. "No, not yet." She set it back down and chanced a glance out the window. "The bear is lying down."

Dylan joined her at the window and looked out.

"What's it doing?" he asked. "It looks like it's protecting the dumpster."

She turned to him. "You don't suppose . . ." She tilted her head. "Did you ever see the video of the three bear cubs that got stuck in the dumpster?"

He groaned. "Shit." He ran his hands through his hair, tugging on it. "That makes sense. She's pissed she can't get to her kid, or kids."

"Does this mean we're stuck here?" She sat down at the table.

Dylan moved to a different window. "I think I could sneak out the back window. Then run and get help?"

"No." She shook her head. "It's too dangerous."

"What do you suggest, then?" he asked.

She thought about it. "Aiden and his crew are bound to come around."

"And what?" he asked. "Be scared away, or worse, surprised by an angry mama bear?"

She hadn't thought of that possibility and stood up to look at the bathroom window near the back of the cabin that he was talking about. "You can't fit through that. Your shoulders are too wide"—she eyed the window—"but I can."

"No." This time he shook his head. "No way." He frowned at the small shoulder-height window.

"Dylan, like you said, it's probably our only choice," she said. "Besides, I'm pretty sure I can run faster than you."

His eyebrows shot up. "Later, we'll test that theory out, but not now." He glanced toward the front. "If she's still there." She could tell he was battling whether to let her go. "Do you think you can head straight through the woods toward the back and get to the trail from there?"

"I know this place better than you do," she said as they looked out the front window. The large bear was still lying in the trash, its eyes glued to the dumpster.

"Go," he said as they rushed toward the back. "I don't know who can help, but go fast and be quiet until you hit the pathway."

She was thankful she'd worn sneakers for the sail last night.

It took her a moment to wiggle her way out of the window. Dylan hoisted her up, and she had to fall toward the ground outside, but the moment her feet hit the ground, she took off, trying to be as quiet as she could.

Anytime she heard a sound, she glanced behind her, afraid to see a black figure crashing through the trees and brush after her. Finally, when she hit the main pathway, she relaxed slightly and made a quick decision to turn toward the nearest building.

The horse barn stood less than a mile from the cabin, and when she rushed in, she ran straight to Carter, the vet from town who occasionally donated his time to help them out. He slowed her motion by gripping her shoulders, and he started to laugh at her until he saw the look in her eyes.

"Bear," she managed to get out in pants.

Carter's entire demeanor changed. "Where?" He dropped his hands and moved into his office.

"Cabin, the new one. Dylan's locked inside," she said between breaths as Carter pulled a gun from a cabinet.

"No, don't shoot it—it's just trying to get to its cub that's stuck in the dumpster." She grabbed his arm, feeling the scrapes from branches she'd gotten during her run.

"It's a tranq gun," he said. "It will do for a bear until the wildlife service can come and relocate it. We can't have one roaming the grounds while you have guests. Call up to the main house and have them put out an alert for everyone to stay inside until it's handled. Tell Jules to call FWC. She has the number for emergencies."

She blinked and shook her head. "Who . . ." She was a little winded from her run, and her mind hadn't cleared yet, as possibilities of the bear breaking into the cabin still held sway.

"Florida Wildlife Conservation. Elle and I prepared for things like this. Remember: vets work with all animals, including bears," he teased. "Now move."

She did as he'd instructed and told Julie to send out an alert and call the wildlife service.

"I'm going with you," she said and followed him out.

"Okay, but you're staying in the truck." He motioned for her to get in.

They drove the truck down the path that Aiden and the supply trucks had cut to get to the new cabin. When they approached it, the bear stood up and started pacing the ground in front of the bin as if it would pounce on anyone who approached.

"Yeah, looks like Mama's in protection mode." He sighed. "Stay put. I'll get only one good shot at this."

She held back as the man slowly climbed out of the truck and took a few steps closer to the bear with the gun aimed. She heard a small pop, and Carter moved back to the protection of the truck door.

The animal went down in what seemed like an hour of terror, but in fact, it had only gotten a few steps toward them before it hit the ground. She held her breath, unsure if it was faking or not. *Do animals fake it?* she asked herself as Carter slowly approached the dumpster.

"There's two of them in here," he sighed. "I'm going to keep them in here until FWC gets here. Nice morning," Carter called out to Dylan and waved for him to come out of the house.

"Yeah"—he smiled—"it is now." Dylan gave the slumbering bear a wide berth and walked over to open the truck door.

"Are you okay?" He pulled her halfway out of the truck for a hug.

"Yes." She touched his face.

"You're bleeding." He frowned down at her legs and arms.

"The bushes were thick." Just then, another truck pulled up behind them, and Aiden and Elle cautiously peered out the windows.

"She's down," Carter yelled. "Should be out long enough for the FWC to get here."

"Are you two all right?" Elle climbed out and rushed over to hug Zoey. "Julie said you outran a bear?"

"I didn't—I just snuck past her. Dylan was the one she chased." The air in her lungs froze up for a moment at the memory.

"It's a good thing you two walked by this morning," Aiden said, looking down at the bear from a few feet away. "I'd hate to think of what would have happened if a guest had stumbled upon this."

Zoey avoided Elle's gaze and nodded. "It's a good thing the place had a door and windows," she said. "Otherwise Mama here would have joined us in the cabin."

"Mama?" Aiden asked.

"Her two cubs are stuck in the dumpster," Carter answered. "They look okay, but we'll want to check them out to make sure. Which is probably why she made such a big mess last night."

"Damn it." Aiden walked around the sleeping mother bear and glanced into the dumpster. "I told my men not to throw food trash in here. The smell of leftovers probably drew the bears in the first place." He glanced over to Elle. "I'll make sure this doesn't happen again."

"Thanks." She smiled at him.

Just then another golf cart skidded to a halt in the dirt, and Owen and Liam leaped out.

"You okay?" they asked Dylan. Zoey could see the worry in both brothers' eyes.

"Yeah." Dylan shifted and looked uncomfortable with the worry they radiated toward him.

Elle broke the silence. "If it's okay, I'll take these two back up to the main building in your truck."

"We can . . ." Liam started but stopped when Elle gave him a look. Zoey made a mental note to ask her friend what that was all about.

"Go ahead. I'll stick around here with Carter until they come and take the family away." Aiden turned to Carter. "You do have more tranquilizers if we need them, right?"

Carter chuckled. "Yes, but she should be out for more than an hour."

"Thanks," Zoey said to Carter.

"Anytime. Make sure you have those cuts looked at," he replied.

They drove back to the main building in silence, with Dylan's brothers following behind them. When Elle parked the truck, Dylan helped her out. Zoey had been so numb with fear and worry that the pain of the cuts hadn't hit her yet. Now, however, since her blood had cooled, she was feeling every scratch.

"I'll help you into the clinic." Elle held on to Zoey's arm.

"I can . . ." Dylan started, but when Elle raised her eyebrows at him, he backed off, much like his brother had earlier. "Let me know how it goes."

"Thanks." Zoey squeezed his arm.

"So," Elle said when they were a few feet away from the three brothers, who stood in the parking lot, no doubt getting the full story from Dylan. "Sounds like you two were very lucky you were there this morning."

"Shut up." She nudged her friend but hissed as the motion brushed a deep scratch.

"Come on. Let's go get you cleaned up." Elle hugged her. "I'm thankful you're okay."

"Me too," she added as they stepped in the front doors. A burst of cheers met her. More than a dozen employees and guests had gathered in the main entryway—locked in, since they were still on lockdown mode.

Her mother rushed forward with a hug. "Hannah wouldn't let us leave. Are you okay?"

"Yes, I'm fine."

"We wouldn't let anyone leave until we knew it was safe," Hannah added, giving Zoey a hug too.

"What's all this?" Zoey asked, glancing around the crowded room.

"I told them you wrestled a bear," Scarlett said as she moved up for her own hug.

"You did . . . what?" Zoey shook her head.

"Stop it." Hannah elbowed Scar. "They heard what you did—running through the forest to get help. That's all. It was very brave of you."

"No," Scar corrected her. "It was stupid of her." The fact that her sister was smiling at her told her that she was proud.

"How about I take a look at those cuts?" Dr. Val asked as she cut through the crowd. "Some of them look pretty bad."

"Yes, please," Zoey added, letting Elle and Dr. Val lead her down the hallway toward the medical offices near the end of the hall.

Zoey sat on the table and let the doctor clean each cut and place small bandages over some of the bigger ones.

When Zoey stepped back out of the office, she found all four of her friends and her mother waiting for her.

"I'm okay—no stitches." She showed them her legs. Then she was engulfed as they all hugged her at the same time.

CHAPTER
SEVENTEEN

It took a few days before talk of the great bear escape died down. Stories of Dylan's heroics had been exaggerated, as had Zoey's great trek through the woods. However, after seeing the bandages on her legs, Dylan quickly realized she hadn't been given enough credit.

All he'd done was hide out in a plush cabin until she'd brought the cavalry.

Still, his brothers had given him shit about it until he was sick of hearing the same tired bear jokes from them.

On the upside, his schedule was full thanks to all the guests wanting to hear the story firsthand. His days flew by quickly, and his nights seemed to drag, since all he could do was stare up at the ceiling listening to his brothers snore and wishing he were lying beside Zoey.

He had scheduled his next days off so he could be with Zoey. They planned to drive into Destin to spend their two free nights at his place.

As new short-term guests came and went, the long-term guests grew more comfortable with the camp and employees.

There were a few rumblings from the cleaning crew about more parties in cabins, but the gossip never reached any of the ears of the "top five"—or so they were being called.

Dylan was even becoming familiar by sight with most of the guests and employees he hadn't met before. He knew which guests caused problems and which ones were in the swingers' group. It wasn't hard to tell them apart. Every time he walked by the pool, the swingers were always there, in a large group, hanging out together. Most of them didn't utilize the zip lines or any of the other fun activities. For the most part, the pool/bar was their main hangout area.

He'd even met the famous Barbara Collins. He'd seen and loved watching most of her movies and had taken a picture with her and her husband, Jamie, as they posed at the top of one of the zip line towers. They had been with another couple and acted as if they were best friends.

It had shocked him a little to see how tightly Barbara, or Barb, as she liked to be called, hung on the other man more than she hung on her own husband. He thought about his relationship with Zoey and wondered how he would feel if he caught her flirting as much as Barb had with a man who wasn't him.

Jealousy wasn't something he normally felt; even though he'd caught Amelia in bed with those other people, he'd never been the jealous type. Every one of his other long-term relationships had all ended on what he believed had been mutual terms. Still, being cheated on had stung.

He doubted from Zoey's experience with her father and mother that she was a cheater. After all, she'd seen the pain cheating caused firsthand.

His father had never really settled down after losing his wife when Liam was born. So he could technically never claim to have cheated on any one person. His father had been with a long string of women, and for the most part, Dylan believed that all the women knew about one another.

Owen had once compared their father to Hugh Hefner. The comparison was pretty accurate. Of course, thinking about his father set him worrying even more, since there hadn't been a day that had gone by in the past six months that the three of them hadn't tried to reach him. But his father's cell phone instantly went to voice mail and then had been disconnected, which had them worrying even more.

Their father's longtime secretary hadn't heard from him either. He knew that Owen was being pressured by the board of directors to get any information they could. The company had been counting on the large investment their father normally made at the end of the year, which was quickly approaching.

The brothers had less than five months to find their father and come up with the lost money, or the board was going to vote their father out completely. Not to mention having to find outside funding to keep the current projects on time and on budget.

Halfway through his workweek, after the last of his daily runs, he was making his way up to the dining hall to have dinner with Zoey when he collided with a very drunk Ryan. The woman practically fell at his feet. If he hadn't reached out and steadied her, she would have landed on the pathway.

"Oh"—when she noticed it was him, her smile grew—"my knight in shining sexy." She slurred her words, and he almost sighed with annoyance.

Since his last run-in with her, he'd been lucky enough to avoid her again. He'd heard from his brothers that they hadn't been so lucky.

At one point, she had cornered Liam at the woodshop building he worked in and had actually ripped his shirt off. Liam had been pissed because Elle had found them and had lectured them about appropriateness in the workplace.

"Ryan." He tried to release his hold on her, but she wasn't stable on her feet yet.

"No." She pushed his shoulder as her other hand gripped his shirt and held him closer. It was almost as if she were fighting a battle within herself. Or trying to put on a show that he was somehow molesting her.

He dropped his hands instantly, just in case someone was watching them.

"I told you," she said, and a wave of alcohol fumes washed over him. He recoiled. "Ryan, let go."

"No," she shouted, "you let me go." She shoved him again with one hand but still held on to his shirt with the other.

He held his hands up in the air, fully away from her, yet she still tugged his shirt toward her, bumping their bodies against one another. He tried to take a giant step back, but she twisted and somehow managed to get her foot behind his, sending them both sprawling toward the ground.

He landed on his back, causing all his breath to whoosh out of his lungs as a groan of pain escaped him when a rather large rock jutted into his ribs.

Ryan's dark hair fell over his face as she giggled.

"Oops." Her hands roamed all over his body, and it wasn't until he pushed her off him that he realized she'd undone several of his shirt buttons. "Oooh." She smiled at the exposed skin. "Wow." Her hands reached up to touch, but he easily caught them and gripped her wrists in his hands to halt her motion.

"This is fun." Zoey's dry voice sounded from directly above him.

He held in a groan and glanced up to her. "Would you help me?"

Zoey's eyes scanned them, and suddenly the anger was replaced with irritation and annoyance.

He couldn't hold in a chuckle when Zoey walked over and yanked Ryan off his lap and stood the other woman on her own feet.

"Are you okay?" Zoey asked him as he stood and dusted himself off and began to rebutton his shirt.

"Just bruised my pride." He met her eyes.

Ryan was rambling on about something and acting offended as she waved her arms around.

"I didn't do anything," he told Zoey.

"Yeah, I get that. Sorry for doubting you," she mumbled as they turned toward Ryan, who hadn't even righted her blouse.

"When do you go on shift?" Zoey demanded.

"It's my day off." Ryan smiled brightly, then turned toward him, all but ignoring Zoey. "I want to have some fun. I've earned it." She started to move toward him again, but Zoey easily stepped between them, earning a frown from Ryan. "I wasn't talking to you. Move. You're in the way of what I want." Ryan teetered on her low heels. "I know things . . . things that they should pay for."

Zoey gripped her arm lightly. "You're fired. I'll walk you back to gather your things, then have—"

Ryan jerked her arm from Zoey. "You can't fire me. I don't work for you. I work for Isaac Andrew!" Ryan screamed.

"Who works for me. I suggest you head back to your room and start to pack your things. I'll have someone deliver you where you need to go, since you're too inebriated . . ."

Ryan's laughter stopped Zoey from finishing.

"Like I said, I know things. If you fire me"—Ryan leaned closer—"I'll expose everything. Things he doesn't want you or anyone else to know."

Dylan watched Zoey tense for a split second, then relax again. "Then we can sue. You signed a confidentiality agreement. Which includes guests and employees alike. If you spill, you're in breach of contract. Dylan, can you call—" She didn't make it any further, as Ryan jumped on Zoey's back, yanking her hair backward as they went sailing through the air. Zoey landed on her hands and knees in the dirt, while Ryan sat on her back, pulling at Zoey's hair.

Two seconds. It took him only two seconds to have Ryan off Zoey. He held the drunk woman up in the air as her arms and legs kicked out toward Zoey, who was still kneeling on the ground.

"Are you okay?" he asked, unsure what to do with the wildcat in his arms.

"Yes," Zoey ground out. "Get her out of here."

"Where?" Still holding the woman in midair, he briefly thought about dumping her in the nearest body of water to sober up. But fear of the woman not being able to swim had him rethinking that idea. After all, he didn't want to have to jump in and save her.

Zoey stood up and dusted off her pants and hands. He noticed a slight tear in her jeans and wondered if Ryan had irritated Zoey's cuts from her run through the forest.

"See if you can get her to go into the clinic until she sobers up. I don't want her on the streets in her condition. After that she needs to leave."

"I'm not fired," Ryan screamed over and over again. "I know things."

He half dragged, half carried her toward the building, while Zoey followed more slowly.

"I know who you are." Ryan dragged her feet in the dirt to slow them. "I'll tell them."

"They already know," he whispered and glanced back to make sure Zoey was doing okay.

"They don't know," Ryan insisted. "They don't know that you're millionaires, each of you, and that you're the heirs to a billion-dollar company!" The latter she shouted. He stilled and glanced back once more. Zoey's steps faltered, but she continued to follow them.

"They know."

"They don't know that you're here looking for your dad," Ryan spat out.

"We know, stupid," Zoey hissed as she passed them. "Give it a break."

Ryan stopped in the middle of the trail; the force of her body stopping almost tipped him over. "I bet she doesn't know you broke into her office?" Ryan crossed her arms over her chest, and he felt his entire body tense.

Zoey stopped walking and turned back toward them. "We caught it all on the surveillance videos." She turned back around and marched toward the main building.

Hearing this, he forgot all about Ryan and rushed after Zoey.

"Zoey," he called out, but she didn't stop until she was inside the back door of the main building. Then she turned on him.

"You forgot your charge." She pointed at Ryan, wobbling her way down the path toward the pool house. "Better go after her before she disturbs the guests." Zoey disappeared down the hallway.

As he chased after the drunk Ryan, he wondered if what Zoey had said was true. Did they already know about his breaking into their office? How long had she known? Before Vegas?

He found Ryan at the pool bar. She'd just ordered a drink, but when she saw him approaching, she reached across the bar and grabbed a full bottle of tequila. Then, she started drinking directly from the bottle as the clear liquid ran in a thin stream from the speed-pourer spout.

Britt, a bartender who was working behind the counter, tried to grab the bottle from Ryan but couldn't reach her across the bar top. When Dylan reached her side, Ryan swung the bottle out as if it were a tennis racquet. The almost full container caught him on the side of the temple with a loud thump that had his ears ringing. He saw stars for a split second; then he was being pushed into a chair as his brother's voice pierced through the loud buzzing that echoed in his head.

He groaned, holding his head in his hands. "Damn it. Did she just bean me with a tequila bottle?"

"Yeah." Owen sighed. "You're not cut, but there's a large knot." He handed Dylan a bag of ice. "Britt says to put this on it until Dr. Val can get here to check you out."

He blinked a few times. "Did I pass out?" He glanced around and realized everything had moved. People were no longer where they were when he'd been hit.

Ryan was being held down into a chair by Britt, who was sitting on the skinnier woman.

Dylan realized he was in a chair under an umbrella by the pool. Even though the sun was down, his eyes were having a hard time adjusting to the bright lights strung around the patio area. He shut his eyes to ease the throbbing in his head, but it didn't really help.

"No," Owen answered. "You didn't pass out—just kind of went dumb for a moment. But hey, what's new?"

He heard his brother chuckle.

"Shut up," he groaned. "Damn, she hit my temple." He touched the spot and felt the growing bump.

"What happened?" Owen asked. "Lovers' quarrel?"

"Shut the fuck up." He groaned again. "She was drunk, had a run-in with me, and then Zoey showed up to help. After she attacked Zoey, she fired Ryan and told me to see her to the doc's office. Then Ryan escaped and . . . boom, whacked me over the head." He wanted to stop talking. Actually, he wanted everyone to stop talking, for all noise to cease.

"Yeah, I saw that part."

Dylan realized that Owen had probably been working behind the bar as well. He and Liam had played bartender when needed. "Britt wants to call the police."

"What?" He sat up with a wince. "Why?"

"Assault," Owen said in a low tone.

"No." He started to shake his head, then stopped when things started spinning and his vision grayed. "I won't give her the attention she wants. I will not have her tied to our name and to the camp like that." He pitched his voice to his brother's low tone.

"Yeah"—Owen sighed—"I convinced her not to call. It's probably another one of her ploys to have her name in the papers."

"Another?" Dylan asked his brother.

"Later," he said. "Here comes the doc." For the next half hour, he was pampered and watched over closely by the doctor, while Ryan was held in another room until she could be removed from the grounds with an appropriate blood alcohol content.

Almost ten minutes after he'd settled down in the office to be watched over, Zoey rushed in.

"I heard what happened." She frowned down at him. "Don't you know you're supposed to drink tequila, not get beaned with it?"

He faked a laugh and then held his head and moaned. Then he reached out his hand for her to come closer to him. She glanced down at his hand, then moved closer and took it easily.

"I'm sorry. I should have told you about searching your office," he admitted.

"Like I said, we knew." She shrugged as she sat next to him on the examining table.

He shook his head. "I don't care. I should have told you what I was looking for . . . I should have told you everything after I kissed you that first time." He reached up and brushed his thumb down the worry line in between her eyes. "Worried?"

"About you?" She shook her head. "I knew you were too hard-headed. Not even a bottle of tequila could get through to you." She touched his face softly and turned serious for a moment. "But yes," she admitted. "You should have told me after Vegas. Let this be a lesson to you to not keep secrets from me." She bent down and placed a soft kiss on his bruised head.

He smiled and pulled her down into an embrace. "I only make mistakes once. I'm sorry."

The door opened, and he watched his brothers walk in. By the look on their faces, he knew he was in deep trouble. Still, he held on to Zoey in defiance. He no longer cared if they were on a mission. He knew in his heart that Zoey had had nothing to do with their father going off the rails and the disappearance of the money.

He'd deal with his brothers later. For now, holding her was making his head feel better. It might have had something to do with the fact that all his blood was leaving his brain and heading to his groin. Whatever the reason, being next to her made him feel unlike anything else he'd ever experienced. And he wasn't prepared to give that feeling up. Not even for his father.

CHAPTER
EIGHTEEN

Firing Ryan was the best thing Zoey had done all week long. She should have not worried about stepping on Brent's or Isaac's toes and gotten rid of the woman long ago. After all, both Hannah and Elle had complained about Ryan getting in their faces as well. What was the use of being boss if you couldn't fire someone like Ryan?

"She actually tried to blackmail Owen," Hannah said. The three of them were standing around one of the first campfires the following night. The weather had been too warm those first weeks they'd been open to have one, but when the evening temperatures had dipped below seventy, Hannah had arranged for their first official s'mores cookout.

By the overwhelming turnout, Zoey was calling it a huge success. Almost every guest, long term and short term, had huddled around the two firepits and enjoyed the gooey treats with containers of hot chocolate and Baileys Irish Cream.

She was sipping her second cup at this point and had downed at least three s'mores, possibly four. She'd lost count, since she'd skipped dinner that night.

"Blackmail?" Elle frowned. "Over what?" she asked as she took her burning marshmallow out of the flames and blew on it to put out the fire.

"He didn't tell me, exactly. I caught them arguing and asked what it was about. He was vague and . . ." Her friend's face turned pink; even in the firelight, Zoey could see the brighter shade. "He changed the subject." Hannah bit into her s'more.

"What did he do? Kiss you until you stopped asking questions?" Zoey joked.

When Hannah almost choked on the bit of graham cracker, Elle laughed. "He did!"

"Remember, they're looking for their father," Zoey whispered. They were sitting around the larger fire, after most people had gone back to their cabins for the night. Now, it was just a handful of employees and a few of the guests left over.

"Did you ask him later?" Zoey asked Hannah.

"Of course." Hannah sighed. "You know me, Mrs. Know It All." She finished off the s'more.

"And?" Elle asked.

"He told me it was personal." She frowned. "Every time I brought it up, he . . . distracted me. Have you seen the muscles on those men?"

"Sucker," Zoey said and giggled as Hannah stuck her tongue out at her.

"Do you think . . ." Elle started. "At one point I had thought that Liam and Ryan were an item."

Hannah turned toward her. "For a while, I thought that about her and Owen as well."

The two of them looked at Zoey.

"Nope. Dylan told me initially that she wasn't his type." She shrugged. The way her friends were eyeing her told her that they had more information than they were revealing. "What?" She set her stick down and drank the rest of her hot chocolate. "What is it you're not telling me?"

The pair looked at one another; then Elle turned toward her.

"Liam kissed me," Elle admitted.

"Owen kissed me too," Hannah chimed in.

"Oooo-kay," Zoey said. "So?"

"After you showed us the video of them sneaking around, well, we started spying on them."

"Well, yeah." Zoey frowned. "I know—we agreed on who was going to watch whom. I got Dylan. Best choice, by the way."

"We think . . ." Elle glanced over at Hannah. "The two of us . . . that it's their way to get us to stop following them. By putting the moves on us."

Hannah jumped in. "Either that or to get more information out of us."

"Do you know why? I mean, I get it—they're looking for their father—but why here?" Elle asked.

"They claim—"

Just then something caught her eye. "Seriously? Here?" She nodded to the couple just outside the fire's light.

Elle sighed. "The Youngs again?"

"Don't they ever give it a break?" Hannah whispered.

"What do we do?" Zoey said quietly. "I mean, she's bouncing up and down on his lap."

Elle giggled. "Say, *Excuse me, can you stop banging in public?*"

Hannah snorted and then covered her mouth. The sound caused both Elle and Zoey to turn toward her.

"What was that?" Elle laughed.

"What?" Hannah sighed.

"You just snort laughed," Zoey said. "You haven't done that since—"

"Ever," Elle finished.

"No." Zoey shook her head. "She did it once, when . . ." Her eyes narrowed as she remembered the one time Hannah's prim-exterior bubble had been burst. When they'd sat around the campfire their senior year and talked about how they had each lost their virginity. "You've had sex."

"What?" Elle gasped and turned to Hannah, the couple going at it a few feet away in the dark fading for all of them. "Is it true?"

"No." Hannah shook her head. "Not sex. Just . . . kissing."

"With Owen?" Zoey asked.

"Yeah. Whatever else they're looking for here, they're willing to go the distance." Her friend smiled.

"Hannah!" Elle gasped.

"Not . . . that distance," she added, her face turning pink again. "I mean, I don't think he'd sleep with me just to . . . you know. He's not a spy. I mean, if they do that—not that I know." Her friend was blushing profusely now, her normally perfect skin burning even with the glow of the fire.

Hannah turned toward her. "You've slept with Dylan. Do you think it had anything to do with why they've been sneaking around?"

"No," Zoey answered quickly. "Nothing to do with it." She knew with everything in her that it was the truth. "Ryan claimed that they're millionaires. The searches I've done didn't say anything specific about their net worth—the three brothers. I mean, sure, the family business is pretty significant, but . . . Dylan, Owen, and Liam millionaires?"

"Then"—Elle set down her mug—"why are they working here? It can't just be because they are looking for their father. How many places could a grown man hide around here? And who is their father, anyway?"

"Remember?" Zoey asked, then related what Dylan had told her about his father's meeting with Elle. "You should know. You were supposedly having a meeting with him."

She was sure her friends had done as much homework on the brothers as she had, but she didn't know if Elle had been a part of that research. Then again, she'd forgotten how busy Elle was around the camp. Whatever Zoey's work schedule had been, Elle's had been easily double that.

"I . . ." Her friend balked and then bit her bottom lip, like she always did when she was thinking; then her eyes grew large. "Costa." She sighed and rubbed her head. "Leo Costa. I never thought . . . I didn't put it together . . ." Elle slightly tugged on her hair. "Shit," she mumbled under her breath.

"Okay," Hannah said. "Care to let us in on the big secret?"

Elle turned to them. "Uncle Leo."

"He's your uncle?" Zoey asked.

"No." Elle shook her head. "Not really, just . . . it's what I've always called him. I never really thought about his last name. Besides, I'd only heard it once before."

"You know Dylan's father?" Zoey finally asked.

"Yes." Elle nodded. "I've known him all my life." She shocked them by standing up. "I . . . have to go. We'll talk later." She started to rush off.

"Nope!" Zoey said, her voice echoing across the grounds. "What's going on?"

Elle turned back around. "I don't know yet, but I'm going to get to the bottom of it. I'll let you know when I find out. I did get a call from Leo a few months ago. He wanted to meet with me, but, well, I was so busy, I told him if he wanted to talk to me, he'd have to come here."

"So did he?" Hannah asked.

Zoey thought about Dylan's father's calendar and held her breath.

"No," Elle answered. "Not that I know of. I didn't really think of it again. We were in the middle of painting all of the cabins. We were all stretched thin, remember?"

"So . . . where does this leave us?" Zoey asked, relaxing slightly knowing that she could pass on that bit of information to Dylan.

"I'm not sure," Elle said. "But I'm going to find out." She turned to go again. "I'll fill you in when I find out something," she called over her shoulder.

Hannah glanced over at her. "What the heck . . ."

"Don't ask me." Zoey shook her head. "I'm in the dark as much as you are."

They sat there listening to the fire crackle for a moment, then heard the couple finish up in the dark. "Let's go," Hannah whispered as Zoey cringed. "There isn't enough Baileys to make me forget that sound."

That night Zoey lay in her bed thinking about Dylan as she waited to fall asleep.

She did another Google search on him and his family, this time adding in the word *millionaire*. Ryan had been right; his family was more than rich. They were richer than Hannah's and Aubrey's families put together.

Zoey didn't have anything against rich people. Hell, before her parents' divorce, she'd been one of them. It was the reason they had attended the camp in the first place. Besides her and her sister, along with Elle and Aubrey, Hannah's family members were the only ones who still financially stood behind their daughter.

Not that Hannah talked about her parents much, since she'd claimed they had temporarily cut her off when she'd declined to marry the man they had lined up for her.

Still, with her trust fund, Hannah had enough money to do what she wanted, when she wanted. Zoey didn't hold that against her.

Over the next few days, guests came and went, and the staff was beginning to wonder when the Youngs would be moving on. Zoey knew that they were booked through the end of the month and made a point to check to confirm that they were too booked to allow them to extend their stay.

She knew that the first six months after opening day, they would find out if they could survive River Camp's first full-blown season—mentally and financially.

Hannah and Elle were working overtime, it seemed, to keep up with the activities lately. She had tried to talk to Elle about Dylan's father, but her friend kept avoiding her and told her that she would explain everything once she knew more. She knew her friend was being elusive about what she knew about Leo Costa. Still, since it appeared at the moment that she didn't know much, Zoey figured her only option was to be patient until Elle found out something more and shared it with them.

Zoey, Scarlett, and Aubrey rushed from one side of the campground to the next every day, making sure everything was in place and that the guests were entertained.

They added a few new activities to the schedules, including hot yoga, evening campfires, and daily fishing trips, all of which happened to be a huge success, especially since most of the women spent their days at the spa or lying around the pool.

Seeing how most couples acted around one another set her to wondering what it would be like to be married herself. She'd never thought of herself as the marrying type, having seen firsthand the destruction deceit could cause in a relationship. Still, now, as the thought slipped to the surface, Dylan had automatically filled the role of husband in her mind, which scared and excited her at the same time.

She had a full day of work before the two-day retreat that she was due to spend with Dylan at his place just outside of Destin.

Since Ryan had been escorted off the premises, things had been quiet. Brent had hired a new server named Lindsey. The woman was, in Zoey's opinion, a hot mess compared to all the other waitresses but a million times friendlier than Ryan. Which racked up more points than being tidy and organized. With Brent's help, Lindsey would learn quickly enough.

There hadn't been any more bear sightings, and the FWC had informed Carter that both mama and cubs had been successfully tagged and moved to the national park less than a hundred miles away.

Since she'd canceled lunch with Dylan to spend it with her mother, she was a little stunned to see Reed Cooper, the man who lived across from the campground, stepping off her mother's porch at the River Cabin.

"Hi," she called out, getting his attention.

His smile grew. "Hi." He walked over to her.

"Visiting?" she asked.

His eyes moved back to the cabin, and then he nodded. "Yes. Kimberly told me you were stopping by for lunch. I didn't want to interrupt your time together."

Her mother insisted that everyone call her by her first name, so the familiarity didn't shock her much. But the fact that her mother was telling the sexy man whose mansion flanked the camp what her plans for the day were did.

"Are you enjoying the camp's grounds?"

"Yes," he chuckled. "I'm getting spoiled being around here. There's so much to do. I'm going to hate being gone for the holidays."

"Oh?" she asked, her curiosity piqued.

"I'll be flying to England to visit my son and his family. I'm going to miss the warmth."

"How long will you be gone?"

"All of December." His eyes moved back to the cabin. "I'll get out of your way—enjoy your lunch." She watched the man disappear down the pathway.

If she were twenty years older, she would have chased him down herself. The sexy accent, the body, those silver eyes . . . She sighed when the image of Reed morphed and turned into Dylan.

Damn, she thought. She was in deep trouble. Sure, she'd enjoyed her time with Dylan, but the fact still weighed heavily on her that he was keeping so many things from her. It wasn't as if she expected someone whom she'd started a relationship with to tell her all his secrets. Still, the things that he was keeping from her had her questioning if she should keep her distance. Her mind kept playing back to all the trouble her parents had gone through. Would something like that happen to her if she trusted Dylan? If she gave him her heart?

Then, on the business side of things, at this point, they couldn't afford to lose the three brothers. They had each filled a role the camp needed, taking on multiple tasks, and were a valued part of making the crazy everyday life around the camp run smoother. She stepped onto the deck and knocked on the door quickly, then opened it when her mother called a greeting.

She was scrambling around the kitchen, putting together chicken sandwiches and a salad for them.

"Mom?" She sat down at the small bar area. "Why was Reed Cooper here?"

"Hmm." Her mother glanced up as she pulled the chicken from the oven. The look her mother had on her face was the same a child would have after being caught with her hand in the cookie jar.

"Why was Reed here?" She leaned over the countertop.

"Oh, he stopped by to give me those." She nodded at the bundle of flowers on the small table in front of the window.

"Why is he bringing you flowers?" Zoey moved over and leaned down to sniff them.

"I don't know," her mother said, setting down two plates on the table, then returning to the kitchen for the bowl of fresh salad she'd made. "We had a good time together the other day zip-lining. Then I ran into him on the Frisbee golf course . . ."

"You Frisbee golf?" she asked, sitting back down.

"I was trying to. I had Owen, Dylan's brother, show me the basics."

She had steered clear of the Frisbee golf course; that was more her sister's area of expertise. Sure, she liked walking the new course that ran through the campground but had never really gotten into it as a sport. To her, a sport meant you walked away either dirty or sweaty. Frisbee golf did neither.

"Why didn't you have Scar take you?" she asked.

"Oh." Her mother sat down across from her and waved the question off. "She was busy. Anyway, I bumped into Reed, and he walked me through the basics."

"Which, apparently, warranted flowers?" She motioned to the bouquet.

"I can get flowers." Her mother narrowed her eyes at her.

"Yes, you can." Zoey dished up some salad. "It's just . . . shocking, I guess."

"Why? That a man would find me attractive?"

"No." Zoey almost dropped her fork. "Mom, no, of course not. It's just . . . I didn't think—"

"No." Her mother's chin rose slightly. "Apparently you didn't think before you opened your mouth."

Zoey sighed. "I'm sorry."

Her mother smiled at her. "Let's not fight. I had a nice time with a man, and he brought me flowers. Nothing more." She tilted her head. "Now, tell me all about your man."

"If your love life is off limits, then so is mine," Zoey said.

"Nope, I'm the mother. You're supposed to do as I say, not as I do." She chuckled. "Now, spill. What are your plans for your days off?"

She told her mother that she didn't know much of what Dylan had planned, other than they were going to stay at his place just outside of Destin. She was excited about spending more time with him and hoped that spending secluded time would answer some of the questions she had. Then her thoughts turned to wondering what kind of place Dylan actually lived in.

"You seem hesitant about something," her mother finally said.

"Mom," she said, "he comes from money, like Dad did."

Her mother was silent for a while. "Not all men are created equal. Your father . . ." she started, then stopped. "Did I ever tell you how we met?"

"No." Zoey shook her head after thinking about it.

"Your grandmother used to take me down to the country club on Saturdays." She set her fork down and pushed her half-eaten plate aside. "She would force me to dress up in these frilly dresses that I hated, and she would roll my hair in tight ringlets." Her mother touched her short-cropped silver hair. "I hated having my hair pulled. I still do, which is why I keep it short. Anyway, she would almost parade me in front of the young boys at the club, as if I were a piece of meat."

"I didn't know that." Zoey frowned at the thought.

"Anyway, I went along with it because, well, that's what kids do to please their parents. She always told me, 'Kimberly, you're going to marry a rich man. You'll get out of the dumps we live in and make something of your life.'" Her mother leaned back. "We had a nice home. My father had a respectable job and made enough money to live comfortably. But it was never good enough for my mother."

"Where does Dad come in?" she asked, pushing her empty plate aside.

"He was there, at the club. I used to sneak away from my mother and head out to the edge of the woods to smoke."

Zoey cringed. "You smoked?"

"Not cigarettes." Her mother winked. "Jean was there one day, leaning against a tree. So handsome, dressed in his tight jeans and a leather jacket. A true rebel. I fell for him instantly. Before I even knew him."

"I bet Gran loved that," she said sarcastically.

"She did, and the first time she caught us kissing under that same tree, she demanded he make an honest woman out of me."

"She didn't! For kissing?" Zoey was shocked.

"She did. She marched us right up to his father, who happened to be part owner in the club, and demanded that his son marry me." Her mother sighed, and her eyes grew sad. "We were married that fall."

"Did you love him?" Zoey asked.

"I didn't have time to know one way or the other. Things were forced on me." She reached across the table and took her hand. "Take your time; get to know your man before jumping in. But I'll caution you: when you do know it, don't take too long to tell him or to show how you feel."

"Mom?" She frowned. "Have you ever been in love?"

Instead of answering, she changed the subject and asked about how things were going with Zoey's father's lawyer.

The lawyer was keeping her up to date on liquidating all of her father's assets, and since her father had been squeezed out of the business, his stock options were being valued and sold off. Of course, the lawyer had suggested she hold on to them, but Zoey and Scarlett had agreed they were done with R&R Enterprises. Besides, the money that was flooding into the joint checking account was going to help settle their mother and them both further. They had even talked about building cabins of their own on the campground so that they could have a little more privacy.

When she'd moved into the apartment on the third floor of the main building, she'd never imagined she'd want to bring a man back up to her place. Now, however, she was looking forward to spending a few nights in Dylan's arms again.

She left her mother's place and walked toward her next appointment at the tennis courts to teach pickleball to a group of guests. As she went along, she thought about Dylan—the man had filled most of her thoughts since he'd shown up that first day with his brothers. She loved being with him and around him. No man had ever made her feel as much as she felt when she was with Dylan.

She knew that there was something deeper than just physical attraction happening between them. It had grown into something much bigger than she could have ever imagined. And the more she thought about it, the more scared she was.

CHAPTER
NINETEEN

There was plenty of time left before Dylan had to meet Zoey at the parking lot the first morning of their joint days off. He had already packed his overnight bag, which sat by the door. Owen was filling him in on the latest news from Joel on how things were shaping up at Paradise Investments.

"So, Joel says that the board meets again at the end of the month to decide if they'll squeeze Dad out." Owen sat on the edge of his bed, his hair messy, as if he'd had a sleepless night.

"If they vote him out, what does that mean for us?" Liam asked as he pulled on a work shirt.

"It means all we have left in our family business is the shares we each hold." Owen tossed his phone down on the bed. "Without Dad, we lose our voice on how the business is run."

Liam paced the small room. "Where the hell did he go?"

"Has his assistant found anything out?" Dylan asked. "Plane tickets? Hotel bills? Anything? She must have found something."

"No, but since Dad pulled out all the cash from the bank, he could be anywhere, paying with cash," Owen answered.

"So, the only thing we do know is that he pulled out the cash, had a meeting scheduled with Elle, but didn't show up?" Dylan could tell Owen was getting frustrated as he stood up. "We'll keep on it. I think Hannah knows something else that she's not talking about. She's been acting strange in the past few days. What about Elle?" He turned to Liam. "Have you gotten into her phone yet?"

"No." Liam shook his head. "It's hard to cross that line. Sneaking around the camp looking for Dad is one thing; breaking into someone's private phone is a different story."

Owen was silent. "What about Zoey. Does she know anything else? Has she talked to Elle yet?"

"I haven't talked to her about it since the last time . . ." he admitted. How was he supposed to tell his brothers that he wasn't going to cross any more lines? That he planned on telling her everything? *Well, she pretty much knows most of it already,* he thought and avoided his brother's eyes by bending over and tying his shoe.

Owen broke in. "What the hell? This isn't a vacation—"

"I know." He held up his hands. "But at this point, I'm with Liam. There's a line I'm unwilling to cross. I really like Zoey, and I'm not going to do anything to jeopardize what we have. Besides, we have to ask ourselves—how important is holding on to Paradise Investments, anyway? How bad could it be? We all have enough in the bank account to retire on. If Dad wants to throw his money away, then I say let him. He's earned it. If he comes crawling back to us, we'll decide what to do then."

Owen pulled his hair, drawing his hands down around his face.

"Between the three of us, we hold about ten percent of the stock." He shook his head. "Ten percent of the business gets us one, maybe two, seats at the table."

"That should be enough," Dylan said, gaining his brother's attention.

"No, it's not. I should have involved myself more in the business when I could. Dad's been on me for years to take over," Owen said, and Dylan could tell his brother was kicking himself.

"Hey, at least you were away at school," Liam started. "We were just jet-setting around the world having fun." Suddenly, Dylan felt guilty for all the years he'd wasted instead of working harder to learn more about the family business.

"I'll ask her while we're away," he assured his brothers.

Owen walked over to him and slapped his back. "Try to have a good time." Then he nodded at his forehead. "How's the head?"

Reaching up, Dylan touched the slight bump that still throbbed every now and then.

"Better," he admitted. "If you find out anything, you know how to reach me." He picked up his bag and left.

Zoey was waiting by her car when he stepped outside. The wind had kicked up slightly, which had vacated the campground at that early hour.

"Hannah has a bunch of indoor activities scheduled for today." She smiled as he tossed his bag in the back seat with her own. "That should be fun," she said sarcastically.

"Some of the greatest Olympic sports are held inside."

"True—gymnastics, ice-skating." She ticked them off on her fingers. "If it leaves you sweaty, I'm up for it. But I just don't see any of our guests doing backflips."

He laughed. "And the Youngs?"

She cringed. "Don't even go there."

When he stopped chuckling, he glanced over at her. "Did you find out anything more from Elle about our father?"

The mood in the car changed instantly.

"No, she keeps putting me off. But I can tell," she added quickly, "that she's working on getting answers. When Elle puts her mind to something, she tends to stick to it until she has all the answers." She reached over and touched his arm. "She's working on it: you can trust that." His chin dipped slightly, and then he shifted.

"What do you want to do? We've got two whole days to ourselves."

She leaned back in the seat. "I'm going to sleep in tomorrow morning. Anything beyond that is a bonus."

He chuckled. "So, no early-morning sunrises on the beach? Or a sunset dinner?" He reached over to take her hand as they hit the main highway—the conversation with his brothers all but forgotten.

"Now, that I can go for," she agreed. "How far is it to your place?"

He glanced over at her. "About an hour. I thought we'd stop at that little place in town for some of those bagels again."

"Hooked, aren't you?"

"They must put something in them. Do you know, I've dreamed about having another one since that first time?"

She giggled. "I know what you mean—I swear, every summer we came back to camp, I'd gain at least five pounds."

"You should figure out how to get them to the guests. I bet your repeat-customer list would grow."

Once they arrived, they sat on the back patio, which looked out over Pelican Bay. Even though it was windy, they enjoyed the hot bagel sandwiches and coffee by huddling together out of the wind.

When they hit the road again, he asked her how things were progressing with her father's lawyer.

"Some of the money has been transferred over to a joint account that was opened for Scar and me." She glanced down at her phone. "Whenever I log in to the bank, the amount is scary. I've never had this much money before. Not that we won't utilize it. There are at least a dozen more cabins we want to build." She set her phone down just as it chimed.

He looked over at it. "Problems with the camp already? We've been gone less than half an hour."

"No, she wants me to ask you something, but it can wait." She set her phone down again.

"Why not now? We're stuck in traffic," he said, causing her to glance ahead, where she noticed all the brake lights ahead of them. "You know how it is: tourist season year round." She was silent for a while. "I'll start. Dylan . . ." The high-pitched sound was nothing like Zoey's, but still, she smiled. "Elle wants to know . . ." He gestured for her to finish. She laughed, taking the edge off the situation.

"Dylan, Elle wants to know if you've heard from your father."

His smile fell. "No. Did you find out if she ever met with him?" Zoey shook her head. "No, she didn't meet with him, or no, you didn't find out?"

"No, she didn't meet with him. She didn't even know he wanted to meet. He called her and asked, but after she told him she was busy with the camp . . . she forgot about it. He never contacted her again."

"Is there anything else you've found out?" She went quiet again. "Are you supposed to keep it from me?"

"No, I'm just trying to figure out how to tell you."

He felt his stomach roll. "Is it about Elle and my father's relationship?" Zoey nodded her head and closed her eyes. "They were having an affair, right?"

Zoey jerked her head toward him, then burst out laughing. She held her stomach while she bent over with hysterics. "Oh my god, that's the funniest thing I've heard all year."

"What's so funny?" He frowned over at her as the traffic started moving again.

"Elle sleeping with . . ." She wiped a tear from her eye. "First of all, I'm pretty sure Elle has only slept with one man before."

"What?" He glanced over at her. "No way."

Zoey nodded. "Yeah, we're all pretty sure she was the last to break that . . ." Zoey made a hand movement that had him cringing. "Sorry. I know men can be squeamish about that sort of thing. Besides, your father must be in his . . . what? Late forties?"

He thought about it and then nodded. "So? He's dated younger women ever since our mother died."

"*Younger*, younger?" Zoey asked.

"Candice, his last girlfriend of almost a year, was twenty-four." He sighed. "Actually, before she started dating Dad, I thought . . ." He stopped when he realized what he was about to admit.

"What? That she was hot for you?" Zoey asked and reached over for his hand. "I'm sorry."

He shrugged. "Dad found out a year later she was after the family money, and since he's the head of the family business . . ." He shrugged again. "You probably know how that feels: Bridgette was a lot younger than your father."

"Yeah." She looked out the window as he turned toward his place. "It's kind of creepy."

He nodded. "Owen had the hardest time with it. She was actually the same age as he was."

"Why do men do that?" she asked as he pulled into his complex. "I can see a few years' difference, but more than a dozen, and . . . what do they even have in common?"

He pulled the car into the parking garage next to his own, in his designated second parking spot, then turned toward her. "Well, we haven't talked music or movies yet." He reached over and ran a hand down her hair, enjoying the softness of it and the way she leaned into his touch. "Favorite band?" he asked.

"What if I said Def Leppard?" she asked.

"I'd ask you to marry me," he joked. "I'm an Ozzy fan myself."

She smiled. "I've been known to enjoy a good Black Sabbath song occasionally."

247

He took her hand up to his lips and kissed her knuckles.

She reached for the door handle and got out of the car. "Where are we?"

"My place, remember?" He pulled their bags out of the car.

"I mean, where? I didn't even pay attention as you drove." She glanced around.

"The Sanctuary in Santa Rosa." He took her hand and walked toward the elevators. "I have a condo here—a three-bedroom place that overlooks the gulf."

"How long have you lived here?" she asked.

"Two years," he admitted as the elevator moved upward. "We all jumped ship when Dad brought home Candice."

"I don't blame you." She followed him out of the elevator.

"Nice pools." As they walked toward his door, they could also see the white, sandy beaches of the gulf in the distance.

"I haven't really gotten to enjoy the pools much lately." They walked down the long walkway until they reached the end. "My place." He punched in his code and opened the door, then quickly reset his alarm inside. He set the bags down on the floor and motioned for her to look around.

"I would tell you to pick your room, but know this"—he stopped her from walking past him into the place—"whatever room you choose, I'll be joining you in bed." He leaned down and kissed her: something he'd been wanting to do since they had left that morning. She melted against him, wrapping her arms around his neck and holding on to him as the kiss turned deeper. Finally, she pulled away; her eyes had turned soft.

"If not, I'd come and look for you." She kissed him back, then stepped away. "I want to see the place."

He followed her into the condo. It was a standard setup: two bedrooms in front with two small bathrooms, a long curved hallway to the kitchen, and a living room; the master bedroom was off the back of the place with a killer view and a bathroom in the middle.

"They have two-story places, but I liked this one." He leaned against the kitchen bar. He had paid to have it professionally decorated after the whole Amelia incident. He'd had zero talent with choosing anything other than a large-screen television, which hung over the fireplace. But the designer he'd picked had done a great job. The place was cozy and actually looked like a man lived there.

"I like it." She wandered through the room. "Best view ever. What about my favorite indoor sport this time?" She nodded to his opened bedroom door.

He laughed as his hands moved down her sides and rested on her hips. "You read my mind."

He kissed her again as, this time, she nudged him backward toward the bedroom.

Just getting her naked again was like seeing her for the first time. Their clothes hit the floor, and he took a moment to run his eyes over her soft skin, followed by his fingertips, then his mouth as soft, low moans continued to escape her.

Her fingers dug into him, pulling, holding, taking what she wanted as he tried to give her everything while getting what he wanted. He had to admit: since the last night they had been together in the cabin, he'd dreamed about being with her again. He wanted to take his time, to enjoy it, but the way she was moving under him had his hands and his body rushing it.

He brushed his mouth over her breasts as he slipped into her. She arched for him, wrapping her legs around his hips, holding him hostage until he started to move, slowly. Her nails dug into his shoulders as her hips begged him to move inside her.

He tried to take his time, enjoy as much of her as he could, but when she circled her hips slightly, he couldn't stop himself from meeting her demands. When he felt her building, demanding more from him, he knew that when she fell, he wouldn't be far behind her.

When she gripped his shoulders and cried out his name, he realized he was lost. He lay there, listening to her heart settle as he tried to figure out what his next steps were. How did he go about telling someone he loved her?

This time as he lay there, holding her in his arms, he questioned everything.

Did he love her? Hell yes. The answer was almost immediate. He'd never told a woman those words before, had never felt it before. Nowhere near it, actually. He'd avoided real intimacy all his life.

She was unlike anyone he'd ever been with before. She was strong and independent and knew what she wanted out of life. She was kind and patient with others. Not to mention the way she treated her friends. The love he saw in her eyes when she talked to her mother was something he had been instantly jealous of.

"I can hear you thinking." Zoey chuckled after a moment.

He leaned up and kissed her again. "I'm thinking about putting on swim shorts and hitting the pool." He smiled. "Then coming up here, grabbing some lunch, and doing this again. Maybe a few more times. Then we'll take a nap before we find someplace to watch the sunset and have dinner."

"Sounds wonderful." She nudged him to move with a smile, then rolled off the bed herself and beelined to his bathroom.

"My god," she said from behind the shut door. "This is an amazing bathroom."

He chuckled and walked over to pull out his swim trunks. He walked to the front hallway and brought back her bag just as she opened the door. She was wrapped in a towel and smiled when she noticed him holding up her bag. She kissed him and grabbed the bag from him.

"I'll be just a minute," she said as she shut the door again.

He glanced around and decided to check his phone messages. He picked up his cell, which he'd heard buzz a few times while they'd been busy, and listened to the messages.

There were a few text reminders from Joel. One he assumed was a sales call, since the person had hung up. But the last call was from his father, which almost made him drop his phone.

He called Owen and played the message for him.

"Dylan, it's Dad. I know I left things tangled for you boys, but I just want you to know that I'm okay. Well, I'll see you soon. Bye." There was a pause. "I love you boys."

"What the hell?" Owen said over the phone.

"Yeah." Dylan sighed and ran his hands through his hair. "No *Hey, I'm alive* or where he was, just 'I left things in a mess.'"

"What's up with the 'I love you boys'?" Owen asked.

"You don't think he's sick, do you?" Dylan asked, running his hands through his hair.

"No, we checked with his doctor," Owen answered. "His last checkup was earlier this year, and he had a clean bill of health."

Dylan relaxed. "Then what the hell . . ." He heard a chair move and glanced over to see Zoey watching him. He'd totally forgotten that she was there. She was sitting at the kitchen bar, sipping a glass of water, waiting patiently for him.

"Ah, hey, I've got to go. We'll talk later." He hung up before his brother could respond. "Sorry."

"It's okay. I'm glad you've heard from your father." He realized she had probably been sitting there listening to them the entire time.

"Yeah. I'm never having teenagers," he joked, "if this is what it feels like."

"It's funny." She stood up and walked over to him. "We chose to open the camp back up to adults because we thought, 'Hey, adults are easier than chasing after a bunch of other people's kids, right?'" She waited, and he nodded. "But after seeing the aftermath of three orgies, running into the Youngs banging around every corner, and finding a bunch of used condoms and spent joints around the camp's grounds, I'm beginning to think kids would have been easier."

He chuckled and pulled her close. "What do you say we grab some beer and food and head down to the pool to relax?"

"I wouldn't say no to some beer and food, if you have it." She smiled up at him.

"I had the place stocked before we arrived. There should be plenty of food." He opened a cupboard, and indeed, there was enough food to last them a few days stacked neatly inside. They made and packed turkey sandwiches and drinks for the pool in a small cooler he had. Then they headed down to the pool, both with beach towels draped over their shoulders.

He enjoyed spending the next couple of hours by the pool—at one point, he believed she'd fallen asleep lying in the sun.

When they finally decided to head back up to the condo, she let him slowly peel the tiny bikini off her and pull her into the shower.

He could tell she melted a little bit inside as he made love to her under the warm spray. Enjoying the feeling of the relaxed motions, he took his time pleasing her until he felt her legs grow weak. He wondered if he could ever get tired of touching her, of being with her.

He carried her out of the shower and then took his time drying her skin and kissing her as she lay out on his bed. Then he pulled the comforter over them, and they grabbed an hour-long nap wrapped in each other's arms.

When he woke, it was to the smell of her hair and skin, which had him instantly hard. His hands, on their own accord, moved over her soft skin as his body grew even harder. Her body was pressed up against his; the softness almost undid him completely. There was no way he was going to be able to sleep without her next to him again. No way he wanted to go one more night without feeling her body when he woke up each day.

Now, all he had to do was persuade her to stay with him.

CHAPTER
TWENTY

Zoey woke slowly as strong hands moved over her body, exciting her. Her entire being vibrated as fingertips traced her nipples slowly, causing them to ache and peak. When a finger brushed her pussy, she moaned and slid her legs farther apart, wanting. When it dipped into her, her eyes fluttered open finally. Her eyes locked with Dylan's as he watched her before leaning down and brushing his lips against hers.

"More?" he asked, his deep voice causing her body to vibrate further. She nodded, burrowing her fingers into his hair so she could hold him to her. Kissing him even deeper as desire slammed into her.

His fingers moved inside her as she wrapped her leg around him and reached for him. She found him hard and enjoyed the way he jumped as she touched him. The sounds he made as she stroked him were music to her ears.

"More?" she asked with a smile.

"God, yes," he groaned out as he shifted, pulling her beside him.

"This was a great idea," she whispered as they continued to move together.

"Great idea," he agreed as he kissed down the column of her neck. When he took her nipple into his mouth, she arched and lost hold of him, gripping the sheets instead.

He trailed kisses down her ribs and over her belly; he took a moment to dip his tongue into her belly button before moving farther down. As he settled his mouth over her pussy, she cried out at the feeling of his tongue against her heated skin. Her legs fell open with his fingers resting on her thighs.

"My god, I could eat you out every day for the rest of my life," he said against her skin.

"Please . . ." She knew what she was begging for—release. "I need . . ."

She heard him chuckle; then his mouth returned to her, along with his fingers.

Lights burst behind her eyes, and she felt herself falling faster than she had ever gone before. She gripped the sheets; somewhere in the back of her mind, she wanted to deny what she was feeling, but by the time Dylan was sliding into her, tears were rolling down her cheeks, and she knew it was too late. She had fallen in love with him.

He stilled, looking down at her, then leaned in and gently kissed the tears away. "For me?" he asked.

She shook her head and reached up to wipe them away, feeling stupid. "I'm just . . . happy." She finished by grabbing his tight ass and forcing him to continue moving above her. "Don't stop." She smiled up at him as she bit the inside of her lips to hold in the words that she feared would burst out.

She would have thought that it was impossible for him to build her up again so fast, but she felt the growing need, and this time when she spiked, she felt him join her.

"I think we need another shower," he mumbled into her hair, causing her to chuckle.

"If we do, we may have to take separate ones; otherwise we'll just end up back here." She was running her hands over his shoulders. "God, I love these." She squeezed lightly as she tried to keep things from turning deeper.

He pushed up and rested on his elbows, hovering above her. Her eyes locked with his, and she couldn't help but smile.

"I'm an ass man," he blurted out, causing her to laugh. He smiled. "I knew the moment you turned around and climbed those stairs that I had to get my hands on this." He moved until his hands covered her butt. When he squeezed slightly, a low moan reverberated from his chest. "Yup, this is the finest butt I've had the privilege of holding on to."

She chuckled. "I've never dated an ass man before."

He stilled, then smiled. "Dated." He wiggled his eyebrows. "So it's official?"

She held her breath as she thought of it. Yeah, they were dating. Wasn't that what he thought this was? Maybe he thought it was just sex? She pushed him off of her.

"What did you think this was?" She got out of the bed and glanced at him over her shoulder, then smiled, trying to keep it light. "Just a booty call?"

He laughed as she walked into the bathroom, then jumped up and rushed after her.

They showered together, this time sticking to just cleaning up; then she took almost half an hour to pull on the sundress she'd brought along and to fix her hair in a long braid that lay over her shoulder. She kept her makeup to the basics, since she didn't want to keep Dylan waiting too long. Besides, she was starving for dinner—it had been hours since they'd had their lunch of sandwiches and beer.

She was a little surprised when, instead of them climbing into her old Honda, he opened the door to the beautiful Tesla Model 3 that was sitting next to her car. She'd admired it when they had pulled into the parking spot before.

She bit her lip and slid into the leather seats as he unplugged the car and then climbed into the driver's side.

"I've always wanted to ride in one of these," she admitted, looking at the computer screen in the middle of the dash. The car was sexy, just like him.

"It's my newest toy. I gave up a 2017 Shelby GT350R for this beauty." He glanced over at her. "I haven't looked back."

"Nice," she admitted. "I'm a bit of a car snob." She nodded to her beat-up Honda. "As you can tell."

He chuckled as he pulled out of the parking garage and drove through the gates. When he turned onto the main road and hit the pedal, she was plastered back into the seat and squealed as the g-forces held her back.

"Wow!" She smiled over at him. "I actually felt my stomach flip, like it does on roller coasters."

"Yeah." He eased off and turned down another road. "It's fast. It does zero to sixty in four point six seconds. But tonight, we won't be going far. Tomorrow I'll take you out on the highway with her."

"Her?" she asked.

"Every sexy vehicle is a she. Her name is Jett." He smiled. "She's got a lot of kick, so she deserves a kick-ass name."

She chuckled. "If your car's name is Jett, what's your jet's name? Roadster?"

He laughed as he pulled into a parking spot in front of the Red Bar. She'd been there more than a dozen times and always enjoyed the music and the food.

"No—that one my dad had already named Stella." He shook his head. "Stupid name."

She bit her lip but chuckled. She watched him rush around the car and open the door for her. It was a good thing because she didn't know how to open the door, since there were only three buttons, and she didn't want to push the wrong thing.

"It's this one." He pointed at the button by her thumb.

"Good to know. I really like your car," she added as they started walking into the restaurant. The place was crowded, and already there was a band playing on the small stage area in the front room.

They found seats in the back, near the bar, where the music wouldn't be too loud for them to talk.

"Have you been here before?" he asked.

"Yes, the eggplant parm is to die for."

"My favorite as well," he agreed, then reached across the table and took her hand. "It was nice of you to change my days off to match yours."

Her eyebrows rose. "I didn't . . ." Then she sighed. "Elle. I thought it was strange that they meshed up this week."

"Well, we owe Elle then." He held up his water glass, and she tapped hers against his.

"To Elle," she said.

"Speaking of which . . ." He set his glass down.

She sighed. "I suppose it was too much to ask to have a few days off from all this, but I understand, after hearing your father's message."

They took a moment to order drinks and food; then he waited for her to restart the conversation.

"Apparently, Elle has known your father all of her life." She felt it was best just to come out and say it.

"What?" He frowned across the table at her. A crease formed between his eyebrows.

"She calls him Uncle Leo. She didn't put it together—the three of you, connected to him—after we found out about your real name. Not until the other night, at the campfire. For most of her life, she just called him Uncle Leo. Not Leo Costa."

"Uncle?" He shook his head. "My father didn't have any family. Well, he had a sister that died when she was young, but . . . no one else.

And," he added, "my mother was an only child. So I don't know of any cousins we might have."

"No," she replied. "Elle made sure to tell me that there is no relation—just that she always called him that."

He was quiet for a while. "So"—he shook his head—"what does that mean?"

Zoey shrugged. "Apparently, your father was an old family friend of hers?"

"You sound unsure."

"I am. After telling us this, she excused herself and rushed away. She hasn't spoken of it since."

He leaned back in the booth. "Did you ask her?"

"Yes." She sighed. "She told me that she'd tell me everything when she found out more. I think that she's trying to find him herself."

"Do you think she knows where he is?" he asked.

"No, she's been too busy with the camp to know anything more than you would. I think she might have an idea, like you. Elle is very . . ." She thought about it. "Determined."

They were quiet, and she sat back to enjoy the music until their food came.

"Elle was raised by her grandfather, correct?" he asked after they had started eating.

"Yes." She nodded and set her fork down to take a drink of her wine. "Her mother died when Elle was ten. The summer before we met, she moved in with her grandfather at the camp."

"Being raised at the camp must have been . . . wild." He took another drink of his beer.

"She wasn't really raised there all of the time. Her grandfather had a house in Pelican Point. She owns it now. That's where she spent her time when they weren't at the camp for the summer. We each spend our days off from work there."

"What happened to her father?"

"Elle doesn't talk about him." She shook her head. "Neither does Aubrey. We all have our own secrets and respect them." She took another sip of the wine. "But we all know that he spent some time in prison when she was young. For what, we never could get out of Grandpa Joe. I don't even think Elle knows."

"Do you have secrets?" he asked, leaning closer.

She smiled at him. "I have you."

He chuckled. "I think everyone in the camp knows what's between us at this point."

"What sort of secrets do you still have?"

He shook his head. "No changing directions. Tell me something you haven't told any of your sisters."

She thought about it, running over things in her mind, then came up with one and leaned closer.

"The night before I injured myself, I broke into the Olympic grounds in the middle of the night and ran around the softball bases, bare-ass naked." His eyes grew huge as she shrugged and leaned back. "It was a dare."

He burst out laughing. "You did not."

She nodded, then motioned to him. "Now it's your turn."

He shook his head and held up his hands in defeat. "I can't top that." He fake-bowed to her. "The queen of the field. I would have paid a million to see that."

She laughed. "I'm thankful no one did. Well, except my team, who dared me. I only did it after I locked all of their cell phones in my locker. To make sure none of them slipped photos of me." She waved the waitress down for another glass.

"No evidence?" he asked, a sad tone in his voice.

"If there was, it would have surfaced by now, especially after that picture of me and Roger Holloway circulated."

"Right." He snapped his fingers. "That's where I've seen you before." He sat forward. "So, what was between you and Roger?"

"Nothing." She sighed heavily. "Only in my dreams."

He reached across the table and once again touched her hand. "Don't make me hunt the man down. I bet he'd kick my ass, no matter what sort of good shape I'm in."

"I bet you could beat him." She thought about it. "You're about the same build."

"Flattery." He finished off his food, then pushed the plate to the end of the table as the waitress refilled her wine and took their empty plates. "It's nice to know that you don't have any problems running around naked."

"Nudity isn't an issue—it's getting caught that's the problem."

"How many times have you been caught?" he asked.

She smiled. "Only once." His eyebrows shot up. "But that was Elle's fault."

"Oh?"

"Yeah. She screamed when a frog jumped into the pool next to her." She remembered that first night they had been at the camp. "We had decided to sneak to the pool and go for a midnight swim. Of course, we had all started out in our swimsuits, with towels wrapped around us like shields. Then, out of the blue, someone, I can't remember who, dared me to do a cannonball naked, which led to more dares." She chuckled. "In the end, we all ended up shedding our swimsuits. It was so liberating, so . . . freeing. To not care about our body images. Teenage girls are the worst." It was so nice, being able to open up to a man. It wasn't as if she'd never enjoyed talking to a date before, but with Dylan, things were different.

She kept forcing her deeper feelings to the back of her mind to keep the mood of the night light. She was trying to convince herself that it had been just the throes of passion. She successfully avoided thinking about the topic for the rest of the night. That was, until they decided to take a long walk on the beach outside of his condo.

She strolled with him down the long boardwalk toward the water and held his hand as they tossed off their shoes and made their way across the white sand. When they hit the warm waters of the Gulf of Mexico, they let it lap at their feet. She had to admit that she felt something she'd never felt before.

The fact was, what was between them meant something. She cared for him more than she'd cared for any other man before. Still, she struggled with knowing he was probably still hiding things from her.

"Is there anything else about your father's disappearance that you haven't told me?" she asked as they made their way back to the condo.

He stopped and pulled her into his arms. "No." But when she arched her eyebrows, he added, "There's a lot of money that's gone with him. Money that was reserved for the business."

She frowned. "How much money?"

"Lots," he sighed. "Each year, Dad invests in the business."

"Like an owner capital account?" They had all learned about the ins and outs of owning a business last year when they'd invested in the camp.

"Yes—for years Dad has been putting extra money into the family business. The board has come to expect that money, but this year, Dad took off with it instead."

She tilted her head as she thought about it. "It's still his money, to do what he wants with."

"But the board is threatening to remove him as acting CEO."

"He's CEO and he's been missing for how long, again?" she asked.

"Almost six months."

She stood back. "I'm surprised the board hasn't voted him off already."

"They've given us until the end of the year." He took her hand and finished walking up the boardwalk.

"To find him, or to force him to invest the money?" she asked as they moved into the light of the condo complex.

"Both." He ran his hands through his hair.

"What happens if he chooses not to invest his money?" she asked.

"Then, we're all left with scraps of our family's legacy and business," he answered as they entered the elevator.

"Property management, correct?" She remembered him telling her in Vegas but thought that it had to be more than just a simple property-investment company.

"Yes, property investments," he answered, stepping out of the elevator. "We own a chain of condos up and down the Gulf Coast."

"These condos?" she asked as he opened the door. She remembered now.

"No." He shook his head. "I didn't want to live in one that we owned."

She walked in, removed her sandals by the door, then followed him into the kitchen, where he pulled out a bottle of wine.

"How about we sit out on the deck and finish off this bottle?" He took two glasses down from the shelf, and she nodded.

"Tell me your magic grocery elves bought something chocolate, and I'm right there with you." She smiled.

He set the bottle down and opened the fridge, where a container of chocolate brownies sat. "Brownies okay?" he asked.

"Perfect," she said, looking at the man leaning over the opened fridge and realizing how fitting the word was for him. He was perfect. Too perfect. She knew that all good things tended not to last too long. Sooner or later, something came along and shook things up. She just hoped it wasn't going to happen during the next two days.

She didn't know how she was going to make it through the next two days and nights without blurting out her feelings for him. But she was willing to fight it as she savored her time with the most perfect man she'd ever enjoyed.

CHAPTER
TWENTY-ONE

Dylan glanced over at her as she drove her car back toward the camp and wondered how he'd go another week without her in his bed.

"There isn't any way I could convince you to move in with me and my brothers, is there?" He'd meant it as a joke, but instead of laughing, she glanced over at him.

"Joking." He held up his hands. "I'm just trying to keep sleeping with you."

Here she did chuckle. "Okay, so, at this stage, we're at the 'move in with one another' part of our relationship?" She glanced sideways at him.

"Sure." He shrugged. "I mean, the last two days were great, right? I mean, I found out in Vegas that you're just as tidy as I am."

"As you? Ha." She smiled. "No one is as anal as you."

"The last two days have been incredible."

"They were great," she agreed.

"Okay." He relaxed. "So, would you?"

"Would I what?" She glanced at him again.

"Move in with me?" He waited, almost holding his breath.

"With you and your brothers in the one room you share at the camp?" She frowned.

"God, no. I mean . . ." He hadn't thought about it. They were still at the camp and were most likely going to be until they found out everything about their father. Even if they did find their old man, he had no intentions of leaving the camp without Zoey, and he knew she wouldn't want to leave. "I mean, shit." He ran his hands through his hair. "How do we do this?"

"I have an idea," she said, getting his attention. "We, the five of us, talked about what happens if we . . . need a night alone. I'll see if I can work something out."

Reaching over, he put his hand on her leg. "I want more than just one night with you."

"I'll see if I can work it out," she said.

"I'm counting on you," he said as they pulled into the parking lot of the camp. She parked her car in her spot under the cover, and he got out and carried her bag into the main building.

He left her to go stash his bag in his room while she climbed the rest of the stairs to the third floor. His brothers were MIA, so he pulled out his phone to check the app for his schedule for the day. He had a run before lunch and one after. Most of the names on the list were new to him.

He changed into his cargo shorts and camp shirt, then made his way down the stairs, hoping to run into Zoey again soon.

Instead, as he walked down the path toward the zip line towers, he ran into Scarlett, who veered off the trail so that she could chat with him.

"So, you guys are back?" she asked. Scarlett leaned closer. "Don't make me regret being nice to you with that scheduling help." She turned on her heel and walked back down the pathway.

All in all, he figured there were worse places to work than a year-round summer camp.

After lunch, he was getting ready for his next group when he glanced up to see Ryan walking toward him on the pathway.

Her again? Holding in a groan, he tried to keep his cool as she stopped directly in front of him. Was she there to get the rest of her belongings or collect a paycheck? Either way, he hadn't planned on running into her again.

"Can I help you with something?"

She squinted at him. "I thought you'd like to know beforehand that I'm going to the press."

"About?" He'd turned so he could continue to lay out the harnesses for the next group, but when he heard her move up the stairs, he glanced over.

"Us," she said directly behind him. "I'm going to tell the entire world about us."

"There is no us." He didn't turn around to give her attention this time. "You know that."

"There is an us. You promised." Her voice had risen slightly.

"No"—he shook his head and finished setting out all the harnesses—"there isn't." When he glanced back, he was shocked to see a black pistol aimed directly at his stomach. He froze, his heart stopping completely in his chest. He blinked once, slowly, to make sure he hadn't been seeing things. "Ryan? What is this about?" He raised his hands, his mind going blank as he tried to think his way out of the situation.

"You think you can just blow me off? All three of you. You played me." The look in her eyes was something he'd never seen before. *Mad* was the only thing he could think. She'd gone crazy.

He watched the gun waver slightly and felt his heart kick hard in his chest at the thought of feeling a bullet rip through his flesh at any moment.

"Easy," he said.

"I won't be ignored." Her voice rose again.

"I'm not ignoring you." Slowly, he moved toward her just an inch. Thoughts of grabbing the gun or making a run for it flashed through his mind. But she was blocking the stairs to the hut. He'd never thought he'd ever have to deal with a gun being pointed at him. He hadn't planned or trained for this. Ever.

"No." She smiled and tilted her head slightly. For a moment, he thought he noticed her take control of her emotions; then her eyes turned again, and crazy Ryan was back. "You aren't ignoring me now."

"No," he admitted and started to move forward again.

"Stop," she warned, the gun rising slightly. Now it was pointed at his chest.

He held up his hands again. "Tell me what I can do."

"You could have not ignored me to start with. Just given me what I deserved," she said, shifting her feet so that she blocked the stairs completely.

He knew that it was almost half an hour before any of the guests for the next run would be arriving. A lot could happen in half an hour. Hell, all it took was one second for things to turn deadly.

"What do you deserve?" he asked in what he hoped was a calm voice, while his heart raced.

"Everything." She narrowed her eyes. "Leo promised me things."

He stilled. "You . . . know my father?" His heart caught in his throat.

Ryan laughed, throwing her head back. "Of course I know him. Why do you think I got this job in the first place? I followed you three in hopes that you'd lead me to him. He took off on me. I had plans for him."

He figured it was now or never, since her eyes were slightly unfocused as she spoke, and he was just about to move, to rush her, when a flash of a movement out of the corner of his eye caught his attention.

He watched in horror as Zoey rushed across the trail and up the stairs quickly, knocking into Ryan from the side.

Their two bodies flew through the air, both of them landing in the bushes on the side of the steps in a heap.

He scrambled forward, crying out Zoey's name, fear causing bile to almost surface as thoughts of Zoey with a bullet hole in her filled his mind.

Then he stood back and watched in amazement as Zoey drew a fist back and punched Ryan directly in the face. In one quick move, the other woman was out cold.

"Bitch," Zoey spat, still sitting on top of Ryan, holding her down. Then she turned to look at him. "Grab that gun, just in case she comes to." She nodded to the gun, lying in the dirt a foot away from Ryan's unconscious form.

He blinked a few times to make sure he wasn't hallucinating it all, and then he picked up the gun and flipped on the safety. He set it on the stairs, well out of the other woman's reach.

Then he moved over and pulled Zoey up from Ryan's unconscious body. He wrapped his arms around Zoey and held on to her.

"My hero—my god, I love you." The words burst from him, and he kissed her. He didn't regret them one bit and said them again when he pulled back and looked into her eyes. "I mean it."

She smiled up at him. "You're just saying that because that was an amazing flying tackle."

"That, and can I say, wow—what a right cross you have? Remind me never to piss you off." He chuckled.

"What the hell is going on?" A voice sounded behind them.

"Call the cops." He turned and looked at the man, then recognized Reed Cooper and pointed toward the hut. "Cell's on the counter."

Turning back to Zoey, he bent down and kissed her again and held on to her like his life depended on it.

"Don't ever do something that crazy again," he whispered into her hair before letting her go.

Ryan was moaning and moving around, and he wanted to make sure she didn't try anything else.

"I called 911; the cops are on the way," Reed said. "I also called the main office. Julie assured me she'd make sure the police were escorted here quickly."

"Help me out?" he asked Reed and grabbed a large zip tie from the drawer behind the counter. Reed had pulled the woman up to stand and was holding her hands behind her back as she jerked in his arms and tried to get free. She stopped and glared at him as he slipped the ties over Ryan's hands and tightened them.

"What do you know about my father?" he asked, turning her around to face him.

Ryan smiled. "More than you do."

"When was the last time you saw him?" he asked. Her smile grew, and she remained silent.

Zoey walked up and tilted her head as she looked at Ryan.

"She's playing you. I doubt she even knows your father." Zoey started to move away.

"I do too—I know he's in Mexico right now," Ryan blurted out.

"Mexico?" Dylan's hands tightened into fists as Ryan smiled up at him. "Where in Mexico?"

Ryan must have realized that she was giving him what he wanted, because her smile fell away, and she shut her mouth.

Dylan jerked her around and forced her to sit on the steps so she wouldn't run away from them. Then, with her hands tied behind her back, she crossed her legs and managed to look like she was sitting there on the steps enjoying the sunny day, instead of waiting for the police to show up and haul her to jail.

"She won't talk anymore," Zoey said. "Like I said, she's bluffing."

"I doubt that will work a second time," Reed managed.

"Oh, I'm not playing her." Zoey chuckled and wrapped an arm around Dylan. "I just no longer care what she has to say."

Less than five minutes later, a golf cart came barreling up the road. Elle and Scarlett rode in the front, while Hannah held on to the back.

They all seemed to jump from the cart and rush them at the same time.

"Is everyone okay?" Elle asked as Scarlett wrapped her sister in her arms.

"You're bleeding again," Scarlett said, pulling Zoey's elbow up to get a look at it.

He hadn't even checked her out after the tackle. He'd just been glad that she hadn't had any new holes that were spewing blood.

"Here, I'll take care of it." He picked her up and marched up the stairs; then, after setting her on top of the counter, he pulled out the first aid kit.

"It's just a scratch," she began, but he shushed her.

Scarlett stood over him, watching him as he cleaned the cut. Zoey filled her in on what had happened.

"I was coming out here to tell you that we talked it over and decided that we could stay in the Bear-Foot Bungalow," Zoey admitted.

"Bear-Foot . . ." Dylan frowned as Zoey laughed.

"Our cabin. Instead of opening it up to guests, we can stay there—at least until my place is built."

"Your . . ." He shook his head. "Wait, you named our cabin Bear-Foot Bungalow?"

"It was Elle's idea." Zoey gestured toward the doorway, where Elle stood, smiling at them.

"You're welcome to it, until Zoey's place is finished. I'll go out and wait for the police. Reed seems to have Ryan under control."

"Thanks." Zoey smiled at Elle.

"I'll go, um, too . . . bye." Scarlett rushed from the hut and shut the door behind her.

"You're having a place built?" he asked her.

"Yes," she answered. "I thought we could talk to Aiden and have him draw us up some plans for our own place."

"You want to build a place with me?" he asked, his hands going to her hips as he stepped closer to her. Her arms wrapped around his shoulders.

"Don't you want to wake up next to me every day?" she asked.

"Every day," he agreed before kissing her.

There was a knock on the door, interrupting them.

"Sorry, the police are here," Reed called out. "They'll need to talk to you both."

He quieted. "Do you think she really knows anything about my dad?"

"No." She shook her head. "Ryan's the type of woman who'll say anything, do anything, to get what she wants. She wanted attention from you, and she got it."

"She wanted more than that. She wanted me to jet her around the world, spend money on her, I suppose, and to be famous."

"I still don't understand how being around you would make her famous?" she asked as he helped her down from the countertop. "I get that you're rich, but—"

"The Costa family is somewhat famous in this area," he admitted. "I guess she figured she could work off that popularity."

"I've done a search on you. You're not that famous." Zoey chuckled.

He shrugged, feeling stupid. "My dad is kind of . . . Anyway. He's donated a lot to the city, he's in the paper a lot, and he's even been on television a few times."

"That doesn't make you famous," she said as they opened the door. "Just being around you wouldn't have given her fame."

"It would have given her something, or at least she thought so."

A female officer was putting Ryan in the back of an SUV patrol car. A male officer approached them.

"Dylan," he sighed. "I heard it was you. Are you okay?"

Dylan glanced at Zoey. "Yeah. Brett, this is Zoey—she saved my life." He nodded. "Zoey, Brett Jewel."

"Officer Jewel." He held out a hand for Zoey. "Dylan and I went to school together."

"Nice to meet you." Zoey shook his hand. "Did you go to school around here?" She frowned up at Dylan.

"Yeah." He nodded. "We all did."

"I bought my house from his dad," Reed broke in.

"You . . ." Zoey frowned. "Why didn't you say anything?" She dropped her arm from his.

"I didn't think that it really mattered."

"You used to live across the camp; you grew up there. It mattered." He could tell she was retreating.

"We moved out when I was sixteen." Then he added, "Moved to Destin." He turned to the man. "Brett, what do you need from us? I'd like to take Zoey back and let her clean up." He nodded to her bandages.

"Oh, right." Brett pulled out his notepad.

Dylan and Zoey answered all the questions Brett had, then took one of the golf carts back to the main building.

He stopped Zoey from leaving him on the stairs by following her up to the third floor. Not giving her a chance to deny him access, he held the door open for her.

"We're going to talk about this," he said softly.

She nodded and motioned for him to sit down.

"Beer?" she asked calmly.

"No." He shook his head.

"Well, I need a freaking case of wine." She walked over, took a bottle and a glass, then sat down and poured a full glass.

CHAPTER TWENTY-TWO

"I assumed you grew up in Destin," Zoey said after swallowing half the glass of wine. It was stupid, but now that she'd cooled off, she found herself shaking. Maybe it was because on the short cart ride back to the main building, her mind had gone over all the possibilities.

What would have happened if she hadn't shown up to tell Dylan about the cabin? Ryan could have shot him.

Or, if Ryan hadn't been distracted, she could have been the one to have been shot. They could both be dead. So many different outcomes.

"I'm sorry. I should have told you." He sighed as he ran his hands through his hair. "Does it really matter?"

She thought about it: about all the years she had spent here, about this place as her second home, while he was just across the water.

"No, I suppose not." She leaned back. "To be honest, I'm coming down from an adrenaline rush." She rubbed her forehead. "I'm not sure what's what anymore."

"Why don't you head in and take a rest. We can meet later." He grinned. "So . . . Bear-Foot Bungalow later tonight to finish our talk?"

She nodded, feeling that her mind was too tired to even focus.

"Dylan." She stopped him when he got up. "I'm sure Ryan didn't know anything more about your dad. I would even question if he's really in Mexico at this point. Anyone who would do what she did has to have a few screws loose."

He took a deep breath. "Yeah, I'm sure you're right. Still, it would have been nice to know more. Just a hint at where he might be."

"We'll find out something. I promise: we won't stop helping you until he's back home, safe." She felt all her energy seep from her.

"Rest," he said. "I'll have Isaac make us something special and bring it to the cabin."

She rested her head back on the sofa and could have just fallen asleep right there. "Okay," she mumbled, then decided the sofa was just as good as her bed. "I'm so glad you didn't get shot." She hadn't heard him move, but suddenly, his lips were brushing hers. "You scared me."

He whispered, "Sleep," and pulled her legs up onto the sofa, removed her running shoes, then covered her with a blanket that Aubrey had knitted one summer.

"I love you too, you know," she said, but she had drifted off and didn't know if she'd thought it or said it out loud.

Scarlett's glare met her as she awoke.

"Oh god," she groaned. "Not what I wanted to wake up to. That ugly mug." She sat up, rubbing her eyes.

"You slept for two hours." Scar sat down next to her. "Dylan stood guard at the door and wouldn't let any of us in here until now. He left to head over to the kitchen to get you dinner. He told me to let you know he'd see you in an hour." She shifted on the sofa, causing the entire thing to bounce.

The thing was as old as the camp was, the springs having broken long ago; they had replaced them with thick pillow stuffing so that it was easily the most comfortable sofa she'd ever sat on. Actually, the entire apartment was packed with furniture that had seen better days but had been turned into pieces of beauty, all thanks to Hannah.

"Did you really tackle Ryan while she held a gun on Dylan?" Aubrey asked from her spot at the bar.

They had another bottle of wine out—her glass got refilled.

"Yes." She glanced down at her watch. "Oh no . . . I have a class."

"Taken care of." Elle waved. "What's the point of being bosses if we can't delegate a little, especially after you stop a murder?"

"Oh god," she sighed, and it hit her again. "She could have killed Dylan." She set her glass down and cradled her head in her hands.

"Easy," Hannah said, sitting beside her. "She's got it bad."

"I love him," she moaned. "How stupid is that?"

The room was quiet, so she chanced glancing up. Everyone looked at her like they had all known the joke hours ago.

"Well? Don't expect us to argue with you." Elle smiled. "Anyone who's crazy enough to tackle a gunman—or gunwoman, as it were—is obviously in love."

She turned to Scar, who just smiled and nodded at her. "Mom's known longer than us. She told me weeks ago. That's why I moved the schedules around. So you could see it for yourself."

"You . . ." Her eyes moved to Elle. "I thought it was you?"

"Nope." Elle shook her head. "No clue until I saw the way he carried you up those stairs at the zip line hut, two hours ago." She slid down into the chair, her glass of wine held tight to her chest. "If only someone would look at me like that."

"What about Liam?" Scar interrupted, causing Elle to laugh.

"Right. He's just horny." She shook her head. "So am I."

Hannah broke in. "Horny could lead to love." Everyone looked at her. "Well, it could." She shrugged. "Can't it?"

Zoey stood up. "I'm going to go shower, then change before dinner."

"So you really are moving into the cabin with him?" Scar asked.

"Yes. You can have the room all to yourself now."

Scar frowned. "I'll miss you."

Zoey chuckled. "I'm going about a quarter of a mile away, not to Japan."

"So." Scar stood up and hugged her. "We've never shared a room before. It was fun while it lasted."

Zoey hugged her back. "Don't make me cry. I'm overflowing with emotions right now."

"Fine, but you still have to do girls' night up here," Scar added.

"Duh!" She playfully shoved her sister.

"Zoey," Elle called to her as she left the room. "If anyone ever pulls a gun on me, I want you to rescue me."

"Me too," Hannah said, followed by Aubrey.

"Super Zoey." They all chuckled as she went to pack up her stuff and shower.

She came out to find her friends waiting for her.

"Stop." She held up her hands after setting her bags down. "Seriously—I'm going across the camp, not the country."

"It's not that, it's just . . . we took a vote, and, well, we have something for you." Elle pulled out a small box from behind her back. "Since you're the first to fall in love."

"You were in love," she countered.

"No." Elle shook her head. "You all knew that it wasn't love too."

"Okay." Zoey moved forward and, taking a deep breath, took the small box from Elle's fingers. She'd never thought she'd be the one to receive it, but now, as she opened the small box, she smiled at the innocents they had all once been.

A small unicorn ring sat tucked inside, much like it had the day the five of them had placed it inside.

"Can you believe that we once fought over this thing?" She pulled it out and placed it on her pinkie, since it was too small for her other fingers at this point.

"For good reason—we all pitched in ten dollars to buy it," Aubrey added as they all moved closer.

She held up her hand and showed the ring off. "We should have bought another pizza," she said. "Not that the ring isn't cool, I mean." She held it up. "By the power of the unicorn . . ."

"God, it's ugly." Scar chuckled. "I'm glad I wasn't the first one to fall in love."

"Shut up." Zoey held the ring to her chest. "It's beautiful." She glanced down at it and smiled, enjoying the way the crystals sparkled in the light. "I earned this." She felt her eyes burn and wiped away the tears before they fell.

Suddenly, she had arms wrapped around her, and she held on to her sisters.

"Stop," she moaned. "I'm just going across the field."

"No." Elle took her shoulders. "It's not the physical distance we're celebrating—it's the leap you've taken." She kissed her cheek. "We're happy for you, and we all voted that Dylan is the one for you. Officially."

She put her hand over her heart. "Oh god." She felt her breath kick. "He is, isn't he?" Full realization dawned on her. She'd known earlier but had tried denying it. Like someone trying to stop the rain. She should have known she was doomed. "He's the one."

Her bags were picked up as she was nudged out the door and down the stairs to where a golf cart waited for her.

"Do you need us to drive you there too?" Elle joked.

"No, I've got this." She'd started to reach up to put the cart in gear when a bottle of champagne was shoved in her face.

"To celebrate," Hannah said.

She set it in the seat next to her. Her bags were loaded on the back by Scarlett and Aubrey.

"Good luck." They all stood back as she pulled out of the parking area.

"Have fun storming the castle," she thought she heard her sister yell behind her, and she laughed as she drove toward her future with Dylan.

She parked the golf cart next to the steps at the cabin and smiled up at the plaque that read BEAR-FOOT BUNGALOW above the doorway.

Then she noticed Dylan standing in the doorway.

"Elle had the code reset for us." He grabbed her bags. "Head on up."

When she stepped into the cabin, she gasped at the beauty of the place.

"Hannah," he said softly from behind her. "Who I suspect had help. But I brought you these." He pulled a bundle of wildflowers from behind his back. "I should have given you flowers long ago."

She took them from him and hugged him, then turned back to the room.

Soft string lights dotted the space. The kitchen table was set up with flowers of every color on a white tablecloth. Dinner was laid out; the food was still steaming.

"They just delivered the meal," he said. He took the bags and set them down and shut the door behind him.

"They also hung blinds." She nodded to the windows as she set the wildflowers into a waiting vase. Then she paused to bury her face in them and took a moment to enjoy the fragrance of them all.

He chuckled. "Yeah, no more bears watching us do it at night. We'll leave the voyeurism to the Youngs."

She laughed as she turned toward him. He took the bottle of champagne from her and set it down on the counter. Then wrapped his arms around her.

"I can't tell you how happy I am to know that we have this to ourselves." He leaned in and kissed her.

"I'm just thankful to get out of the same room as my sister." She laughed. "She snores."

He chuckled. "You don't know the half of it. I was sharing a room with my two brothers." He kissed her again. "How about we eat this meal before it gets cold?"

She turned around and took a seat when he pulled out the chair for her. She sat back as he opened the champagne and poured two glasses, then sat across from her.

They each took a sip, and she picked up her fork. The chicken cacciatore looked amazing, and she dug in.

"So, I was thinking," Dylan said after a moment. "After we find my father . . ."

His pause caused her heart to go crashing down in her stomach. She hadn't thought that far into the future. Only now, only tonight.

"I want to put the condo up for sale and move out here with you."

She felt like she could breathe again. "Really?" She set her fork down. "What about your work? Your family?"

He reached for her hand. "I work here, remember?"

She chuckled. "I'm sure you have something else you were doing before you came here."

He shook his head. "A few odd jobs at the family business, but nothing major. Actually, it's really Joel who runs the business while Dad's off . . ." He motioned. "Wherever, doing whatever. Owen knows more than I do. Out of the three of us, he's the one we always expected to take Dad's place."

She relaxed. "You wouldn't mind staying at the camp? Really?"

He squeezed her hand. "As long as you're here."

"I'm not going anywhere," she said. Then he shocked her by turning her hand around and frowning down at the ring.

"What's this?" he asked. He had been playing his thumb over the ring.

She chuckled. "My prize for rescuing you today."

He glanced up at her. "From your sisters?"

She nodded. "The Wildflowers." She glanced down at the ring.

"Fitting name for the bunch of you." He held up his glass. "To the Wildflowers," he said and joined her in a sip.

"So, I was thinking, with the sale of the condo, we could have a house built instead of just a cabin." He picked up his fork.

"I like the way you think." She started eating again and smiled across the table at him.

By the time they were done eating, the champagne was all gone, and they stepped out on the front porch. She had grabbed a light jacket to ward off the chill in the night air.

"Looks like we're in for more rain." He nodded to the dark sky; the clouds blocked out the moonlight and the stars.

"You can feel it in the air." She leaned against him as they watched the dark waters across the small grassy area.

"This view is a lot better without the dumpster and the black bear chasing me," he joked.

She turned in his arms and hugged him. "It seems like only yesterday, doesn't it?"

He brushed a strand of her hair away from her eyes. "Would it freak you out too much if I told you how much I love you?"

She shook her head, reached up on her toes, and kissed him. "I love you too."

His lips covered hers again.

"I don't know what my future holds, as far as my father or the family business, but I know that here, now, at this place and time, I've never been happier than I am holding you, being with you."

"Me too." She laid her head on his chest.

"If I could, I'd hold on to this moment for the rest of my life," he said into her hair.

"Then let's do it." She leaned back. "Hold on to this forever."

"Okay, I'm game." He nodded. "Forever it is." He kissed her.

"I mean . . ." she started, but he stopped her.

"Yeah, I know what you mean, and when we can, we'll go into town and pick you out a ring that . . ." He pulled up her hand and played with the unicorn. "Doesn't have a horse on it."

"It's a unicorn," she corrected.

"One with a diamond, then."

She looked into his eyes. "Not too big, though. I tend to play rough."

He laughed. "Right. Besides, it would probably get in the way of that mean right swing you used to lay out Ryan."

She hugged him. "I love you," she said into his chest, then leaned back and said it again when their eyes locked. "I love you. I never thought I could be so happy."

"I had always hoped. It's a good thing I persuaded you to take me on." He smiled.

She squinted at him. "You didn't have to persuade me. I took one look at those broad, sexy shoulders and knew I had to get my hands on them." She threw his words back at him.

She ran her fingers over them now and smiled when he reached around and hoisted her up, his hands firmly on her butt.

"Then that makes two of us," he said, walking them up the stairs and back into the cabin. "Why fight it anymore?"

"Yes," she said between kisses. "Why fight it?"

ABOUT THE AUTHOR

 Jill Sanders is the *New York Times* and *USA Today* best-selling author of the Pride Series, Secret Series, West Series, Grayton Series, Lucky Series, and Silver Cove romance novels. She continues to lure new readers in with her sweet and sexy stories. Her books are available in every English-speaking country and in audiobooks and have been translated into several languages.

Born as an identical twin to a large family, Sanders was raised in the Pacific Northwest and later relocated to Colorado for college and a successful IT career before discovering her talent as a writer. She now makes her home along the Emerald Coast in Florida, where she enjoys the beach, hiking, swimming, wine tasting, and—of course—writing. You can connect with Sanders on Facebook at http://fb.com/JillSandersBooks, on Twitter @JillMSanders, and on her website at http://JillSanders.com.